HEART
in the
CLOUDS

HEART
in the
CLOUDS

JENNIFER MISTMORGAN

HEART in the CLOUDS © 2023 by Jennifer Mistmorgan. All rights reserved.

No part of this publication may be reproduced, stored in a retrieval system, or transmitted in any way by any means—electronic, mechanical, photocopy, recording, or otherwise—without the prior permission of the copyright holder, except as provided by USA copyright law.

Cover design by Roseanna White Designs.

ISBN 13: 978-0-6458566-1-3 (Paperback)
978-0-6458566-0-6 (ePub)

*Romance for Mum and aviation for Dad.
Along with all my love for you both.*

I believe in the cause for which we are fighting and I am equally sure that our actions are justified in the eyes of God. . . . Faith in God is a wonderful thing—it dispels your doubts and misgivings and replaces them with a feeling of contentment. I want you to know therefore that if I should die I shall not be afraid because my heart is at ease. Please don't think I am pessimistic but I do realize what the odds are and I have seen too many of my friends pass on without leaving any words of hope or encouragement behind.

—RAAF Flying Officer Colin Flockhart of 619 Squadron,
RAF Bomber Command
in a letter marked "to be posted in the event of my death."
The letter was mailed to his family on January 8, 1945.

CHAPTER ONE

Above Frankfurt
26 October 1942, 12:45 a.m.

Two and a half minutes.

That was how long Flight Sergeant Alec Thomas held his aircraft steady in enemy searchlights. Not just one light either. Three searchlights locked on to him just as he opened the bomb bay doors of his Avro Lancaster. All he could do was hold the aircraft steady while Jimmy Hardie, the bomb aimer lying in the nose of the rumbling aircraft, dropped their payload. Every gun on the ground and every fighter defending the sky above Frankfurt focused attention on Alec's aircraft for those agonizing minutes.

The longest two and a half minutes of his life.

"Bombs gone." Hardie's voice came over the intercom.

Alec didn't wait to check if they'd hit their target. He pulled the plane into a corkscrew—diving, banking, and changing altitude, an evasive maneuver to shake the searchlights.

Lighter now that it wasn't laden with explosives, Alec could control the aircraft more easily through the flashes in the sky from the antiaircraft fire. The drone of the engines drowned out any sound the flak made. If not for the smell of cordite hanging in the air, he might enjoy the light show.

That was one thing he hadn't been prepared for when he'd enlisted in the Royal Australian Air Force. That from above, a whole city burning looked quite beautiful—if you could forget the horror happening on the ground.

He rarely could.

Alec managed to dodge the lights, but a fighter had already locked on to the aircraft.

With orders not to waste ammunition, the gunners—three in all, now that Hardie had done his job aiming and could use the guns in the nose turret—were only meant to fire as a last resort. But this fighter was as persistent as a mosquito in summer. Skillful flying didn't shake him.

The sound of guns rattled through Alec's headgear, and the smell of explosives reached the cockpit. "Rear Gunner to Skipper—we got him."

He leveled out the aircraft, letting his heart rate recover from the perverse thrill of the chase. "Skipper to Navigator—what's the course?"

Up here, they only addressed each other by their roles. They hardly ever used their names. Apart from it being the protocol hammered into them during training, it helped to think of themselves as part of the machine. It wasn't far from the truth anyway, Alec thought. They were plugged into a mechanical monster, dependent on it for communication, oxygen, and heat in the subzero sky. The aircraft united them so they could serve it to Hitler, flying as one being with one purpose, across occupied territory and into enemy airspace night after long, cold, lonely night.

He stayed on edge, watching for enemy fighters, as he guided the aircraft northwest over Holland and the English Channel. A full "Bomber's Moon" hung silver in the sky, reflecting off the inky water below and lighting their way until Alec spotted the beacons that told them they were above England now.

"Another one over, chaps." Alec touched down on the barely lit runway of their Royal Air Force station in Lincolnshire, England.

He switched off the intercom and powered down the engines, which closed down into silence, or more accurately, absence, as his body stopped vibrating from the noise. He disconnected the oxygen supply and intercom and jumped down from the aircraft while the ground crew took control of the plane.

He'd done this postop routine many times before—twenty-one times, to be precise. A number to be proud of considering the fifty-fifty odds facing him each night.

The seven of them caught a ride on the transport wagon back to the kit room. The Women's Auxiliary Air Force corporal collecting their flight suits grinned at them.

"Welcome home, boys."

The WAAFs performed every non-flying duty imaginable on an air station like this. Unlike some men he knew, Alec didn't mind the female presence, especially when it met him with a smile at the end of an operation. That smile meant he'd survived.

Together, they headed to the locker room to peel off the layers of excess clothing. Sleep called, but he couldn't head to bed just yet. He was too hungry, with too much adrenaline still in his veins and too many postop rituals to complete. First there was the cup of rum-laced tea to warm them. The station chaplain—Padre, they called him—spoke with them while they drank it. Alec had little to say but accepted the chaplain's prayers. He happily grasped at any straw that might keep him alive in the sky.

Then an intelligence officer sat the crew down and peppered them with questions about the operation. Did they hit their target? What guns fired as they flew over occupied territory, and where? What were the time and coordinates of aircraft they saw go down? What else did they see? At least, answering these questions now meant he didn't have to write up a report later.

By the time this was all done, Alec was well and truly starving. He made a beeline for the mess and ate in silence amid the familiar clatter of the room, until the hot meal thawed him out.

He slunk toward his dormitory just as the first gray light of dawn stole in. The adrenaline was long gone, and fatigue made every limb heavy. But before his head could hit the pillow, he took out his logbook and a red-ink pen. After filling out the details of the aircraft and crew, he wrote in the duty column, *OPS—FRANKFURT (coned in searchlights for 2 1/2 mins)*. Then he wrote *22* and circled it.

His twenty-second mission. If he survived eight more, he'd have finished his tour and could, perhaps, go home.

Survival wasn't statistically likely.

But he got through tonight. That was a sweet enough dream for now.

The Vicarage, St. John's Church, Kenilworth, England
20 November 1942, 8:02 a.m.

So many kisses.

Not the passionate kind. The well-meaning, peck-on-the-cheek kind.

Maggie supposed grief did strange things to people. To the parishioners of Kenilworth, Warwickshire, grief at the sudden death of their beloved vicar's wife made them want to embrace and kiss her daughter. She couldn't explain their lack of reserve. Where was the famous British stiff upper lip when she really wanted it?

She frowned at herself in the mirror as she fidgeted with the corner of an embroidered cloth on her dressing table. In the reflection, she saw her childhood room behind her. A simple, modestly sized wardrobe sat in front of pale wallpaper flecked with a small floral pattern. Neat quilts, knitted pillows, and even the teddy with a missing eye she'd had since she was four adorned the comfortable bed.

For the past three and a half weeks since the funeral, it was a luxury to sleep on those soft pillows. After today, she would be back to the hard straw mattress and scratchy blue blankets in the WAAF sleeping quarters of a Lincolnshire RAF station.

"Hurry up, Maggie! Breakfast is getting cold!"

Maggie shook her head to clear it. How long had she been sitting here staring, unaware of the passing time? It wasn't like her to be so still for so long. But then, grief did do strange things to people.

"You don't need to shout!" Maggie shouted back down the hall to her sister. It was their private joke from childhood, when they were constantly chided by their mother about their noise and lack of propriety.

Their mother. The one they'd never see again. Not in this world anyway.

Her father's firmly closed study door rebuked her as she passed it on the way to the dining room. She would have to work up the courage to knock before she left.

"Do you really have to go back?" Rosie slumped in her seat at the breakfast table as Maggie took a bite of national loaf. She'd coated it with margarine and enough of Mrs. Bickham's apricot jam to make it palatable.

"You know I do. The war didn't stop when Mother died."

"No, but Father did."

Poor Rosie had been the one to find their mother sitting in her usual chair with her Bible in her lap. At first she'd thought Mother was reading, but when she didn't reply to Rosie's cheerful greeting, the sixteen-year-old had realized something was wrong.

Her heart, the doctor said. Probably an underlying weakness that no one had known about.

"Be kind to him, won't you?" Maggie glanced down the hallway toward the closed study door. "He's hurting."

Rosie nodded, but her frown deepened. In the past few weeks, their father had distanced himself from them. After the funeral he disappeared into his study, leaving Maggie and Rosie, along with their housekeeper, Mrs. Bickham, to receive the steady stream of callers paying their respects. If Maggie transcribed the entirety of the conversations she'd shared with him in her weeks at home, the words would fit neatly onto one foolscap page.

Maggie's finger rapped on the breakfast table as she considered what she would say to him now.

"Will you be all right?" Rosie asked.

"Once I get back to the aerodrome, I'll be busy. Grace said the new squadron has arrived, so I'll have no time to think about anything else." Maggie could see her sister was bursting with questions, but she had already said too much to Rosie. "Now don't ask me anything else about my job—you know I can't say!"

She stood, smoothing down her uniform, as if it would steel her to speak with her father, just as Mrs. Bickham walked into the room. Round and warm and lovely as usual.

"Oh, you do look lovely in that uniform, my girl. How it makes your blue eyes shine! And your hair all done up like that suits you so well."

Maggie reached up to touch the braids tied at the back of her head. She much preferred to curl it and wear it out, trying hopelessly to imitate Greer Garson. But plaiting her dead-straight locks and pinning them in a dark clump behind her head was much more practical, even if it did make her look closer to Rosie's sixteen years than to her own twenty.

"I have to keep it up off my collar." It came out like the apology it was.

"Let me get one last look at you." Mrs. Bickham held her at arm's length, her hands clamped on Maggie's upper arms. "You're a brave girl, Maggie Morrison. You remember everything that your mother ever told you, and don't go getting into any trouble with those Brylcreem Boys."

"Any *more* trouble, you mean?" Rosie piped up from the breakfast table.

Maggie shot her a glare.

"We all have to have our heart broken once." Mrs. Bickham smiled. "But once is enough, mind."

Maggie broke away. "I should say goodbye to Father."

She knocked and waited for his answer before she entered his dark-paneled study, feeling like a four-year-old about to be scolded. Even though it was early, he was already at his desk reading.

Her father had a broad range of literary interests, but this morning he had several of what looked like Spurgeon's sermons open on the desk. His face looked gaunt and ghostly in the light from his desk lamp.

No hint of a smile in his eyes, he glanced up briefly, registering her blue uniform before returning to his work.

"You haven't changed your mind, I see." He fixed his eyes on the page.

"No. This is what I signed up for."

"Well then. You've made your choice. Goodbye."

His cold and final words were like a slap in the face. She couldn't even plead with him for compassion, because he wouldn't lift his gaze from his desk. She swallowed to stop the prickling tears from fully forming.

"Goodbye, Father," she whispered.

Mrs. Bickham gave her an apologetic look when Maggie returned to the breakfast table. "Have you got something to keep your hands busy?"

Her sister and Mrs. Bickham were some of the few people who knew the strategies Maggie had honed to keep anxiety at bay. Even now, living as she did in a dormitory full of strangers, she was able to disguise that she sometimes felt the irrational beast of panic clawing at her chest.

Knitting was her mother's idea originally. "To keep your hands busy and give you something to focus on." Maggie and Rosie had spent a good deal of the last week unraveling cardigans and vests. Some old things of Father's and one or two of Mother's less fashionable items that they couldn't bring themselves to wear were sacrificed into the multicolored balls of yarn that Maggie stuffed into her bag.

"I'll be fine. Really, I will," she said as she hugged them both. Maggie hoped she was right.

CHAPTER TWO

The Savoy Hotel, London, England
20 November 1942, 1:00 p.m.

Sipping her hot tea, with a double-tiered plate of petit fours in front of her, Maggie let the cares of the last few weeks slip away.

"These are so pretty—it's a shame to eat them. But it won't stop me." Maggie grinned as she popped an intricately decorated cake into her mouth and savored its rich sweetness.

Her dearest friend, Grace Deroy, sat opposite her. Two years older than Maggie, Grace had already completed most of an art history degree at Oxford when she'd enlisted in the WAAF. They'd only met during training, but Grace was the kind of friend who had walked into Maggie's life and made her feel as though Grace had always been a part of it.

It was Grace's idea for Maggie to travel back to the aerodrome via London. Maggie insisted that it didn't make sense to go so far out of her way, but Grace was adamant Maggie needed cheering up. Maggie had hesitated. Grace hailed from one of the wealthiest families in the country, so she never thought twice about mundane things like wasting money on extra train fare. However, Grace had met Maggie at Charing Cross station and whisked her straight to the tea room at The Savoy.

"It's a jolly surprise to bring me here," Maggie said. "Do you think we'll see any film stars?" She glanced around the opulent space, trying not to look like she was gawking. She loved the cinema and relished the thought a real star might be somewhere close by.

"Well, the surprises don't end there." Grace grinned. "Father booked us a room here for the night."

"He didn't!" Maggie widened her eyes in disbelief.

"He's at some sort of a meeting and won't even be able to meet us for dinner." Grace's eyes sparkled. "I've got the whole afternoon and evening planned."

Never had Maggie thought she would be able to stay even one night in the same hotel where film stars and even royalty stayed. She could never afford this kind of luxury, no matter how much she yearned for it.

"I can read your mind, but you mustn't worry." Grace interrupted Maggie's racing thoughts. "I'm treating you to a glamorous little London adventure before we get back to that mud at the aerodrome. Now eat up, Corporal. That's an order!" Grace called over the smartly suited waiter to order another pot of tea.

"So what have I missed while I've been away?" Maggie's eyes swept over the tiny treats as she made her next selection.

Grace prattled on for a few minutes about the new Australian squadron at work and how interesting it was to meet airmen from far-flung places. Apparently the new squadron included airmen from New Zealand, Canada, and Rhodesia. But they'd been greeted by truly abysmal English weather, and according to Grace, that made them all tetchy.

"They're bored, but the sky just won't clear for them. They aren't bad company though, and several are very handsome!"

"Grace Deroy!" Maggie chided playfully.

"Oh, I wasn't thinking for myself! I thought another romance would cheer you up."

Maggie laughed. "I'm no good-time girl, Grace. And neither are you, for that matter. Besides, you know how terribly things ended with Ralph."

"Yes, but surely one kiss wouldn't hurt? I mean, what a wonderful distraction!" Grace teased.

"No, I've now sworn off airmen for the duration."

When their giggles subsided, Grace asked, "Did you write to Ralph about your mother?"

Maggie nodded. "He didn't reply." She glanced at her hands to avoid Grace's sympathetic look.

"He was a coward to break it off in a letter."

A few months ago, Maggie would have defended him with every breath in her body. Grace had never liked Ralph Archer, said he was all bluster and show, only after one thing. She'd told Maggie directly that a man who flirted with other women when the girl he was stepping out with wasn't in the room was bad news. But Maggie insisted he was no philanderer, just the outgoing, charismatic sort who couldn't help the attention he got from women. She'd kept telling herself that, even when he'd been posted to a new air station and the letters trickled to nothing.

Maggie shrugged. "Poor form, but not cowardice." Her fingers twitched, with a sudden urge to reach for knitting needles, so she changed the subject. "So what does our afternoon hold?"

Grace explained her plan. Her pleasure at seeing Maggie's jaw drop when she told her they had an appointment at a hair salon on The Strand showed in her grin.

"You look like Gene Tierney with your hair set that way!" Grace complimented Maggie as they looked at their reflections after visiting the coiffeuse.

The hairdresser's magic fingers had coaxed Maggie's dark-brown hair into curls and an elegant roll at her temple. Still off the collar and able to accommodate her cap, but this time with more glamour than practicality.

"Hardly," Maggie said, but she was still pleased at the woman staring back at her from the mirror. Her face had been quite plump before the war, but it had slimmed down like everyone else's had in the last few years, making her look more sophisticated.

If her mother knew how much Maggie enjoyed the compliments about her looks, she would roll in her grave. A strange feeling passed over Maggie, a dull ache at the idea her mother would never again scold her for her vanity.

Grace put her hand on Maggie's forearm. Maggie tried to force the corners of her mouth up, but with a friend like Grace, she didn't need to pretend.

"She's in a place with no more pain and no more tears. That's got to count for something during this blasted war, doesn't it?" Grace said softly. "Now, lipstick."

Grace passed a deep burgundy crayon for Maggie to apply. Living with her parents, Maggie was never allowed to go near makeup. Grace had introduced her to the idea. Maggie still remembered the first time she'd worn it.

"Do you mean to tell me that you've never worn lipstick before?" Grace's incredulous expression had been reflected back in the mirrors that they had shared with so many others in the bathrooms of the barracks during WAAF training.

"My mother said I was vain enough without it," Maggie had mumbled.

Grace had given a wry smile. "It's not vain to draw attention away from these awful, thick stockings. It's simply humane."

Now, two and a half years on, Maggie outlined her lips with expert precision, handed the crayon back to her friend, and watched her apply it. Grace by name, graceful by nature. Grace was blessed with the type of tall and elegant figure that not even the clunky WAAF uniform could fail to flatter, and her honey-colored hair always did exactly what she asked it to even without the help of a professional.

When they stepped back on The Strand, a man in air force blue whistled. Maggie thrilled at being admired by a stranger, but she held her chin high and tried not to look delighted. She was sure Gene Tierney, had she been here, would do the very same thing.

The Strand, London
20 November 1942, 4:25 p.m.

"So what's our poison tonight, gentlemen?" Jimmy Hardie turned to face the group and walked backward a few steps. "Booze, cards, or loose women?"

Jimmy waggled his eyebrows until Al Graves gave him the answer he so clearly wanted. "All three if we can manage it."

"But can either of you afford any of those things?" Alec draped his arms across their shoulders and leaned his face between theirs, hoping to move the conversation on. "I thought I just cleaned you both out."

They had just left the billiards table at the Boomerang Club for Australian servicemen, and Alec's pockets were full of their money.

"You can shout, Thomas," Davis chimed in. "Since you are the one with the promotion."

"Not yet," Alec said.

It was just the suggestion of a promotion, and he wasn't even sure he wanted it. What he wanted was to get the final eight ops of this tour done before his luck ran out, and never risk his neck flying over enemy territory again. But his possible promotion was the reason they were picking their way through the bombed-out streets of London and not the muddy airfields of Lincolnshire. He'd earned the crew a transfer to a new squadron and three days' leave between postings.

Less than a week ago he'd been called into his wing commander's office and told the news. The top brass were forming a new and mostly Australian squadron.

"There's a whole lot of new blood coming in too, of course, but they also need more experienced crews, which aren't as easy to come by as we'd like them to be. You and your crew are being transferred to Bottesford," his commanding officer had said.

Alec had protested. He liked the idea of having Australian commanding officers, but changing to a newly formed squadron, even a RAAF one, would mean slowing down the number of operational sorties he flew while the new crews got up to speed.

"Sir, I'm so close to the end of my tour. I don't want to be transferred to babysitting duty," he'd said.

"If I wanted you to babysit, Thomas, I'd have sent you to be a tutor at a training unit. You're going to lead by example. I'm recommending you for a commission too, so try not to make me regret this." He'd been dismissed before he'd had a chance so say anything more.

"Why don't you want a commission, Alec?" Jonty Ables asked in his rich Edinburgh accent.

The question brought Alec out of his memory and back to the present.

"Don't you want us all to salute every time we see you?"

"Well, with you, I would insist on it, Ables," he said.

Joking was easier than thinking it through. There were plenty of perks to being an officer, but his focus was on surviving this tour.

Eight more ops.

They'd been lucky so far. He didn't want to risk change in case it threw off the delicate streak of luck they enjoyed as a crew.

Months ago, fresh from a conversion unit where they'd been upgrading their flying skills, the assessors had tossed the seven of them into a room to see if they could put up with each other long enough to complete a few simple tasks. Since then, they'd enjoyed the military privilege of eating, sleeping, living, and working in one another's company all day every day. Brothers in arms. Changing something might end their lucky streak.

They headed west along The Strand, carefully skirting the craters opened by German bombs during their blitzkrieg and the sandbags lining the streets, reinforcing the buildings. He hadn't seen London before the war. Others claimed it was a glorious city, but he found it difficult to picture the streets in a better time, a sky without huge gray barrage balloons defending it. Not without a lot of imagination.

"It's getting dark. Soon we won't be able to see a thing. I vote we head to the dance hall," Jonty said. "Then it's every man for himself."

Jonty prattled on, provoking the others into speculating about the girls they would meet. He reminded Alec of a puppy bounding at the heels of its owner. Jonty's enthusiasm never waned. Alec and the others had had trouble understanding Jonty's accent through the intercom on their first few ops. But he talked enough that they'd soon learned to grasp it.

When they were in the air, Jonty had the loneliest job of them all. Positioned in the tail of the aircraft, far away from the rest of the crew, he was the one most likely to cop a German bullet during an operation. But his irrepressible attitude to life in the face of that meant Alec forgave him his relentless, unnecessary chatter.

"I just hope there's enough girls to go round," Hardie said.

"I can't help it if you miss out when the ladies flock to my side, Hardie," Jonty said. "I have a certain wounded-soldier appeal."

Early in the war, when Bomber Command's aircraft were not up to the job they'd been given, Jonty had survived a crash landing that killed the rest of his crew. Not even that could stop him flying. He never tried to hide the fierce scars on his neck and face that testified to his lucky escape.

Alec enjoyed the banter surrounding him as he and his crew continued up The Strand with purposeful, confident strides.

Three days' leave, then eight more ops.

Alec pushed the thought from his mind, determined to enjoy the night ahead. A young woman, probably his little sister's age, passed by on the arm of her mother. She caught his eye with her striking red hair and pink-lipped smile. He sent her a wink as she passed, and enjoyed the blush that colored in her freckles.

He chuckled. As much as he enjoyed it, he didn't do anything to attract female attention. He just made the most of it when it came. He hadn't had a real sweetheart in all the time he'd been over here. Not the kind he wanted to write home to his mother about, anyway.

The voice of his little sister scolded him in his head. *"One day, big brother, someone will come along who isn't fooled by your charm. I hope she breaks your heart into a million little pieces so you can know what it feels like."*

His crew mates teased him about it too, but it worked in their favor more often than not. How many times had he single handedly found dates for all seven of them?

As they passed The Savoy, a young woman in a WAAF uniform opened the door of the kind of fancy hairdressing salon his sister loved, and stepped onto the street with a confident laugh.

Her smile caught his attention. It lit up her features and made her eyes sparkle, transforming her plain face into something beautiful. He whistled in appreciation, but she didn't seem to notice. A pity. She looked ready for a night on the town, and she had a friend with her. There was no harm in trying his luck and asking if they were free this evening, was there? With the thought barely finished, he slammed into Jonty, who'd suddenly stopped like a statue in his path. Alec cringed at their unintentional Abbott and Costello routine.

Alec's irritation flared at Jonty for making him look like a fool in front of a beautiful woman on the London high street. "Jonty? What on earth . . ."

His anger dissolved when he saw Jonty approach the sparkly eyed woman and her friend like he'd known her forever.

Alec grinned. The night ahead just got interesting.

CHAPTER THREE

"Maggie Morrison?"

Maggie heard the soft accent behind her and whipped around to see who had called her name. She furrowed her brow at the lanky, thin-faced man. Then her eyes traveled to his neck, covered in dreadful scars from what she guessed must be skin grafts. They made his face look like it had melted to one side, his smile crooked. But there was no mistaking his grin. He stood beaming brilliantly, though she wasn't sure why.

"Is it really you?" he asked.

When he took off his cap, Maggie saw a shock of bright-red hair clipped close to his head.

"Jonty Ables?" she cried out, struck by the surge of an awful memory. She'd only been at her first station for a matter of weeks when she'd witnessed an accident on the runway. She should have waited for the fire tenders but, because she'd walked outside to escape the fug of smoke in the break room, she was the closest to the wreckage. Close enough to see that the rear gunner, protected from the impact of the crash, was alive! She'd surged forward, running across the tarmac and into the radiant heat to help.

When she'd understood by his fearful mime through the Perspex that his escape doors were jammed, she'd edged her fingers into the gap in the hot metal and used her body weight to drag the doors open. The man had clawed at his parachute harness as the flames licked his ammunition supply. She threw herself farther into the heat to help. His clothes burned as they worked to free him. The tangible memory of the intense heat ran through her mind the moment she recognized the man in front of her.

"Jonty Ables? How are you still here? You must have nine lives!" She threw her arms around him to prove he was real and not a ghost. He'd been in a hospital bed that last time she'd seen him.

He grinned from ear to ear, flanked by several airmen in inky-blue Australian uniforms.

"Everyone, meet my guardian angel, Maggie Morrison!" Jonty announced her like he'd just been the victor in a prize fight.

She scanned their eager faces one by one. They all clamored to shake her hand and share their names as Jonty told the story of the night they met.

"Alec Thomas." The pilot among them, distinguishable by the wings on his uniform, stepped forward with the kind of smile that made her stomach do flips. He held out his hand for her to shake.

For a brief moment, she stared. His voice told her he wasn't a film star who'd stepped straight from the silver screen onto a London street. It contained the lazy vowels of the colonies rather than the sophistication of Hollywood.

But his face!

If it hadn't been for the deep-blue RAAF uniform, she would think she was standing in front of Clark Gable. The dark hair. The blue eyes. The smile. Even the slightly sticking-out ears.

And the charisma. Oh yes. Unmistakable. Only when Grace elbowed her could she stop herself from staring.

"Pull yourself together, Maggie," Grace muttered.

Mere hours ago she'd made a vow to swear off airmen entirely.

She would not let herself come undone at a smile from the first pilot who came her way.

Steeling herself, she shook his hand and tried not to notice the current of warmth his touch sent up her whole arm. To stop herself from becoming a puddle of goo at his feet, she snapped her hand away.

She was not about to fall for another pilot.

At least, that was what she told herself over and over as she moved her attention to the next of Jonty's friends waiting to shake her hand.

The 400 Club, Leicester Square, London
20 November 1942, 8:30 p.m.

The 400 Club was his natural environment, Alec decided as he took in the atmosphere of the dimly lit club in the heart of London's West End. The bomb-scarred streets outside were a mere memory in here.

The place oozed with understated elegance. A jazz quintet played in the larger room next door, accompanying a songstress with a smokey voice that made a man never want to stop listening. Society doyennes floated into the room in shimmering gowns, and peals of confident laughter rang out from the men. The drinks were barely even watered down! And the food—well, they couldn't do much about that, he supposed.

Jonty's new friend, Grace Deroy, daughter (it turned out) of Air Marshall Sir Henry Deroy, had signed them into the club, dropping her father's name. Although judging by the number of uniforms like his in this room, the patronage wasn't as strictly upper crust these days as it might have been in the past. Grace seemed at home here. Her companion, Jonty's rescuer, seemed more wide eyed with wonder.

Now, there was a mystery. The easygoing, self-possessed smile he'd spotted coming out of the hair salon had disappeared the moment she'd set eyes on . . . well, him. She'd snatched her hand away from his like a prim schoolmarm, tilting her chin defiantly. But not before he'd seen the flicker of something else in her eyes.

Admiration perhaps? He couldn't be sure. Whatever it was, he wanted more of it.

All night he tried to find an opportunity to talk with her again, but she wouldn't have a bar of him. When he bought the drinks, she declined them. She barely met his eye in conversation. Every time he moved close enough to ask her to dance, she flitted away to swing merrily on the arm of another man with her broad, beaming smile.

He'd understand it if she were angry at him, but she didn't even know him. She couldn't possibly be angry with him. Not yet, anyway.

"I owe her my life," Jonty said as they finished their meal, watching couples make their way onto the dance floor.

"You're exaggerating, Jonty," Maggie said several times as he repeated the story of her heroism, talking up her bravery and painting her as a regular Florence Nightingale for visiting him in hospital. "I just did what anyone would do."

"I don't think so, Maggie darling. That's why you got a bravery commendation for it," Grace said. "Give yourself some credit."

"Would you like to dance, my guardian angel?" Jonty asked, his smile permanently lopsided.

She took his hand. He swung her onto the dance floor as the band picked up the pace.

WAAF uniforms were designed to keep a man's mind on the job. They did everything they could to detract from the womanly figures underneath them. But even in sensible shoes and twill that had no grace or give to it, she cut a fine form on the dance floor.

Alec enjoyed watching the two enjoying themselves so fully as they danced. Especially given the way her strangely colored eyes—blue, with flecks of gold in the center—were alight with the fun. He watched as Hardie cut in on Jonty, and then Graves on him. Alec tossed back a drink for courage to confront this puzzle head on.

"May I?"

He tapped Graves on the shoulder and held out his arm to Maggie, whose face fell. Actually fell. No other woman had looked at him with such distaste after knowing him such a short time. Maddening.

She glanced around like she was looking for some kind of rescue. When she didn't find it, she reluctantly took his outstretched hand. As they moved to the music, she avoided his eyes by staring at his shoulder with such grim resolution it was almost offensive. If it wasn't for the fact that she smelled divine, like the first peaches in summer, he might have been put off. Actually, no. Now that he was so close, he didn't think anything could put him off this intriguing creature.

"I've decided something," he said when she didn't speak.

"You have?"

That got her attention, or at least drew her eyes to his, even if her expression was just like his little sister's when he annoyed her.

"I have decided I'm not the problem."

"I beg your pardon?" She looked at him as though he were speaking another language.

"You've been avoiding me all night, but there's nothing wrong with me. Therefore, I am not the problem."

She opened her mouth to speak, but only squeaked a little. "I haven't been—"

"Aha! I knew it!" He cut her off triumphantly before twirling her under his arm.

When they came face to face again, she shook her head. "You airmen are all the same, aren't you? Arrogant, conceited, and self-absorbed. You think you are God's gift to women."

He barely took the breath to mount his defense, when fire flared in her eyes and her insults gained momentum. "And anyone with wings on his uniform seems to be ten times as bad as the others. Do they teach you all how to be beastly as part of pilot training?"

"I think you have me mistaken for someone else." For a moment another dreadful possibility occurred to him. "We haven't met before, have we?"

She let out a little "pfft," as though what he'd just said confirmed her suspicions about him.

"So what happened?" He turned on his charm. "And more to the point, how can I make it up to you? Is there any way I can restore your faith in the blue uniform?"

They danced closely enough to feel her breath quicken. He liked having that effect on a woman. For one moment he thought she might show that genuine smile from out on the street. Then he'd have a chance at making her laugh. After that, he knew from experience, she'd be putty in his hands. But she kept her dour expression in place.

"You can't," she said, so quietly that it was almost under her breath. If they hadn't been dancing, he might not have heard her. "Excuse me."

She dropped his hands, leaving him standing alone on the dance floor. His arms had never felt so empty.

The Savoy Hotel, London
21 November 1942, 12:30 a.m.

Maggie fell backward onto the bed and spread her arms wide, smoothing them up and down on the bedclothes the way a child might play in the snow. She relished the feeling of her skin against the satin.

"Perfect luxury." Maggie sighed. Sadness crept into her heart when she thought about how her mother would chide her craving the finer things in life too much.

"Thank you for all this, Grace." She waved her hand round to indicate the elegant decor, all dark-green hues with gold trim, and the subtle sumptuous touches—the gramophone, the fruit bowl—that made her feel like royalty. "It's very thoughtful."

Grace soaked in a deep tub in the adjoining bathroom, with

the door ajar so they could talk. She hummed quietly to the gramophone playing "Moonlight Cocktail" in the corner of the room.

"What on earth did that pilot say to you to make you so rude?" Grace called out.

"He didn't say anything. He just *was*."

"He was?" Her friend laughed. "What on earth do you mean?"

"He was handsome and clever and a good dancer and charming. He *was* everything that Ralph *was*! I wasn't about to do it to myself again. I thought that if I could just put him off for one evening, I'd never have to see him again."

"Didn't you even think to ask where they were stationed or what squadron they were with?"

Maggie heard Grace step out of the bathtub, and she meandered into the bedroom, wrapping herself in an elegant kimono robe.

Unable to ignore her mother's voice in her head, Maggie tried not to envy Grace's beautiful things and the poise with which she wore them.

"You know they can't say," Maggie said. "And besides, I got the impression from Jonty they had a new posting."

"Yes!" Grace laughed. "To us at Bottesford!"

Maggie stared in incredulity at her friend.

"Steel yourself, Corporal Morrison. You might have survived tonight, but it's about to get a whole lot harder!"

CHAPTER FOUR

RAF Bottesford, Lincolnshire
2 December 1942, 4:25 p.m.

Alec took a long, final draw of his cigarette, then stubbed it out. He'd lost track of time. Whenever stationed somewhere new, he tried to find a quiet spot with a decent outlook where he could sit and write letters to his mother and sister. The words came easier when he wasn't surrounded by a hundred other men.

But finding quiet during a war was easier said than done. There wasn't much to be found on the weeks-long sea voyage to get here, although he sometimes managed to pen a few words while above deck, staring out at the steel-blue sea. There was no quiet in Cairo, where he'd spent a few weeks as part of his journey. But then he'd filled his letters with the strange things he'd seen and heard, knowing those letters would delight them.

This place had a decent patch of woodland at one end that served his purpose. It wasn't exactly quiet, what with all the inevitable thrum and rumble of aircraft. But he'd been able to finish a long-overdue update for his sister.

He mounted one of the station bicycles and headed for the officers' mess, hoping to make it across the airfield before the ever-threatening gray sky opened upon him. As he pedaled the rickety bike, issued to help personnel get around the extensive perimeter track, a few thick droplets fell across his face. Apart from the break this afternoon, the rain here was constant. It had kept them grounded for the past two weeks. Alec had only a handful of entries in his logbook—all training flights, not operations that counted toward his tour.

Still eight more to go.

Bottesford airfield sat across the border of two rural counties, and he thought the engineers who selected the site must have been city dwellers. They'd obviously never experienced what happened to the rich soils in the English countryside when they became sodden. The whole place became a quagmire when it rained.

The concrete runways, dispersal pans, and perimeter track linking everything together ensured the heavy aircraft stayed out of the mud, but the people who worked with them enjoyed no such luck. He'd spent the last two weeks permanently cold, wet, caked in mud, and feeling further away from completing his tour than he had ever been. He'd also seen no sight of the pretty WAAF with the intriguing eyes he'd met in London, even though Jonty assured him that she was one of the almost three thousand personnel here.

At the administration buildings, he stopped to take a brief look at the notice boards before heading inside, happy to dodge the worst of the rain when it began in earnest. Nothing on the board he needed to pay much attention to, just a few notices about missing equipment.

Someone wrote an "Ode to My Missing Wrench." Clever. Playful without having the aggressive quality of the note about missing gloves next to it. Both took a backseat to the notice about a social event later in the month.

Mercifully, he arrived at Wing Commander Palmer's office only a few minutes late and a little bit damp. A smile easily quelled the disapproval of WingCo's secretary, and she let him through with one of her own.

"At ease," his commanding officer said from the seat behind his desk.

Alec relaxed his stance, lowering his salute and resting his hands behind his back.

He wasn't the only one in this meeting. His squadron leader, Flight Lieutenant George Bowles, sat opposite the WingCo, about as "at ease" as was possible. He leaned back in his chair, with one ankle resting on the other knee as he puffed on his pipe.

Known for his abruptness and efficiency with words, Wing Commander Samuel Palmer waved his hand, indicating that Alec should sit in the chair next to Bowles. Alec had already seen the man be stern and exacting, but this seemed casual. Cheerful, even.

They were both about a decade older than him, with graying temples. He hadn't seen Bowles in the air yet, but if the rumors were true, he was an exceptional pilot with a clever, strategic mind. Alec liked the way his ability with the men on the ground was as good as his reputation in the sky.

Alec didn't mind Palmer either. He appreciated having an Australian in charge now. The RAF was egalitarian compared to the other services in Britain, but he didn't like the jibes about being a 'colonial' when he was on secondment to them. That didn't happen here. Or, at least, they were all colonials so it didn't matter as much.

"You've been recommended for a commission, Thomas," Palmer said, avoiding small talk. "Bowles here says you're reluctant to take it. I want to know why."

Alec glanced between the men. Where did he begin? He started with the easiest reason. "I don't want to abandon my men, sir."

Becoming an officer would mean separate sleeping quarters and a separate dining area from his crew, all enlisted men. All much nicer, of course. But it didn't seem right to ask them to take the same life-or-death risk in the air when all things weren't equal on the ground.

His explanation didn't sound articulate, but Palmer and Bowles got the idea.

Palmer shrugged.

"Then don't. Stay in the same barracks and eat in the sergeants' mess. If you want to slum it through the war, go right ahead. Makes no difference to me. Anything else?"

Palmer was nothing if not to the point.

"I just want to get through the thirty, sir. I don't know if my luck will hold beyond that."

That was the heart of it.

He wasn't humble. He knew he was a good pilot, but that was only part of what brought him and his crew home every night. Each operation was a gamble. A toss of a coin. Heads they come home, tails they didn't. His run of heads was good until now, but sooner or later the coin would land on the other side. He only wanted to throw that coin eight more times.

"It's more than luck on your side. I can see from your records that you are a good pilot, Thomas. One of the best. In fact, your previous CO has recommended that you talk to Bennett about Eight Group."

He nodded at the compliment. The "Number Eights" were elite squadrons that led the missions over Germany. These pathfinders marked the targets with red and green flares before the rest of the fleet came in. Nothing less than perfection was expected of the crews. If they missed the target once, they were sent on their way.

But to be selected, you had to survive your first thirty operations, and then you had to have the fortitude to agree to do thirty more.

Bowles took a different tack.

"A commission won't automatically mean you have to keep flying after this tour." He sucked thoughtfully on his pipe. "But it will open up more doors for you once it's done. It's worth considering, Thomas. There is life after this war."

But that was exactly his point.

For many, there wasn't.

"You'd be a fool to turn this down, Thomas, but it's your decision. I want an answer either way in ten days' time. Dismissed. Close the door on your way out."

RAF Bottesford, Lincolnshire, England
2 December 1942, 4:55 p.m.

Maggie hated crying. It made her head hurt—and her eyes were so heavy and achy afterward that all she wanted to do was sleep. She avoided it wherever possible and certainly never cried in public if she could help it. Besides, she told herself she wouldn't cry any more tears now she was back at work.

Most of her letters since she had been back at work had been from Rosie. Her sister poured out her sadness and frustration at their father in lengthy epistles. But when Maggie saw this letter, in an elegant copperplate with a mysterious return address, curiosity had compelled her to tear into it before she was out of the post room door. Once she realized what the letter was, she should have stopped reading and taken it to her own room or, at least the Map Room, where the only person she'd see was Grace. It was a small mercy when the tears welled up that she thought to step away from the path and lean against the side wall of the building.

Dear Maggie,

This is a letter that no sister wants to write, more so because I know that things didn't end well between you and Ralph. I don't know how you will receive this news, but I have to tell you, or I am afraid no one will.

Ralph has been killed in action. We got the telegram last week. "Over the Channel, in service to his country," it said. Mother and Father are desperate with grief.

It was lovely getting to know you at the beach that day, and I am sorry for the way he treated you in the end.

I hope that you receive this knowing that I meant to let you know this news out of kindness. I do hope we can meet again sometime.

Sincerely,

Annie Archer

PS: I just read the letter you sent him about your mother. Again, I am so sorry.

Maggie didn't think that she could feel so many conflicting things all at once.

She wanted to be angry at him still. She wanted to be happy he was gone. But she couldn't keep the tears from falling. A sob escaped before she could stop it.

She balled the letter in her fist and shoved it into the deep pocket of her overcoat. She needed to get out of this public space before someone she knew came along and started asking questions.

Her feet fled toward the WAAF accommodations before her brain had time to check the way was clear, ploughing her straight into a solid chest clad in a smoke-scented blue uniform wrapped in an Irvine jacket.

"Steady on!" the head above the jacket said while the feet below it took a step back.

She looked up into a pair of gray-blue eyes. Alec Thomas. The pilot from that night in London.

The one who made her feel gooey when she daydreamed about what it would be like to step out with Clark Gable.

She gasped, partly in recognition, partly at the awful realization that her face must be tear streaked. She hastily wiped her cheeks.

"Are you all right?" He took his cap off in politeness, his features filled with concern.

"Yes, yes. I'm sorry. Bad news from home, is all. Excuse me." She pushed past. Why did it have to be him?

Maybe he wouldn't recognize her. He'd obviously been as distracted as her when they'd collided. Her heart raced. Of all the times and places she could have met him again, why did it have to be now?

He caught hold of her arm as she was about to flee. "Maggie! It *is* you! Alec, remember? We met in London. You told me all pilots thought they were God's gift to women."

She winced. "Yes, I did say that." She sniffed. The mortification of that comment made her face flush. Then the thought of Ralph—the proper recipient of her harsh words, who would never hear them now—brought a lump to her throat.

"Give me a chance to prove it's not true. Let me walk with you to wherever you are going."

If she tried to make a sound, a sob would escape, so she wordlessly assented by glancing in the direction of the WAAF dormitories. She focused on her breathing as they walked, swallowing the lump in her throat to keep herself from acting like a weeping fool.

"I just got word that a friend died," she explained when she felt calm again. "Killed in action."

"I'm sorry." He gave her a sly sideways glance. "A pilot?"

"Of the worst kind."

He grinned. The effect was almost enough to distract her from her sorrow. But Ralph—who'd also had a rakish grin that made her insides go gooey—tumbled back into her mind.

She willed her lip not to tremble. "Thank you for your help, but I will be fine from here." She turned up the path toward the WAAF quarters, hoping he wouldn't follow.

"Will you be at the social on Friday?" he called after her.

She refused to look back.

―――⊷∞⊶―――

She slipped into the privacy of her own room and threw herself facedown on the hard bed.

Flight Officer Hillary Carver, the most senior WAAF at the aerodrome, had granted Maggie the privilege of a private room on her first night back. Known to the girls as Queen Bee, most of the WAAFs in Carver's charge thought of her as a fiercely strict matron. Maggie knew differently. Carver kept her face in an unfailingly serious expression, with her silver-flecked hair pulled back severely, exposing frown lines burrowed across her forehead. But Maggie had seen the light of kindness in Carver's eyes when she'd broken the news of Maggie's mother's death. It was there again when Maggie returned after her personal leave.

"I've missed your sensible attitude, Morrison," Carver had said. "The weather has kept the airmen grounded, and that causes havoc for me. On top of that, the girls are losing their trinkets left, right, and center. I'm looking forward to your more rational influence over the girls. You can have Bosworth's old room."

Queen Bee had given Maggie some pastoral responsibility in the past, and the private room was to augment that. Since the dormitories slept up to twenty women, Maggie relished the thought of being able to close the door on them all—even if the room itself was no bigger than a shoe box.

"What happened to Corporal Bosworth?" Maggie had used the formal title for the friend she knew as Lizzie.

"Dismissed, I'm afraid, for being PWP," Queen Bee had said.

Pregnant without permission. *Poor Lizzie*, Maggie had thought as she studied Carver's expression to find some clue about what had happened to Lizzie and her baby. She found none.

"You're a good radio operator, Morrison. Steady character but with a light touch. I do hope that this . . . sadness . . . hasn't changed that," Carver had said.

At the memory of those words, Maggie sat up on her bed, trying to make them true by wiping away the tears as she reread Annie's letter.

They'd met when Ralph had driven her all the way to Whitby for the day. She remembered how glamorous she'd felt in the car beside him. It had been a glorious summer day. The top of the borrowed Austin 7 had been down, so they'd soaked up as much sunshine as possible. She'd seen enough movies to know that she should wear a scarf to keep her hair in check, but by the time he'd parked the car at the hotel, he'd looked thoroughly tousled by the wind. She'd reached up to smooth his hair before they met with his sister, and he'd pulled her in for a kiss so intense it felt indecent.

The memory of doing such a thing in public brought on a flush of humiliation. She grabbed the wool and knitting needles and cast on stitches. She didn't count them—she just watched her hands work.

Ralph had treated them both to lunch at the Seaside Hotel, where the dining room had an expansive view of the sea. Afterward, they had strolled along the part of the promenade that wasn't blocked off. With the water so gloriously bejeweled by the sun, it was almost possible to ignore the barbed wire and concrete barricades strewn across the beach to impede any amphibious attack by the Germans.

It would have been a perfect day if it had ended there. But Ralph had expected her to go back to the hotel with him after his sister left.

Maggie's knitting grew more frantic as she remembered the conversation.

"Come on, Maggie. Don't let our trip up here be for nothing." He'd circled his arms around her waist.

"It's not for nothing! It's been a lovely day." She'd wriggled out of the embrace.

"Maggie, don't be a drag after I bought lunch and used all those petrol coupons!"

In her head now, he sounded like a sulky child, but at the time he'd befuddled her with his languid gaze and the exquisite feeling of his hands on her waist as he leaned in to kiss her again. She'd felt bad he'd gone to so much trouble. Perhaps she'd given him some kind of indication she intended to stay the night when she agreed to the trip.

So she let him take her up to a room. Let him press her body against the doorframe as he planted eager kisses on her neck. She pushed him away when he started untucking her blouse, but even then she'd had to insist several more times that she wanted to go home before he finally registered the message.

Shame brought a lump to her throat as she tried to concentrate on the stitches fast appearing in front of her.

"It's not your shame—it's his." Grace always reminded her of that when Maggie worried about it.

Afterward, he'd offered to drive her back to the aerodrome like she was some petulant child having a tantrum, even though he was quite clearly the one sulking. She'd caught the train home by herself.

The conversation had been decidedly cooler when she'd seen him again. She'd only learned his squadron was being transferred away through station scuttlebutt.

"Cheer up, Maggie. You can always write to me," he'd said as a farewell.

She did, on an almost daily basis, until she got that one letter from him in reply.

Maggie,

There's no easy way to say this, so I'll just come out with it.

I've met someone else at my new station. Another WAAF. She's a capital girl. I'm sure you'd be friends if you knew her.

I'm breaking things off between us, but please don't be mad. I don't think it would have worked out anyway.

Sorry.

Ralph

The tears that came out now were angry ones. She still felt the sting of receiving this letter, but now she was furious at Ralph for dying so she would never have the satisfaction of slapping him across the face for being an absolute, irredeemable cad.

"Pull yourself together," she told herself under her breath, glad for the privacy of this tiny, simply furnished room. She set her project on the desk with a sigh, a large piece considering the brief time she'd been knitting, but she knew tomorrow she would undo it all.

She walked to the corner basin and tap. Not quite as glamorous as her night at The Savoy with Grace, but the height of luxury around here. Even though the water from the tap was so cold it might as well have come straight from the North Pole, anything was better than traipsing outside to the hand pump every morning.

She ran some water to splash on her face so the others wouldn't ask questions about her puffy red eyes. As she looked at her reflection in the tiny mirror Grace had given her, she wondered about Lizzie Bosworth.

Had Lizzie been tricked, as Maggie knew she nearly was, into an encounter with some self-centered pilot with only one thing on his mind? Maybe she was talked into something by a too-eager young man desperate for comfort before flying out again on the thankless task of bombing Europe? Perhaps Lizzie was truly in love and went willingly?

Maggie might be in the same situation if Ralph had had his way. And that was why she would stay well away from Alec Thomas and any other handsome pilot who crossed her path. No matter what his smile did to her insides.

CHAPTER FIVE

WAAF Dormitories, RAF Bottesford
5 December 1942, 3:45 p.m.

The first trick was to pay attention. Listen to the planes as they moved overhead. Work out the difference between the number of planes on an operation and the number that routinely did practice. Count the planes out and in. Watch the people as they went about their work. Discern how their energy changed when they were preparing for one thing or when they were winding down from another.

Get friendly with the guards at the gate. Listen to their gossip and understand when they were likely to be busy or when their shifts were likely to change.

Smiling helped too. It reduced people's suspicion.

No one expected thieves to grin and whistle conspicuously as they went about their pilfering.

He'd been paying attention for the past six months. Listening, watching. Learning the rhythms of the place.

It was a setback when the latest squadron arrived and he suddenly had a whole new set of rules and habits to get used to. But now he moved around the station without turning a head. He was simply the delivery man for the local farm.

No current night ops meant that most of the WAAFs would be on day duty, so he headed toward the women's sleeping quarters.

"Morning." He tipped his hat to a pair of uniformed women as they strode past, and they didn't even give him a second glance.

He peered through the window to ensure no one was inside before pushing the door open, stepping in and surveying the room. One time he'd stealthily worked a room over while a girl was sound asleep in her bed, but today he was definitely alone.

The second trick was to make sure you didn't take anything too important—anything someone would miss almost immediately. The longer people doubted themselves, by wondering whether they had simply misplaced that thing they couldn't find, the better.

That was where his expert eye came in. He could find the things that weren't so important to their owner that they would be missed straight away but still had value enough they could fetch a decent sum or be traded or melted down.

He hurried now, careful not to disturb things about the room. The top drawer of the small bedside table next to each cot was usually where he discovered the good stuff. He would also carefully look through any suitcases tucked under the beds.

Stockings and silk underwear were valuable, but women quickly noticed they were gone. Still, he loved running his hands across their softness.

Slim pickings in here today. He pocketed only a hairbrush from a bedside stand, and a small gold locket from inside a toiletries bag. All easy to conceal.

Perhaps he'd stop by the post room and see if he could lift anything from there. You couldn't see what you were getting, but this close to Christmas there should be some interesting knickknacks sent in the post.

He heard a stirring in a nearby room. Damn.

He hadn't checked the side room to see if someone was in there. Hiding himself until she left was too risky. Besides, there was no telling how long she'd be in there, and it would look bad if he didn't return in good time from his morning food deliveries.

He crept closer toward the door of the side room, keeping to one side so he could watch her without being seen. The door was slightly ajar, enough to see a dark-haired girl in uniform, head bent in work over her small desk. He didn't think he'd seen this one around before. She paused in her work, shuffling some papers. Did she feel his presence?

He drew back his lips in a thin smile as he watched her, heart pounding with the thrill of knowing that if she turned, or if someone came in, he would be discovered.

Time to go. He didn't want to jeopardize all the opportunities he'd built for himself here.

When she did turn around, probably after feeling the skin prickle on the back of her neck, he'd be long gone.

CHAPTER SIX

Squadron Dormitories, RAF Bottesford
6 December 1942, 11:00 p.m.

"Where've you been?" Alec demanded as Chris Fisher entered with a gust of wind and rain, supporting a disheveled-looking Jimmy Hardie.

"*I've* been visiting a local farm," Fisher said, maneuvering Hardie, who couldn't seem to stand for himself, onto his pallet bed. "I don't know about Hardie, but I almost ran over him in the middle of the road on the way home."

In the air, Fisher acted as Alec's right-hand man. He sat next to Alec throughout every flight, helping him control the aircraft and troubleshooting technical problems. On the ground, he was quiet and philosophical, with a kind heart and a big crush on a local farmer's daughter.

"He reeks." Alec stood from his bed, where he'd been reading a months-old copy of *The Sydney Morning Herald*, sent over by his mother, by the light of a kerosene lamp. He felt a little light headed from the fumes as he moved closer to Hardie, now lying facedown and groaning.

"My guess is Hardie got word that the publican at Normanton sells sly grog." Fisher wrestled off Hardie's shoes.

"He's going to have a blinding headache in the morning," Jonty commented from the far corner of the room, where he ironed his uniform while wearing his undershirt.

Alec ran a hand over his face, trying to decide what to do with Hardie. Alec was their leader on the ground as much as in the air. He couldn't let this kind of behavior go unchecked, but at the same time nothing would get through to Hardie in his present state.

"Boyd," he said to one of the men looking at Hardie over his shoulder. "You're in charge of waking him up in the morning. Two buckets should do it."

Two buckets of bone-chilling cold water in the face, fresh from the hand pumps outside, at five in the morning would sober him up before the presentation parade. Alec would also allocate latrine duty to Hardie for the next two weeks.

Boyd grinned mischievously. "Aye aye, Skipper."

"Jonty," he called, "do Hardie's shirt for him. I'll do the shoes."

Under normal circumstances, Alec wouldn't let Hardie get away with this. But he'd heard the head of Bomber Command, Sir Arthur Harris, was personally recommending any lapses in discipline—particularly those that risked venereal disease—be punished by the airmen having to start their whole tour of operations again. Alec didn't know what Hardie had been up to tonight, but Alec wasn't going to start his tour over again because of Hardie's alley-cat morals.

He scooped up Hardie's muddy boots and joined Bill Davis, seated on a stool near the coal heater in the middle of the room. The light from the single bulb hanging from the ceiling was brightest there. Of all the men in his crew, Alec had most in common with Bill.

"Feels like we're back at basic training." Bill buffed the toe of his shoe.

Alec agreed. To make up for the lack of real action, the wing commander had ordered every single man and woman to be up at the crack of dawn, turned out in full, pressed uniform and polished shoes. The inertia of being sucked away from nightly operations over Germany and grounded in the Lincolnshire mud frustrated everyone. The daily parades were meant to keep routine so this kind of drunkenness didn't happen, but Hardie couldn't seem to help himself.

Dark-haired and stocky, Hardie looked like trouble personified. Although he did his job well, Alec found him unpredictable when they weren't working. Too prone to going off by himself or getting into dust-ups with the locals. Bill, on the other hand, was Hardie's opposite in every way. Not just because he looked sun bronzed, tall, and athletic. He was also reliable and dependable.

Alec had met Bill when they were new recruits back in Sydney. They hadn't talked much then and had taken two separate journeys to England. But when they'd met up again with a bit of wisdom and experience under their belts, they'd cemented their friendship. Alec enjoyed Bill's quiet, whip-smart intelligence and trusted his ability to apply it in subzero temperatures. No matter where they were in the sky, Bill could find them a way home.

"So, Fisher, what's 'visiting a local farm' code for?" Jonty asked as he wandered over with Hardie's shirt on a hanger and hooked it over the shelf that ran above their beds.

They all knew what Jonty was getting at. Fisher didn't speak much about it, but he was investing most of his free time romancing a local girl he'd met at the pub. He stood strong through the whistles and hollers his crew mates directed at him, shaking his head at them as he got to work on his own shoes next to Alec and Bill. Alec knew Fisher wouldn't give away any details, but the way he smiled as he smeared the polish on his shoes told Alec all he needed to know.

Good for him. There was precious little happiness to be had during this war, and he wouldn't begrudge Fisher for finding some. Wasn't that what he himself was chasing when he had tried to find out more information about Maggie Morrison earlier in the week? Distracting himself with the kind of happiness only a girl could provide?

"So what's her name?" he asked Fisher quietly as he rubbed in the polish.

"Lucy," Fisher grinned. "Lucy Mathis."

"Ah yes. The chatty one with blond curly hair. I remember now."

He'd been there when the two had met. The crew spent their free time on "reconnaissance," earnestly sampling the beer in every pub within driving distance of the aerodrome to find out which one was the least watered down. Lucy peppered them with questions about Australia, the thrill of flying, and every other topic in between.

Fisher grinned sheepishly and nodded.

"Good for you, Chris," Alec said. "She's a lucky girl."

For the first time in his life, Alec envied another man's foolish, lovesick smile rather than wanting to mock it.

Map Room, RAF Bottesford
7 December 1942, 2:00 p.m.

"Another day clouded in." Maggie groaned, entering the Map Room, where Grace worked.

"You might not be busy, but I haven't sat down all day! These training exercises they are planning are triple the work for me!" Grace said.

Maggie pressed her lips together, amused at the sight of her elegant, poised friend looking so harried. "Well, I'll just be in my corner. You know I don't bother you there."

She sank onto the chair she called her own, tucked behind the tall shelves. She and Grace had worked together to find this clever spot where no one at the counter could see Maggie so long as she sat still and quiet.

The bell on the counter tinkled, letting Grace know another request had come in.

"Duty calls." Grace grimaced her apology.

Maggie took her sister's latest letter from her pocket and broke the envelope seal.

Dear Maggie,

It is entirely unfair that you won't be at home this Christmas. Absolutely rotten. There's already no lights, no paper, no presents, thanks to the war. No mother. And now no you. Can't you try to get more leave?

Everything is so wretched here. Father is not himself. He haunts about the place, looking lost. I haven't seen him pick up the Bible since you left. Can you imagine that? Father without a Bible? He usually carries it about the place, tucked under his arm, ready to hold court on some theological matter if you give him the slightest opening. He's even arranged for a visiting curate to share some of his Advent services. See what I mean? Christmas is his favorite time of year. "My time to shine," he usually says.

I am writing this while listening to the wireless, because that is all he will let me do. There are Christmas carols playing, which feels a bit unfair, since I'm banned from going to any celebrations. Actually, I'm banned from going anywhere or doing anything. Clara's mother made a point of asking if I could visit for a few hours tonight. Father declined on my behalf without even asking me. He said I should stay home out of respect. That would be easier to swallow if he talked to me. Instead he barely looks at me, and lets the radio fill the silence.

If you were here, you could talk sense into him. You are his favorite, after all. Mrs. Bickham does her best to tempt him out of his study with carrot cake and ginger biscuits, but it's not the same as having you here. Or having mother to smooth things over.

I can see her chair—the very one she'd been sitting in when she died—empty, apart from a blue cushion I embroidered when I was six. She said it was her favorite, but it's so very ugly. Every time I pass it, I see her as she was on that day . . . Father won't let me sit in it in the evenings, but sometimes when he is in his study, I curl up in the chair, catch a scent of her perfume, and try to draw her memory deep inside me so I don't forget it.

Maggie stopped reading. She shared Rosie's fear about losing the details of her mother's presence in the fog of memory, and she had less to trigger the memories in her day-to-day life. Closing her eyes, she tried to bring to mind her mother's smile, her look when she puzzled something out, the expression she wore when impressed. She saw her mother pouring tea and talking with Mrs. Bickham in the kitchen. She saw her wearing the elegant blue dress with tiny red flowers she'd been laid out in.

Feeling the tears coming on, she reached into her standard-issue bag and pulled out her knitting, needles, speared through a tightly wound ball of olive-green wool. Those needles were getting more exercise than a cadet in basic training since the night she'd read Annie's letter, and Maggie needed them now to stop the tears from flowing.

She desperately wanted to be busy doing her job, but rain and clouds kept the aircraft grounded, and fewer flights meant less need for wireless operators in the control room. She ached to be doing something more than listening to prattling gossip. Or worse, talking the younger WAAFs through broken hearts that reminded her too much of her own. When she tucked herself away in the Map Room with Grace, she could knit without being interrupted. She much preferred the dusty smell of the shelves—like the pages of a book that hadn't been opened for years—to the draughty dormitory or the crowded common rooms.

The men called Grace their "map queen" because she oversaw the library of maps used for planning and navigation at the airfield.

"Not so much a queen. More like a benevolent dictator," she would say as she handed the highly classified documents over. Grace joked this job was all her father's doing, that he'd used his influence in the RAF to have her confined to the library. However, she was undeniably suited to the role. Scrupulously neat and meticulously organized, she could locate any map within seconds. She also loved the maps themselves. When she wasn't busy with requests or orders, Grace made herself a cup of tea, sat at the small desk next to a tiny electric heater, and scoured the maps for interesting places to visit.

Never once did Grace let slip information about intended targets, even though she usually knew well in advance of the aircrews. They would try to wheedle information about WingCo's plans out of her.

"You can't charm details out of me, Bill Davis. I'm the daughter of a military man. I know when to keep mum!"

How did Grace manage to say no so firmly while still being so completely charming? Maggie sometimes practiced an effortless smile with polite evasion in the mirror, but she could never do it as well as her friend.

The constant requests flustering Grace didn't bother Maggie. The small, rhythmic poking and twisting movements that kept her hands busy and calmed her mind helped her tune out the world around her. The background hum was almost relaxing, until the sound of Grace teasing an airman intruded on Maggie's thoughts like an air raid siren in the night air.

"Finished the first ones I gave you already, Bill? You're improving!"

"Say, do you know where I can find that friend of yours? The dark-haired one who shoots daggers from her eyes every time she sees me?"

Maggie's hands froze mid-stitch as she recognized Alec's voice.

"She has a name, flyboy." Maggie heard Grace sniff at him. "And if you haven't learned it yet, I don't see why I should tell you."

"Fine. I don't suppose you know if Maggie Morrison"—he leaned on the words for effect—"is going to be at the social on Friday, do you?"

Maggie held her breath, willing Grace to keep her location behind the shelves secret. Grace paused, probably waiting to see if Maggie wanted to reveal herself.

"Well now, I don't know." Maggie could hear mischief in Grace's voice. "But I'll certainly let her know you asked."

Later that evening, Maggie leaned against the wall as Grace locked the door to the Map Room after her shift. Together they headed to the wing commander's office to hand in the key.

"I can read your thoughts, Grace, and I'm not going."

"It's just a dance. I hate to see you shutting yourself up like this. I know Ralph was an absolute cad in the end, but that doesn't mean everyone here is."

"I am not even interested in finding out!" Maggie declared.

"Your feelings are just mixed up. You're angry at Ralph for treating you so badly and angry at yourself for being sad that he's dead. But you can't take that out on every man you meet from now on!"

She glared at Grace's perceptiveness.

"Not every man. Only the airmen . . . especially the pilots." She sent Grace a tight, sarcastic smile. Grace made a face back at her in response before returning the key to the WAAF on duty.

"Scissors, paper, rock," Grace said suddenly as her father's car pulled up next to the administration buildings. Martin, the driver, climbed out and walked around to open the door for her.

"What?"

"You heard me. Scissors, paper, rock. If I win, you have to go to the social. If you win, you can spend the entire evening as you wish, probably knitting like a crazed old lady."

"Are you serious? The children's game?"

"It's decided many an argument before—why not this one?" Grace said, as though it were the most reasonable thing ever.

Maggie sighed. There was no putting Grace off when she wanted something.

"All right. After three. One"—they raised and lowered their balled hands at the same time—"two, three."

Maggie extended her index and middle fingers to shape scissors, but Grace kept her hand balled up into a rock.

"Ha!" Grace was gleeful in her triumph.

Maggie rolled her eyes. "See you there!"

CHAPTER SEVEN

WAAF Dormitories, RAF Bottesford
11 December 1942; 5:30 p.m.

Maggie carefully dabbed the beetroot juice onto her lips with the corner of her handkerchief, using the mirror of a small, nearly empty compact. The look wasn't nearly as appealing as Grace's lipstick that she used in London, but it would do. Unless they were as wealthy as Grace, only girls dating US servicemen had access to proper lipstick these days, and they guarded their supply jealously. She applied a thin layer of powder, hoping to make the rest of her makeup stretch. She didn't know when she'd be able to get more.

Happy chatter and banter filled the dormitory as the girls prepared for the social.

"Has anyone seen my hairbrush?" asked Eadie Carol, one of the kitchen girls, her head popping up from beside her bed, where she was on her hands and knees looking for something.

"Honestly, Eadie, you'd lose your head if it wasn't screwed on,"

Katie Baines called from where she jostled with Agnes Clare for glimpses in the small mirror tacked to the wall.

"But that's just it. I'm sure I left it on my bedside." Eadie frowned.

"These stockings make my legs look twice their normal size!"

Every woman in the room groaned in sympathy. It was bad enough wearing thick, ugly, military-issue hosiery during the day. Having to wear it on a night out—or worse, a date—was one of the worst things about life in the WAAF.

"We're all in the same boat." Amy Snee pressed her lips together to smooth her lipstick and turned away from the mirror. She always seemed to have a steady supply of Victory Red in her handbag. "But trust me, it's not worth trying anything sneaky. We've all tried to get away with nylons or gravy browning, but Queen Bee knows and sees all!"

Maggie once tried to sneak out on a date with Ralph, wearing nylons she'd persuaded Amy to sell to her. That transgression earned latrine duty for three days in a row when Queen Bee caught her out of regulation uniform.

"May I?" Maggie indicated the mirror Amy was using. When Amy nodded, she stepped up and fixed her hair.

No reason to do more than a quick tidy. She was only going tonight because of Grace's childishness. Using hot tongs and setting clips, the way she'd done to get compliments from Ralph, would be pointless.

"Here, try this." Amy handed her a tin of styling wax. "You just need a little, but it helps all the stray hairs stay put."

She took up Amy's offer, trying not to feel intimidated, as she usually did, by Amy's worldliness. While Maggie desperately wanted to look like a Hollywood star, Amy did look like one. With beautiful eyes framed by long dark lashes, high cheekbones, and a captivating smile enhanced by the bold lipstick, Amy reminded her of Hedy Lamarr, the silver-screen starlet. Amy knew exactly how to act and what to say to the airmen to make them fall over themselves to dance with her. Every man on the station was a little bit in love with her.

Maggie had to admit, this quality made Amy a good intelligence officer. She could debrief the aircrews after their operations while distracting them from the horror of what they'd just done. As she plied out the details of what they saw as they flew over Germany, she loosened even the tightest lips with her smiles and soft words.

As Maggie rubbed the beeswax out of the tin and worked it through her hair, a sudden recollection made her hand pause mid-stroke. Once, when Mother caught Maggie counting her coins, agonizing over whether she had enough to go to the pictures as well as buy mascara, Mother had sat her down at the kitchen table for a lecture.

"You worry too much about your looks and wanting to be swept off your feet by a Hollywood hero! But the men who do the sweeping are rarely worth keeping."

Maggie knew her mother's axiom well enough to be able to recite it. But then Mother had wanted Maggie to marry her father's curate when she turned eighteen, not join the WAAF.

"Ready to go Maggie?" Agnes asked.

She threw on her overcoat, grabbed her umbrella, and followed the group out of the dormitory toward Hangar Five, grateful for drizzle rather than heavy rain. After all the work getting ready, it would be a shame to turn up looking like a drowned rat.

"Do you think you'll see your Rhett Butler tonight?"

Maggie overheard Agnes's comment to Katie as they walked behind her along the perimeter track, using torches to guide their way.

"Jonty said Alec would be here," Katie replied.

"He's so handsome." Agnes giggled. "Do you think you'll kiss him?"

"Who knows?"

From the sound of her voice, Katie was beaming from ear to ear at the possibility.

Good for Katie.

Grace shouldn't have so hastily claimed that Alec was interested in Maggie.

Not that she was jealous. He and Katie would make an attractive couple. She had the cutest, plumpest lips that formed a perfect cupid's bow, giving her an angelic look. Like a china doll. But she was almost as childish as one too.

Alec Thomas seemed just the type to hedge his bets. He probably asked after Maggie so he'd have someone to chat up if Katie didn't show. How very much like Ralph of him.

Still, as long as she didn't have to pick up the pieces when it all went wrong, she didn't care what Katie Baines did.

Hangar Five, RAF Bottesford
11 December 1942, 7:30 p.m.

"God bless the NAAFI!" Grace declared, who'd met them on the walk across to the hangar. "Where would we be without them?"

It was the Navy, Army and Air Force Institutes' job to keep up the morale of the troops. They held dances and ran canteens and clubs all over the country, just like the American Red Cross did for their servicemen. They normally used town halls for their dances, but Wing Commander Palmer had invited the NAAFI to put Hangar Five to a different use tonight.

Grace seemed to think they had done a fine job. "I will take any distraction they want to throw my way. The weather is ghastly, and if a night of dancing doesn't help us forget about it, then nothing will."

"Ladies! Can I take a photograph?" A man holding a camera with a large flashbulb approached them as they entered the hangar. "It's for the local paper."

The girls linked arms and posed just inside the entrance, laughing and blinking when the bright light of the flashbulb burst out.

"Who thought of a hangar dance in December?" Maggie rubbed the backs of her fingers against her palms and blew on her hands to keep them warm.

"I think the idea is that if everyone dances, everyone will be warm," Grace said. "Plus, there's mulled wine!"

The NAAFI had done a fine job of setting up the hangar with bunting, hanging lanterns, and sprigs of greenery. There seemed to be a lot of mistletoe about.

"It's a little early to start celebrating Christmas, isn't it?"

"I think the men had some decorative input." Grace pointed to one of the green-and-red sprigs. "My guess is they've hung it up in all the discreet and darkened places they can find."

"Because who can refuse a kiss under the mistletoe at Christmas?" Maggie caught on.

"Something like that."

Strictly speaking, fraternizing between the male and female services on an air station was strictly prohibited. The RAF and WAAF had separate dining halls, sleeping quarters, and common areas. Queen Bee was particularly keen on having the sexes separated, determined to keep everyone's focus on defeating the Germans.

"WingCo ordered this dance because the airmen are getting into all sorts of trouble with locals," Amy Snee said over her shoulder. "It's a matter of public relations more than anything. Better to provide distraction on the aerodrome so they don't go looking for it anywhere else."

Amy would know.

Maggie's fingers drummed against her thigh to the music of the seven-piece band playing on a makeshift stage on one side of the hangar. Mostly locals with a few ring-ins from the RAF, their sound filled the entire hangar and most of the countryside beyond it, lifting everyone's spirits by playing "In the Mood."

Her friends peeled away with dance partners, and Maggie gave herself a moment to let the feeling catch on.

"Care to?" Alec Thomas appeared next to her, holding out his hand.

She hesitated, frowning.

"I wouldn't normally ask someone whose face looks like thunder the way yours does, but it's freezing in here. We should do something to warm up."

She rolled her eyes and shut down that warm feeling across her middle.

"Please tell me the 'we need to do something to warm up' line doesn't work on all of the WAAFs here."

"Come on. Humor me."

She looked around for Grace. Anything to avoid those intent steel-blue eyes.

Go on, then, Grace mouthed from where she was dancing with one of Alec's friends.

Why couldn't Grace be more supportive of Maggie's ban on airmen? Maggie sighed. She wasn't a mannerless monster, so she took his hand, and they worked out the beat of the music.

"That line is surprisingly reliable," he said. "But then it is also very cold—so I'm never sure whether you WAAFs are truly affected by my magnetism or just want to be warm."

She refused to smile. "The latter."

But standing so close with his strong, confident hand on her back, she couldn't be sure that it wasn't magnetism, whatever she tried to say.

He led her through the dance so well that it felt effortless, like she was Ginger Rogers and he was Fred Astaire. Even when the music sped up, one song bleeding into another with increasing pace, it felt like a dream. When they'd danced in London, she'd been stiff and awkward. This time she let herself give in to the fantasy that she was dancing with Clark Gable.

By the time they spun back to the side of the dance floor, she was laughing with him. They ended up across the dance floor from her friends, who, she was mortified to see, were all looking her direction. She didn't need to hear them to know what they were saying.

Katie Baines looked stricken.

"Well, you're right. Dancing is a wonderful way to warm up. I feel perfectly toasty now," Maggie teased.

"What about the other ways to warm up?" He glanced up at one of the strategically placed mistletoe sprigs hanging from a winch above where they stood, then back down to her face.

Her lips, to be exact.

She recognized that look.

The one that made a flutter dance across her middle.

The one that told her she was about to be kissed.

"Well, there's your answer." She glanced back down from the mistletoe into his face as he leaned in.

"To which question?" he breathed.

"I simply wanted to warm up. I'm not affected by your charm at all. Good night, Flight Sergeant."

She took a few steps backward before turning away and pushing through the dancing couples. Her heart raced, and her cheeks flushed red.

From the dancing. Definitely not from the thought of being kissed by Alec Thomas.

A glance back at his confused face told her he'd never been so close and yet so comprehensively turned down. She smiled at the strange tingle that gave her.

"He's all yours, Katie," Maggie said as she passed her.

Katie did not need to be told twice. She hurried across the dance floor to offer what comfort she could.

"What did you say to him?" Grace asked. "He looks despondent."

"He'll get over it. I made it clear that I wasn't likely to fall for the whole charming-pilot nonsense."

"Really?"

Grace arched her eyebrow in a way Maggie knew too well. She didn't believe a word Maggie was saying.

Hardie suggested it.

He'd heard Maggie turn him down and had watched her walk away.

"You too?" Hardie said.

Hardie leaned into Alec's ear. Alec's eyes followed Maggie through the crowd of dancers, and the corners of his lips turned up. He'd never had a thing for chins, but her stubborn one, defying his every attempt at charm and held high as she strode away from him, was really quite something.

"Sorry," Alec replied, annoyed that Hardie shook him out of the magic that was Maggie Morrison.

"It's infuriating when they won't follow up a dance with a kiss, isn't it?"

He scowled at Hardie. Alec wasn't even offended at the way the dance had ended, just deeply intrigued. The electricity in their banter left him wanting more.

"Still, it's a reason for the rest of us to be optimistic. If she's turned down the famous good looks and charm of Alec Thomas, then perhaps there's hope for us lesser beings."

Talk about ruining the moment. Hardie continued to goad him. "Ah, but you think you can persuade her into your arms? I'd like to see you try!"

Alec's scowl grew deeper at Hardie's snakelike style. He opted for a joke to shake his crew mate off. "All I need is time, Hardie. Give me time."

"You have until New Year's Eve, then."

Alec didn't like the way this was going. His joking turned to irritation. "What?"

"I bet you five quid that you can't sneak a kiss from her by New Year's Eve. A willing kiss, mind you. The lady has to be fully cooperative."

Alec rolled his eyes to avoid the challenge in Hardie's.

"I don't gamble on girls, Hardie."

He should walk away. Hardie, Graves, and a few others had established the Sweetheart Sweepstakes as soon as they'd arrived at Bottesford, a sinister competition that had them competing to see how many different romantic conquests they could consolidate before the end of the year. Although, despite the name, the conquests they planned were more carnal than actually romantic. They certainly didn't sound sweet for the women involved.

"Sounds like something that can only end in trouble," Alec had said when they'd asked him to be part of the pool.

"Or disciplinary action," Jonty had added, declining.

"Or venereal disease," Bill agreed, also disassociating himself from the trio.

A bet like this wasn't quite as sinister, was it? It was just a kiss. He was as bored as the rest of them, and chasing Maggie Morrison would be a happy distraction while they were grounded. Mostly, it would be a great pleasure to relieve Hardie of his money.

"Just a kiss. And just one girl," he confirmed, not wanting to be pulled into anything more tawdry.

"Suit yourself."

With the flame of competition under him, Alec held out his hand for Hardie to shake. "You're on. It'll be too easy."

"Your cockiness will be your downfall, Thomas," Hardie said, as a gaggle of WAAFs led by the ever-smiling Katie Baines approached them.

But Alec wasn't listening. Even as he asked Katie to dance, he was thinking about exactly how he was going to get Maggie to plant her lips on his.

CHAPTER EIGHT

Outside the WAAF Mess, RAF Bottesford
12 December 1942, 7:09 a.m.

Maggie followed Queen Bee along the line of bleary-eyed women. Despite the drizzle, all stood at attention, turned out in their uniforms with their hair pinned neatly off the collar under their caps. Most willed away yawns while they stared straight ahead, waiting for Queen Bee to announce her verdict on their appearance. No one complained to her about having a presentation when it had been canceled for the men. No one dared.

The post-dance analysis had continued well into the early hours of the morning, filtering through the thin walls of the dormitories. In normal circumstances, hearing their chatter was useful. It taught her which girls were likely to get into trouble with airmen, which could give good counsel in a crisis, and which was likely to spout dubious health advice. She learned to predict who she should hand aspirin to before they began their duties the next morning. But last night the talk just irritated her, no matter how many pillows she stacked over her head to block it out.

"I kissed Alec Thomas." Katie's words had penetrated the walls and slipped under Maggie's skin.

"He's so dreamy," Agnes squealed. "What was it like?"

"*Very* good." Katie sighed for emphasis.

Before Katie could begin with the details, Maggie had flown out of her bed and flung open the door. The group gathered to hear Katie's story whipped round in surprise. The power of the stripes Maggie usually wore on her sleeves meant they all reluctantly murmured apologies and scurried to their own beds.

"You obviously didn't get kissed tonight." Katie's smugness and the little giggle it evoked in one of the others hit Maggie square in the back as she turned to leave. She couldn't tolerate that kind of comment.

Maggie had summoned all the big sisterly piousness she could and directed it right back at Katie. "You can clean the privies this week, Baines. The rest of you go to sleep, or I will move presentation to five a.m.!"

She'd warned everyone that Queen Bee was likely to be extra fussy as a warning not to let their standards slip the morning after a dance. Maggie even helped some of the girls with their hair when they'd overslept. But not Katie, who simply scowled at her in just the same way Rosie would do.

As Queen Bee inspected each woman one by one, pointing out every crease and crumple, Maggie looked up the line, trying to anticipate what Carver would criticize. Maggie couldn't let her big-sister instinct go. Each of these women was her responsibility, and she took it personally when Queen Bee found fault in them. Even though each was required to stare straight ahead, Maggie tried to warn them with her eyes if a hair was out of place or a button missing. Of course, she tried to catch these things before they got to the presentation line but figured it was better to warn them to brace against the coming wrath if she hadn't caught it in time.

As Queen Bee approached Katie, Maggie noticed a ladder in Katie's stockings, up one side of Katie's calf. Should she try to warn her? It was so small. Perhaps their superior wouldn't see. Katie raised her chin ever so slightly when Queen Bee got to her. Maggie held her breath.

"Stockings, Baines. Not good enough. Don't let me see that again."

"Yes, marm."

Maggie released the breath she'd been holding slowly when Queen Bee moved on without proclaiming any kind of punishment. Katie scowled at her as she passed.

At the end of the line, Queen Bee dismissed the others to breakfast but pulled Maggie aside.

"I saw a lot of sloppy mistakes today, Morrison. We can't let standards slip, even if this airfield is doing more dancing than flying. You are responsible for these women. It's your responsibility, your duty, to see that they are turned out properly no matter what they got up to the night before. You understand?"

Maggie fumed underneath the contrite expression she wore, thankful only that Queen Bee hadn't said this within earshot of the others. Her steps felt like sludge as she headed to the mess, no longer hungry for breakfast. Not one of dry toast and powdered egg, anyway. She shouldn't take Queen Bee's words personally. Her superior was only being extra strict as a vain attempt to keep them disciplined. But something about her words echoed her father's on the day Maggie had left home. Without thinking about where she was going, Maggie turned away from the mess while her conversation with her father bounced around her mind.

"I need you here, Meg-girl," he'd said. She picked up pace as the drizzle hardened into rain. Why did he use his special pet name for her as a manipulation? It didn't seem fair.

"I can't, Father. You know that." She'd tried to be gentle, because he'd seemed so lost. *"Rosie is here for you. And Mrs. Bickham. And a whole parish full of people who care about you, if the last few weeks are anything to go by."*

Gravel crunched under her feet, and morning cold crept up her legs like the ladder in Katie's stockings as she recalled the host of truths she had recited to him. Truths that her father would usually offer to his parishioners at times like this. That God hadn't changed just because circumstances had. That even though his world was spinning out of control, the Lord still held it firmly in his palm. The words didn't have their intended effect.

"You are the oldest, Margaret. It is your duty to look after your family. It's your responsibility. I need you at home."

She stopped, taking shelter under the eave of the infirmary building as the rain picked up. How could the roles they had played for a lifetime reverse so completely? It should be her making unreasonable demands and him spouting passages of Scripture, not the other way around! Seeing her father this way, with grief eroding what she had thought was rock-solid faith, bruised her own soul. Where had the unshakable man she knew gone?

She glanced at the gray sky, trying to judge if she should wait out the rain or make a dash back to the mess for breakfast. It showed no sign of clearing, so she rounded the corner to head back to the WAAF quarters. In the common area, she stopped in her tracks at the sight of an airman in his sports kit doing pushups. Not just any airman. The one she least wanted to see.

Alec Thomas sprang from the ground after completing his exercise.

She pivoted, retreating back around the corner and bracing against the infirmary wall so he wouldn't notice her. The sight of him in his sports kit brought to mind the screening of *It Happened One Night*, which she'd seen with Grace. Her cheeks flushed. She held her breath, expecting him to jog around the corner any moment. When he didn't, she figured it was safe to peek and make sure he was gone.

The common area was empty. She released her breath, then jumped a mile in the air when his voice came from the other direction, right next to her ear.

"Need more warming up, Corporal?"

RAF Bottesford
12 December 1942, 7:16 a.m.

Alec pressed through the cold air, pumping his legs and arms to find rhythm in his run. He couldn't sleep, and exercising in the morning chill was better than lying awake with Bill snoring in the cot next to him. Their presentation had been canceled this morning, so expecting another day clouded in, Alec took advantage of a break in the weather for some exercise.

He pumped his arms and legs faster, thinking he'd take the outer perimeter behind the sleeping quarters and officers' mess. Guilt had chased sleep away last night, but the running helped him untangle his thoughts. A bet wasn't exactly a gentlemanly reason to chase a woman. It wasn't just guilt at the bet. He had another thing on his conscience. He'd kissed Katie in a dark corner of the hangar just before the end of the evening. He cringed, shaking his head at his own stupidity.

Jonty knew Katie from the armory and had introduced her a few days ago. Hardie immediately nicknamed her "Keen Katie." She'd been fawning, and there was mistletoe above them. He'd had kissing on his brain and just let it happen. So much for his "just one girl" rule. Hardie had even asked him if he was planning on competing in the sweepstakes after all. Definitely not Alec's proudest moment.

His long strides meant he got around the perimeter track in a matter of minutes, coming to a stop near the infirmary. He threw himself on the ground, then pushed himself up on straightened arms, feeling the burn in his muscles as he bent and stretched them in pushups. Doctors had ordered him to do fifty a day after he'd recovered from bronchitis last winter. He counted them as they became harder, trying to concentrate on the numbers, not the ache in his arms. His counts appeared as condensation clouds at his mouth.

Twenty-three. Twenty-four. Twenty-five. . .

Wouldn't he be furious if someone made a bet over his sister or kissed her in a darkened corner of an airfield hangar? His mother usually sent off a letter each Monday containing seven days' worth of collected naggings. "Be sensible. Don't get killed. Remember to go to church." In the batch that had arrived last week, she'd mentioned his sister had started writing to some bloke from the US Navy and he was going to join them for Christmas this year. Alec would have to write back and tell her to make sure there was no mistletoe around.

He let his mind slip back into her letters, which included her detailed plan of the Christmas menu, the seating arrangements, and her expectations of how the day would pan out. His sister would be enlisted to help with the preparations. Reluctantly, of course. But once his aunts and cousins arrived, the kitchen would be all busyness and gossip while they worked to get the meal ready, faces flushed and flustered. Sydney weather didn't lend itself to a hot Christmas meal, but his mother insisted on all the English-style trimmings and kept the oven lit all day. The thought warmed him, even as the sky drizzled. His father would be, as usual, conspicuously absent. As a kid he'd hoped every year his father would come home on Christmas Day, arms full of presents and a heart full of repentance for the drinking that made him an unbearable bully. It never happened.

Forty-two. Forty-three. . .

Odd to be thinking about the warmth of an Australian Christmas while doing pushups in the English mud. He forced his mind back to the night before. The bet he'd made with Hardie wasn't his finest decision, but it was made now five pounds was five pounds. He had to work out exactly how he was going to win it. And he might as well have a little fun at the same time.

Forty-seven. Forty-eight. Forty-nine. . .

He scrambled to his feet when he reached fifty, wiping his hands on his sports kit. Despite the hardening drizzle, he was warm through and, now he thought about it, ravenously hungry. He jogged back toward his breakfast. Before he had taken a few strides, his attention snagged on a woman rounding the corner. He only caught a glimpse, because she ducked back around the side of the infirmary as quickly as she had appeared. But he would bet much more than five pounds it was Maggie.

No time like the present to begin winning Hardie's money.

With muscles already warm, he sprinted around the infirmary. If she had headed the other direction in order to avoid him, he'd intersect her path. In the end, he had to make a complete circle of the building in the rain. He found her pressed against the wall of the building, under the eave, like she was terrified to peek around the corner again. She was so preoccupied, she didn't even notice him.

He suppressed a smile as he slowed his pace and crept toward her. "Need more help warming up, Corporal?"

Her head snapped in his direction so fast she probably suffered whiplash. Her wide-eyed surprise gave him the most gratifying view of all the blues and golds in her irises, before she slammed her eyebrows down into a glare and pushed past him without saying a word.

"You keep running away from me!" He called after her to no avail, then huffed out a chuckle. Never in his life had he repelled a woman. It was like they were two like poles of a magnet. The harder he tried to move toward her, the harder she flung herself away.

He shook his head as he jogged towards the mess.

This might not be the easiest five pounds he'd ever won. But it was shaping up to be the most enjoyable.

CHAPTER NINE

Sergeants' Mess, RAF Bottesford
14 December 1942, 4:15 p.m.

The atmosphere in the sergeants' mess was so tense that it slapped Alec in the face as he entered. A card game held the rapt attention of the twenty or so airmen inside, even though only two were playing.

Hardie sat opposite Martin Macpherson, his stocky legs stretched out under the table. Hardie leaned confidently back in his seat. Macpherson worked in the ground crew, maintaining the aircraft. As an Irishman in England, he suffered through many jokes about the quality of his work, but Alec had no complaints about him.

Bill was able to tear his eyes away from the game long enough to catch Alec's eye. He nodded him over.

"Poker." He leaned his head close to Alec so he wouldn't distract the play. "It's ground versus air—and Hardie has two aces."

Alec didn't play poker much. The game had only become popular when the US Eighth Air Force arrived in the area. Still, two aces was usually a good thing, wasn't it?

Alec fell in with the others, crossing his arms as he concentrated on the game. He could only see Hardie's hand, and both men held their faces steady in benignly confident expressions. They faced off across a pile of coins and a few other items left on the table by desperate men who had bailed out of the game. Alec's fingers itched to add his wager to the others.

"Call," Macpherson said.

"Are you sure?" Hardie returned. "I'm going to clean you out."

"I'll take my chances." The Irishman grinned as he revealed his cards. "Straight flush."

Hardie cursed and threw down his cards. The rest of the room let out a collective breath. Some cheered, some moaned, depending on what side wagers they'd made.

Alec moved forward to get a closer look at Hardie's cards. As he did, Flight Lieutenant Bowles walked into the common room. At Alec's last posting, when one of the highest-ranking officers walked in, every single man shot to his feet and stood ramrod straight, fingertips to their foreheads in salute.

Bowles didn't insist on this but still managed to command the immediate attention of the men.

He got straight to the point. "It appears that, until the weather clears, WingCo needs to do something to save the local villagers from the attention of a couple of hundred bored airmen. So you boys just got homework."

He handed out folders filled with typed sheets of paper, explaining the plan to occupy them all with drills and exercises they could do without being in the air.

"Navigators, you're with me," Bowles said. "Gunners need to go out to the shooting-in butts."

A groan arose from the gunners when they realized they'd be working outside.

Alec glanced over the shoulders of the others. Graves had radio drills, and Hardie had some kind of technical exercise using photographs to mimic what he could see as a bomb aimer. Alec's document said he and his flight engineer needed to problem solve a series of in-flight emergency scenarios.

Alec flicked through his papers, with Fisher looking over his shoulder.

"When's the weather expected to clear, sir?" Alec asked, trying to gauge how long he'd have to put up with this theoretical work.

The BBC didn't provide forecasts since the powers-that-be declared the mysterious art of weather forecasting to be a military secret. Despite listening for the warnings to farmers about weather events that might affect food production, no one had any idea of when they might be up in the air again.

"We may very well be stuck like this until Christmas," Bowles said.

Alec groaned internally but fought against it when he saw his crew looking at him to gauge his reaction to the task at hand.

"Any decision, Thomas?" Bowles asked as the room around them broke into groups to start their exercises.

Alec glanced back at the rest of his crew, gathering round a table and opening the folders that Fisher brought to them.

"Not yet, sir."

"You're worried that any change will affect the status quo, aren't you? Worried that a change in circumstance will change your luck."

Bowles had seen straight through him. He nodded.

"Thomas, do you really think that's the way the universe works? Do you think it's our superstitious rituals that keep us from dropping out of the sky? Our stupid rabbits' feet and lucky dice? Or kissing a photo of your girl for good luck? Do you think any of that has power if God decides it's your time?"

Alec bit his tongue so as not to declare that he wasn't sure he believed in God to his commanding officer, who obviously did.

Bowles sighed. "WingCo expects an answer in the next few days. You'd be a fool to knock it back, Thomas."

He nodded again. Not in agreement, but so the flight lieutenant would know that the conversation was over.

He turned back to his waiting crew. "Back to flight school, boys."

The Bottesford Arms
16 December 1942, 7:15 p.m.

Maggie preferred to sit at the table farthest from the fire, no matter what season it was. Since she'd pulled Jonty from that burning aircraft, she'd become paranoid about flames. When she sat farther away, she could enjoy her conversation instead of constantly focusing on how near things came to the fireplace or chastising her friends for getting too close. The Bottesford Arms had two fireplaces—a large one in the main room and a smaller one to heat the side area—so she had few tables to choose from. However, as the weather grew colder, the other patrons drew their chairs toward the fire. She and Grace had adopted a table under a blacked-out window as their usual spot. Maggie felt comfortable here, even if her friend sometimes looked cold.

The pub hummed with happy chatter. Grace had told her that the publican couldn't believe his luck when Bomber Command converted nearby farmland into an airfield. He'd sensed a business opportunity and immediately modernized the facade to help make it the watering hole of choice for the airmen.

"He served in the last war, you see? He knew they'd be determined not to think about their work when they weren't on duty."

The proprietor might have made over the outside, but apart from the electric lights illuminating the interior behind the heavy blackout curtains, the inside of the pub remained firmly in the eighteenth century. Dark wood paneling lined the walls, and the carpet might well have been original, given its threadbare state. The dim lighting, along with dark nooks and alcoves, facilitated romance, as she well knew from the nights she spent here with Ralph.

"What do you know about Alec Thomas?" Maggie wondered aloud to Grace, leaning her head on her hand and watching the flames dance in the grate from this safe distance as Grace reviewed the cinema guide.

"Hmm? I thought you had sworn off pilots," Grace said without looking up from the guide.

"I have. Completely."

"But not irreversibly, it would appear, if you are seriously asking questions about Alec Thomas." Grace examined her from under raised eyebrows. "Well, let's see—he's a pilot, isn't he? So he must be on the clever side."

The pilots in Bomber Command, as well as the navigators and flight engineers, had to understand advanced mathematics, meteorology, and flight theory to be considered during recruitment.

"And I know he's a very good pilot," Grace continued. "Bill told me he's being looked at for a spot with the Number Eights, but he has to finish this tour before they'll consider him." Grace grinned. "And I know that he looks remarkably like Clark Gable."

"He appears to have the same morals as Clark Gable." Maggie huffed. "He's as arrogant as they come, and a shocking flirt to boot!"

"Yes, but doesn't that just mean he is waiting for his Carole Lombard to come along?" Grace said dreamily.

They had both obsessed over the headlines when their favorite star's wife was killed in an air crash at the beginning of the year.

"Actually, I've changed my mind. He doesn't have the same morals as Clark Gable. He has the morals of an alley cat. He tried something on me and then kissed Katie at the end of the dance," Maggie said. "The walls of the dormitory are very thin, and he's all she can talk about at night!"

"Are you sure you aren't talking about Ralph?"

"What do you mean?" Maggie asked, even though she knew what Grace was saying. Ralph was a flirt too. An outrageous one.

"Ralph broke your heart in lots of different ways with his appalling behavior. Believe it or not, I know exactly what that feels like. Exactly."

Maggie shifted in her seat under Grace's gaze. She only knew a little about Grace's heartbreak from before they'd met, but not the whole story. Grace's knowledge of the world seemed so much wider than Maggie's.

"I know that right now you see Ralph in everything and everyone. I can't say that it will go away anytime soon—especially because it's so much harder to get any kind of resolution now that he's dead. But you need to forget and move on. Not all the airmen here are as worthless as him."

"Yes, but when it comes to airmen with a hint of charisma or a whiff of good looks, I am like a moth to a flame." Maggie laughed at her own expense.

As if on cue, the energy in the room shifted. A group of airmen walked into the pub's main room and gathered around the fireplace.

She wasn't the only one who noticed.

"Katie, stop being so keen!" Agnes hissed from her position by the fire.

"Speak of the devil, and the devil appears," Grace said.

Maggie rolled her eyes. "I'm getting us drinks." She headed to the bar.

She preferred cider to beer—although it really didn't matter since everything was so watered down these days. She ordered a half pint of each. One for her and one for Grace.

"Allow me," said an Australian voice over her shoulder as she went to pay.

Alec pushed some coins across the bar to pay for her drinks, at the same time as ordering one for himself.

"Thank you" She forced politeness and a reluctant, close-lipped smile.

A moth to a flame. She should get out of here right now. Run away as fast as she could.

She drummed her fingers on the counter as the publican moved ever so slowly to pour the drinks. Stooping to lean on the bar, Alec's face was almost the same height as hers. She willed her heart not to do that jumpy thing in her chest as she tried to avoid his eyes, highlighted by the dark blue of his uniform and the ridiculous grin he shot her way.

Without being asked, and before she could stop him, Alec carried Grace's drink back to their table, where Grace was talking with Bill and Jonty in that easy way she had with everyone.

Jonty was finishing a story involving some kind of scrape with disaster.

"I hate to think what would have happened if it had been a real op, Ables. Your brain would have frozen solid," Bill added.

"I attribute my luck, hypothetical or otherwise, to meeting the lovely Maggie Morrison again." Jonty grinned, raising his glass and tipping it slightly toward her. "She is, after all, my guardian angel."

"I'll drink to that," Alec said at her elbow. "To Maggie Morrison, the good luck charm of 467 Squadron!"

The others lifted their glasses and chinked them together. Maggie rolled her eyes at them to hide her pleasure at Alec's toast.

A moth to a flame, she mouthed helplessly at Grace.

It was lucky he liked puzzles. Because that's just what Maggie was. He mustered all the charm in his reserves to use on her this evening, thinking that the cozy pub would be just the place to get to know her better without her running off.

He loved English pubs. They were softer, more civilized places than the ones at home. Serving food and sharing the space with everyone—women and children included—made them comfortable and comforting. At home, women were relegated to a "ladies lounge," and even then they couldn't buy drinks for themselves. But here, probably because of the weight of history, they were truly public places, where everyone came to eat and drink and laugh and cry and talk.

Despite the inviting atmosphere, getting Maggie to open up was hard work. Even harder when he saw Hardie smirking at them from another table, over a plate of mushy peas with a dubiously filled sausage.

"I was sorry to hear about your mother," he said after the others dispersed to their own conversations. Maggie, whose set face told him she would rather be anywhere else other than talking to him, kept glancing at the door. Now her eyes flitted back to his.

At least he had their gold-blue attention.

"How did you know?" The question sounded like an accusation.

"Jonty told me. I think Grace told him."

Her rigid posture softened. She took a sip from her still-full cider glass. "Thank you. It was very sudden." She spoke into the glass.

"You aren't spending Christmas with your family?"

"No. I took a considerable amount of leave when . . . it happened, so it's better that I stay here for Christmas. My little sister doesn't think so though."

At last, here was some common ground.

"Ah yes, little sisters. I have one of those at home too. Mine's eighteen. Yours?"

"Sixteen. She was a girl when the war began, and now she's grown up without me."

"I know the feeling, believe me. Is your father still around?"

"He's the vicar of a parish in Warwickshire. We live just outside Coventry. That's what made me want to enlist. I couldn't believe the Germans would flatten the cathedral, so I joined up on my eighteenth birthday." She clamped her mouth shut, looking like she regretted divulging that much information.

"Much more noble than me. I joined to get free flying lessons." The fleeting feeling that he was making some headway with her evaporated as the conversation fell flat.

He glanced at Hardie. This would be the hardest Alec had ever worked for a kiss. His eyes wandered to the cinema guide on the table between them. "You like the cinema?"

"Very much. They are replaying *Gone with the Wind* tonight in Grantham. Grace and I thought we might go, but we were too late for the session."

He used this opening to start a conversation that got somewhere at last. They discussed their favorite films and film stars. She seemed to know all the leading lights of Hollywood as well as their associated gossip, so he didn't have any shame admitting that Jimmy Hardie had styled the woman in the nose art of their kite on Betty Grable. "We're all mad for her."

"You and every other airman in Britain," she chided, but couldn't seem to help but say more about what was clearly her favorite topic. "The cinema is my one vice. I wasn't allowed to go when I was at home because my father thought that it would rot my brain and ruin my morals. But I believe no such thing, and you could say I am making up for lost time."

"You only have one vice? That's impressive, Corporal Morrison."

"Why? What are your vices, Flight Sergeant? And for that matter, how many of them are there?"

He leaned in, enjoying her quick wit. When he won this bet, it would be sweet indeed.

"Come to the cinema with me, and I will happily show you."

She scoffed. "You are a flirt. And I'm not interested. Haven't I made that clear?"

There it was again. The flicker in her eyes, as though a light wind had blown over coals and fanned them into flame.

"Of course. You only have once vice, and I, apparently, am not it. But it's not Flight Sergeant anymore. It's Pilot Officer. Or at least it will be soon."

Making a decision that might ruin his luck in order to impress a girl was not a smart move. He knew that. But his mouth had acted before his brain.

"A commission? Well done, you! But I'm still not interested."

Still, he thought she looked impressed.

"Katie! Won't you join us?" Maggie spoke over his right shoulder.

He winced. He'd given Katie the cold shoulder after the dance, but she couldn't take his hint. She was as persistent as Maggie was reluctant. Especially now, which was doing him no favors with Maggie.

Katie beamed at him. Between the admiring gleam in her eyes and the sparkle of merriment in Maggie's, he felt unsure of his next move. He was remarkably uncomfortable.

"I'll leave you two to catch up. Pity there's no mistletoe here," Maggie said, making Katie blush and shooting a meaningful glare Alec's way.

He opened his mouth to speak—although he didn't quite know what he was going to say—when Maggie stood so quickly that he barely had time to jump to his feet. Why was she always walking off on him, leaving him gaping and, quite frankly, wanting more?

Katie encouraged his attention back to her with one of her appealing smiles. Outwardly, he appreciated that smile as much as ever. But his thoughts walked out the door of the pub with the dark-haired WAAF corporal.

WAAF Mess, RAF Bottesford
17 December 1942, 8:30 a.m.

The weather report might be a national secret these days, but Maggie didn't need it to know that the clouds would continue until the new year. Queen Bee had granted Christmas leave to almost everyone. Day by day the mess was becoming quieter as women said their goodbyes and hurried off to catch trains that would deliver them to their families.

Maggie ached to be one of them, especially after receiving another letter from Rosie pleading for her to come. Looking beyond Rosie's exaggerated descriptions, she saw the depth of her sister's pain. Maggie, at least, had distractions while she was here. Her sister had none.

She took advantage of fewer women vying to book the one telephone booth in the mess, and placed a call to her home. Given what Rosie had reported, she was hoping to catch her father in his study. Perhaps then she could do as Rosie begged and exert her big sisterly influence.

"Kenilworth 6-5-1, please." She held her breath as the operator connected her. After two rings, someone picked up. But it wasn't her father's voice on the other end of the line. It was a distinctly female one.

"This is the vicarage." Mrs. Bickham sounded like she was trying to keep her voice low.

"Mrs. Bickham! It's Maggie. I've called to speak to Father."

Mrs. Bickham had worked with their family since she was a girl. Even though Maggie was entitled to call her Harriet now, she couldn't bring herself to. The vicarage was not so big that a single woman couldn't maintain it on her own, especially with only two children to look after. Nevertheless, when Mrs. Bickham had accepted the role of housekeeper, she'd become an important part of their family. For Maggie, hearing Mrs. Bickham's voice was almost as good as hearing her mother's.

"Oh my girl, it does me good to hear your voice. But your father is asleep, I'm afraid."

"Asleep? In the middle of the day?" Maggie's heart clenched.

"I know, dear. The grief is eating at him. It's the way of it sometimes."

"Was it this way for you?" Maggie ventured into such a personal conversation in the desperate hope that Mrs. Bickham would have some solid advice. Mr. Bickham had died during the last war, when they were still newlyweds. Like many of the other women of her generation who had waved their sweethearts to their doom, Mrs. Bickham hadn't remarried. Instead, she had made a living looking after other families. She'd lived in Kenilworth all her life and had only been to London one time in all her fifty-three years. Perhaps she knew something about shutting yourself away after death.

"Not quite." Mrs. Bickham paused. "I don't suppose you can come home for Christmas, can you?"

Maggie heart tightened to breaking point at the request. "I'm so sorry. That's what I was calling to say. Is Rosie there?"

"No. I sent her to do the shopping. Thought she might like to get out for a bit. I'm making gingerbread. They were my husband's favorite. And your mother's too."

"I remember," Maggie whispered.

She could practically smell the sweet Christmas spices as she imagined Mrs. Bickham asserting herself over a batch of dough with a rolling pin. Warm and inviting, Mrs. Bickham always made sure her kitchen was a pleasant place to linger. Maggie wanted to be there now.

"We have to cherish the memories. I started making my gingerbread men at Christmas to help me remember his smile. When there is enough sugar, I decorate them with hats and coats made of icing. Your mother loved them, so this year I am making them to remember hers."

It was true. Mrs. Bickham's gingerbread men had been part of Maggie's family's Christmas for as long as she could remember. For as long as Mrs. Bickham had been with them. Each year her mother would look at the crazy, colorful icing clothes that Mrs. Bickham decorated them with and say, "You've outdone yourself, Harriet!"

"I only have currants, this year, so they look a bit naked, I'm afraid."

"I'm so sorry I can't be there." Maggie closed her eyes, fighting back the tears that came with her longing to embrace her family.

"I know, my dear. But telephone again soon. Rosie needs it. And you always bring sense with you."

CHAPTER TEN

St Mary the Virgin's Church, Bottesford
20 December 1942, 9:30 a.m.

He appreciated that some of the people in this church on the river bend took comfort in the words expelled from the imposing stone pulpit at the front of the centuries-old church, but for him it was just another chance to watch people. Pilfering what he could about their habits and mannerisms, even if he didn't pick their pockets directly.

Showing his face at church on Sunday lent him credibility on other days of the week, which was invaluable in this line of work. He sowed nods and smiles here and reaped them elsewhere.

The turnout was larger this week. Probably due to it being so close to Christmas. Even the notoriously agnostic wing commander made an appearance.

As the preacher droned on, he inspected the parishioners from his position toward the back. Lots of military hairdos, of course. Short back and sides for the men and off-the-collar styles for the women, with hats on or off, depending on gender.

He scanned them all, making judgments about how they felt depending on the posture they held.

Three rows ahead, he saw that same hairstyle he'd seen a few weeks ago when he was in the WAAF dormitory. She sat straighter now—she wasn't fixated on her writing. Impossible to tell what she was thinking from the rigidity of her shoulders, but she gave her full attention to the preacher in the pulpit. The man next to her seemed much less at ease with his surroundings.

He always made sure he made it out of the church without shaking the hand of the preacher, but once outside, he turned his collar up against the cold and looked around to see her talking to the vicar. She had warm, happy eyes.

He studied her friendly attitude to the curate. Even at this distance he could see she shared an intimacy with him that few others in the parish did. She laughed with him and placed her hand on his arm.

A dark-haired pilot stood waiting for her a little distance away. He seemed intent on the girl but no more comfortable out here than he was inside the church.

Something to keep an eye on.

Where there were romances there were often trinkets—small, valuable ones that were easily concealed. And since he knew where to find her, he'd know exactly where to look for them.

CHAPTER ELEVEN

St. Mary the Virgin's Church, Bottesford
20 December 1942, 9:30 a.m.

Alec hadn't set foot in a church for months. One of the delights of enlisting was that he didn't have to put up with his mother's nagging him about going.

He went through his entire basic training with the Royal Australian Air Force without so much as a second thought about God. He didn't doubt the existence of one, just the relevance of one to his life. The irony—that this bet had driven him straight into a pew at the local parish church—did not escape him now.

Amy Snee gave him the idea outside the WingCo's office. When Alec emerged after telling Palmer he would accept the offered commission, she bummed a light for her cigarette. He was already thinking about how he would use this new development to win his bet with Hardie, and as they talked, he turned the tables to see if he could get some intelligence out of the intelligence officer.

Amy hadn't spoken at first, just looked at him thoughtfully. "I was at school with Grace and met Maggie when we were in training together. Grace is so pious now, but she hasn't always been."

"I'm more interested in her friend."

"Her little protégé, you mean? Yes, she takes a personal interest in making sure her little friend doesn't wander off the straight and narrow the way she once did."

The sneer on Amy's face didn't suit her. But he wasn't interested in finding out more about Grace.

"Do you know what Maggie does on her days off?"

Amy raised her eyebrows as she drew on her cigarette.

"I wouldn't have thought she was your type. Too straight laced and homely."

Best not to mention the bet with Hardie. Besides, he was genuinely curious.

"Well, there's nothing those two like better than going to church. I would have thought that she would want to enjoy her freedom. But she's a vicar's daughter, and the apple doesn't fall far from the tree, I suppose. Word has it Maggie is sweet on the new vicar."

That was how he came to be sitting between Grace and Maggie in the ornate village church, listening to a sermon that had digressed from the nativity to something more general about the grace of God. Alec might not have been to church for a while, but he knew sermons were meant to be seasonal. He should be hearing about angels, shepherds, wise men, and the rest of it.

The young, curly-haired man who spoke from the pulpit had glasses so thick that they made his eyes look twice their normal size. Alec's mind continually wandered. He kept dragging it back in case Maggie brought up the sermon in conversation. For the last twenty minutes, Alec fought the good fight with his own concentration until the curate said something that seemed all too relevant to his circumstances.

"The creator of the world is pursuing each of us the way a man pursues a woman when he is interested in her. This miraculous nativity event, where His power is on full display—in His control over all aspects of creation from the virgin's body to the stars in the sky—is like the beginning of a courtship that culminates in a declaration of love."

Flowery language, but Alec shifted in his seat at the metaphor.

"So can I encourage you over this period of Advent to think about the great love story that is on display here and focus on how you will respond to Jehovah's love for and pursuit of your soul."

The preacher might have said more, but Alec didn't listen. He pondered the idea of his soul being pursued the way he pursued Maggie. Did God work that way, subtly trying to get inside your life so that when the time was right, He could step in and steal a kiss from your soul? The unsettling metaphor had its weaknesses, he supposed. He tried not to seem too relieved when the final hymn began.

Nothing delighted Maggie more than teasing Oscar Williams on her way out of church. Once her father's curate, he was her first-ever crush. Young, enthusiastic, and fresh out of seminary, he used to spend hours in deep conversation with her father about weighty theological matters. She would listen from the kitchen, trying to absorb just a fraction of their scholarly thoughts.

Her mother did everything she could to fan the spark of interest into a romance by inviting him into the family and constantly putting Oscar and Maggie in situations where they could talk. As a result, she respected him for being both kind and clever and knew him the way a sister knew a brother.

But as should have been clear to her mother, settling for the life of a vicar's wife was not what Maggie wanted. Not before she'd even seen what the other options might be. When he took on a new curacy, they'd parted as good friends. She still held warmth in her heart for Oscar.

"Margaret," he'd said the first time he shook her hand at the door of the church on her way out.

She almost snorted at his use of her formal name. He usually called her Meg.

"Reverend," she'd replied sternly, leaning on the formality to tease him.

Now it was their private joke as she left the building each Sunday, earning them both strange glances from the other parishioners.

"This is my friend from the aerodrome, Alec Thomas. And of course, you know Grace."

"Ah. A pilot, I see?" He nodded toward the wings on Alec's uniform. "Welcome. It's nice to meet you."

Oscar's eyes bounced between her face and Alec's. She could see his mind ticking, trying to work out exactly how close they were. As Alec shook hands with Oscar, she shifted uncomfortably. This was the second time she'd introduced Oscar to a pilot, and he was probably getting the wrong idea about this one.

"I've not seen you here before," she said to Alec as they walked down the path toward the road. Embarrassment made her more snippy at him than she meant to be. In truth, her heart had raced a little when Grace had asked him to sit with them. She'd resented it, but she couldn't deny it.

"Church is not my natural environment. But you seem in your element."

"Oscar Williams is the closest thing I have to an older brother. Having him here is such a comfort." she said as they approached Grace, who stood next to her car, talking with her driver.

"Actually . . ." Maggie turned to look at the vicar, still farewelling people at the vestibule. "I need to speak to him about my father. Do you mind waiting, Grace?"

Grace nodded. Maggie walked back up the path and lingered while the vicar spoke with the other parishioners filing out of the building.

"Have you spoken to Father?" she asked Oscar when everyone dispersed. "He was in a particularly bad way when I left him."

Concern colored the vicar's features as he frowned. "It is natural for him to be sad at such a sudden loss. Your mother was a very special woman, with a kind and generous heart."

Maggie wasn't going to let the threatened tears spill out in public. "I know that, and we are all aching. But he . . . he is despairing. His letters since have been despondent too. And I worry for Rosie, who is left alone with him. I am worried that he will suffocate her."

"Your father isn't a man given to violence, is he?"

"Oh, I didn't mean that! No, I am speaking metaphorically. The burden of the house has fallen on her at such a young age, and Rosie has even less of a temperament for homekeeping than I do."

Oscar nodded, his eyes soft and encouraging as always. "I will be in Coventry next week on a personal errand. I can extend my stay and check in on them if you like."

Maggie gave him a shining smile. "I would be so grateful."

"It will be my pleasure. I would like to see him. Now go away, Maggie. I am new here, and if I spend too long speaking to the pretty WAAFs in my parish, the old ladies will gossip. You know how they talk."

Her heart felt much lighter when she walked back down the path to Grace and Alec.

Above RAF Bottesford
22 December, 1942, 10:15 a.m.

They finally got in the air again just before Christmas. It wasn't an operation, but it was something to put in the logbook. The newer pilots gratefully accepted any practice they could get, even if it meant all hands had to shovel snow off the runway and line it with salt.

It felt good to be in the air, even if this kind of practice was about learning and embedding automatic responses and muscle memory. Alec concentrated on the mechanics of the plane, the numbers on the dials in front of him.

Altitude.

Fuel consumption.

Which direction was north.

He hoped that all this thinking now would mean when he had

to take evasive action he wouldn't have to think at all. Just act.

"Cleared for takeoff."

He recognized Maggie's voice in the control tower giving him permission to take off when the light at the end of the runway turned green. Her clear, professional, and non-distracting instructions came through his headset in a most distracting way.

As the aircraft surged along the runway, he and Fisher held the throttles open to lift the tail and get the massive craft off the ground. It was always easier during practice, when the Lancaster wasn't laden with thousands of pounds of bombs.

He'd done this hundreds of times in his career by now, but he could still remember the first time he flew solo. Every pilot remembered that exhilaration. The feeling of complete freedom as the aircraft lifted off the ground as well as complete control because he was the one making it do so.

Back then he flew in a sputtering Tiger Moth running up a grass runway on a training airfield a few hours' drive from Sydney. He'd looked down on the orchards and farmland as he circled the area twice, then came in for landing. The sky had been jewelish-blue, and the trees and fields below had looked golden—a world away from the gray on gray of England's winter.

The squadron flew in formation, practicing low-level maneuvers somewhere above the Peak District, enjoying the brief break in the cloud.

"Skipper to Rear Gunner—what can you see?"

"The sprogs are finding it hard to keep up, Skipper."

"Wireless Operator to Skipper—message from Squadron Leader. He says to show them how it's done."

Alec grinned.

Bowles had just given him permission to fly the plane the way he wanted to instead of the way he had to. No flak to taunt them. No night fighters to chase them. No munitions weighing down the aircraft.

He showed off by flying so low he skimmed the top of the trees. With no fear grabbing at them, all seven whooped and hollered with the exhilaration.

"Wireless Operator to Skipper—Bowles says you can quit mucking about now and head home."

"Roger that, Wireless Operator."

Alec laughed heartily as he banked, bringing the plane around in a graceful, swooping arc and heading back to their aerodrome.

On the ground, Alec filled out his logbook to record the flight in black ink. If the flight was an operation, he would have used red ink and capital letters to distinguish it in the record. He closed the log with satisfaction.

"Pub?" Bill asked.

"Definitely."

He always said yes to the pub these days, even though he was drinking less than ever. Hope that the elusive Corporal Morrison would be there kept him sober.

He scanned the room when he arrived. She wasn't among the WAAFs happily chatting with Jonty by the fireplace. But then, she never sat there, did she? But she also wasn't at her table by the blacked-out window.

He took a step to join the crowd by the warm fire but quickly pivoted when he saw Katie was among them. She didn't need any more encouragement than he'd already given her.

Bowles was at the bar ordering a meal. Something called Rabbit Hot Pot was spooned into a bowl for him by the publican's smiley daughter. It looked greyish and watery but smelled good enough for Alec to ask for the same.

"You made the right choice, Thomas," Bowles said as they sat down in the smaller of the pub's two rooms. "About the commission. What finally swayed you?"

Alec couldn't admit that after weeks of indecision, he'd accepted the commission on a whim to impress a girl. So he said the next most true thing. "I suppose I'm gambling that my skill improves my odds."

Bowles nodded. "Well, you are good—I'll give you that. That was some impressive flying today."

Alec shrugged, although he took the compliment. "Well, it's

fun when you don't have to worry about being shot out of the sky."

Bowles grinned. "It sure is."

"Oh, Alec, there you are!"

He looked up as Grace said his name. His eyes immediately flicked to see if her friend was with her. No such luck.

"Excuse me, sir, but I was hoping to speak with Alec." Grace smiled at Bowles, impeccably polite.

"Go ahead, Corporal," Bowles replied.

"Do you have plans for Christmas Day, Alec? Only if you aren't already busy. I thought perhaps you and Bill would like to spend Christmas night at my home. My brothers will be there. They're both in the RAF, but they'll butt heads with my father if I don't give them enough distraction."

"Just Bill and I?"

"Maggie will be there too."

"Well, I'm in! I know Bill isn't going to turn down your offer in favor of the fare in the mess." He grinned. "We'd love to come."

"Wonderful. Father will send a car, so be ready around three." She disappeared as quickly as she came.

Alec looked back to Bowles, who was regarding him with no small amount of amusement.

"And accepting the commission had nothing to do with impressing a girl?"

"Now why would you say that?"

CHAPTER TWELVE

Broughton House, Lincolnshire
25 December 1942, 3:25 p.m.

"Hello, ma cherie! Joyeux Noelle and Merry Christmas." Lady Elaine Deroy met Maggie and Grace outside her stately home. Tall and slender, like Grace herself, she moved with slow, careful poise. The gray flecks in her dark hair and smile lines creased around her eyes did nothing to diminish her beauty.

Grace moved toward her mother, arms outstretched, ready to greet her with the triple kiss that the French reserved for dear friends and family. First on one cheek, then the other, then the first again.

Maggie's eyes almost popped out of her head, seeing Grace's family home for the first time. The sprawling house was so big, she was surprised it wasn't requisitioned yet, like so many of the other grand houses about the country. Even without climbing the grand entry stairs and seeing inside, she could tell Broughton House would have many rooms that the War Office could convert to use as a military hospital, operational base, or barracks of some kind.

The drive itself had seemed to go on forever before the car pulled up to the house, along a tree-lined avenue, past several smaller cottages and outbuildings, before climbing a little hill to the main house.

As Grace greeted her mother, Maggie looked out over the grounds. Much of what might be rolling open fields, separated by hedgerows in happier times, was now given over to potato fields. She recalled Grace once claiming her family grew the potatoes eaten in the mess at the base. Maggie understood what she meant now, but the thought of Grace herself—or her mother, for that matter—knee deep in a potato field brought a smile to her lips. That was no doubt a job reserved for the Land Army girls billeted in the estate's other buildings.

"Is this Maggie who I hear so much of? It is lovely to meet you!" Lady Deroy's French accent only increased her warmth. "It is so lovely to have you here." She greeted Maggie with the same familiar kiss.

With the brief press of Lady Deroy's cheek to hers, Maggie felt a pang of longing for her own mother. She fought against the lump in her throat. What kind of a first impression would she make on Grace's mother if she blubbered all over her? But despite the thrill of seeing Grace's home, her heart was far away, in a little vicarage in Warwickshire.

"Now, girls, you must go and get changed out of those awful uniforms. I cannot stand them. A man in uniform is one thing, but ladies must dress properly for Christmas dinner! Grace, you will find Maggie something to wear, non?"

Grace pulled Maggie by the arm into the house. The stateliness of the entryway blurred by as Grace hauled her up the grand staircase.

"Mother doesn't like to be reminded there's a war on. Father says she is still recovering from the last one," Grace whispered as they climbed the stairs.

Maggie barely listened as she took in all the details of the portraits and landscape paintings in ornate frames lining the wall.

"She was dead against me enlisting. At Christmas she likes to pretend the world isn't upside down. Not that I mind. It's a pleasure to get out of these awful things." She indicated her stockings.

Grace flung open the door to what was obviously her bedroom. "Maggie?"

She shouldn't gawk, but she couldn't help it. Grace's bedroom was a world away from the Map Room. To think that her friend spent her days in a dank, cramped library of an air station but came home to this! Intricately detailed wallpaper with blue and gray flecks lined the walls. The curtains and duvet on her enormous bed matched. Maggie had no doubt that the sheets were made of as fine a satin as she enjoyed at The Savoy.

A ludicrously big wardrobe dominated one wall, and Grace rifled through the hangers inside, making judgments about each item her hands came across. "Too gray. Too old. Too shapeless."

After wandering around the room to marvel at the luxury, Maggie sat gently on the giant bed. She tried not to sigh at its softness as she did.

"Ha! Maybe this." Grace held out a burgundy dress toward Maggie with one eye closed, trying to assess its color against Maggie's skin.

"It's lovely," Maggie said, about to take the gown, when Grace snatched it away.

"Yes, but it's not perfect. Aha! This is it."

Grace returned the wine-colored dress and pulled out a blue-green one with a draped waist and exquisite details sewn into the shoulders. The tiny pleats and voluminous sleeves used a decadent amount of fabric given the current rationing.

"It's the perfect color for your skin."

Maggie fingered the silk, light and soft in her hands.

"Really? You'd let me borrow this?"

Grace's broad smile told her yes. "Come on, let's see it on you."

Maggie stripped down to her slip, and Grace helped her slide the dress over her head. As her friend secured it in place with several mother-of-pearl buttons at her waist, she gave a wide-eyed smile to the mirror set in the wardrobe door. Never in her life had she put on something so beautiful. Forget movie stars—she felt like a princess.

She swallowed back her fears about whether her father would approve of what she was doing. He would make some remark about her strutting about like a proud peacock. But twisting and turning to see her reflection from all angles, she didn't care. She wasn't trying to impress him tonight. She wasn't trying to impress anyone. Although if Alec liked it, then that wouldn't be so bad, would it?

The dress clung and skimmed in all the right places. Flattering, elegant, alluring without being revealing. The blue complemented her complexion, lifting her pale skin rather than making it seem sallow under her dark hair. She was ashamed to say now that the color of the uniform was the reason she'd chosen to enlist in the Women's Auxiliary Air Force. She'd thought blue would suit her more than the ugly khaki the other services wore.

She remembered the day it was issued. As a bunch of giggly new recruits at a training school in Gloucestershire, she and her friends had filed into a storeroom. Tall shelving units held piles of neatly folded uniforms, and protective helmets stacked one on top of the other next to sturdy pairs of military-issue shoes grouped by size. As they passed, a stern-looking sergeant with her hair pulled back severely looked them over from head to toe.

"Size two with shoes in size thirty-six," she'd said. Her helper selected the right items from the shelves and placed them on the desk in front of Maggie. "I am never wrong," said the sergeant, seeing Maggie's dubious look.

Apart from a few weeks of home leave, Maggie had worn the same regulation-issue clothes (including shoes and underwear) every day for the past two years.

But not tonight. She smiled at herself in Grace's mirror.

"You look gorgeous! Now go and grab some proper stockings out of the bureau over there. The shoes are in the other wardrobe." Grace waved her hand around as she spoke, indicating all the places. "Be a dear and fetch the lilac pumps for me, would you?" she said as she busied herself with undressing.

If the house and the grounds hadn't been an indication of the extreme wealth of Grace's family, the sight of an entire drawer of silk underwear and fine hosiery would have been the giveaway. Maggie had never seen so many together. Not since the war began. Even if she didn't have to wear WAAF-issued ones day in and day out, there were no stockings to be seen in the stores, as all the country's silk was being used to make parachutes.

Grace pulled and twisted her golden hair into a victory roll with speed and expertise, then set to work unpinning Maggie's braids from the back of her head and working on her hair with curling tongs.

"A bit of makeup and we're done!" She spoke like an artist about to complete a masterpiece.

After Grace dusted Maggie's face with powder, Maggie looked at her reflection in the mirror for longer than she had done at one time since joining the WAAF. The woman she saw there looked so grown up. So much more sophisticated than the girl she was when the war had begun. Surely her mother would approve of her if she could see her now, in such an elegant gown and understated makeup. Wouldn't she?

Her eyes threatened to tear up, but she wasn't going to let crying ruin her mascara. She pushed her sad thoughts of Mother aside and, glowing, followed Grace down to dinner.

The thought of a Christmas dinner that didn't come from an air station kitchen excited Alec almost as much as spending Christmas with Maggie. He'd heard rumors about the Deroy estate, and he wasn't about to pass up the chance to see it. Besides, what else did he have on this Christmas apart from losing money at poker to Hardie? Again.

"Stick to bets you can win, Alec," Bill said as they each leaned over a small basin of water toward tiny mirrors that gave them just enough of a view of their foam-covered faces to shave properly. "Hardie's too good at cards."

"Speaking of bets you think you can win, how's everything going with Corporal Morrison?" Hardie called over from where he was reading on his bed.

"Swimmingly." Alec dropped his razor in the basin and grabbed his towel to wipe the soap off his face, shooting Hardie a warning look over his towel-covered fingers. If word got out about his bet, all he would be kissing was his chances with Maggie goodbye.

At the mention of Maggie's name, Jonty piped up. "What's going on with you and Maggie Morrison? You haven't drawn her into one of Hardie's sordid schemes, have you?" He asked with narrowed eyes.

"Relax. I'm not part of Hardie's sweepstakes. Besides, nothing's happened. Yet." It stung to admit in front of Hardie when Alec had been so confident of a quick victory.

"Well, I doubt she'd be interested," Jonty said.

"Every girl is interested in Alec." Bill snorted. "It's been that way from the moment he got his wings, and it will be worse now he's got a commission."

"You got one too, Bill," Alec said. "Things might finally start looking up for you on the romance front."

Bill teased back. "I will say, despite the commission, Maggie does seem more interested in her knitting than in you, Alec. I see her at it like a mad thing in the corner of the Map Room most afternoons."

"Let's just see what the magic of Christmas brings me tonight, shall we, chaps?" He'd better find a way to kiss her soon, or he'd never live it down.

Cleanly shaved and dressed to impress, he and Bill enjoyed being chauffeur driven to Broughton House. Dark had fallen by the time they arrived, but he didn't need light to understand just how big the grounds were. A butler showed them through to a drawing room, and Grace's mother, Lady Deroy, made the introductions.

"This is my eldest, Peter." She indicated a tall man with Grace's coloring and the same athletic frame, evenly proportioned face, and broad smile as his sister. He wore an RAF uniform with pilot's wings on his chest and flight lieutenant's stripes on the sleeve above the hand he held out for Alec, then Davis, to shake.

"Good to meet you, Pilot Officer," Peter said.

His military eye had discerned Alec's new rank immediately, although hearing himself addressed that way still surprised Alec. He'd only just managed to get the new badges sewn on.

"And this is my youngest, Edward."

Lady Deroy held out her hand to a boyish-looking man standing behind Alec, next to a crackling fireplace. This brother was shyer and quieter, with more of his mother's darker coloring and gallic features.

"And I'm Olive." A peevish voice demanded his attention. He looked down to see a girl, not more than eight, insisting on an introduction.

"Alec." He held out his hand in all seriousness. "Pleased to meet you."

Lady Deroy, who paled when the child addressed one of her guests, regained her power to speak. "What did I say about being seen but not heard, Olive?"

Olive pouted, rolled her eyes, and reluctantly withdrew to a seat in the corner.

"She's an evacuee from London," Lady Deroy said with a tight-lipped smile.

The Deroys hosted graciously, offering their guests drinks from a well-stocked cart. The men fell easily into conversation about their work. Peter held the room with his tales of bravado, flying spitfires with Fighter Command. Bill and Edward had enough in common as navigators to keep their own chat going.

Alec enjoyed the camaraderie but missed seeing Maggie and Grace. He was about to ask where they were, when the pair walked through the stately doorway.

"This is better than having to see those horrible uniforms all night, is it not, gentlemen?" Grace's mother said as the pair fluttered in.

He couldn't disagree. He could barely speak.

Grace looked fine in a willowing lilac number that showed off her natural refinement, but the sight of Maggie in a spectacular shimmering dress made his jaw drop. And not just him, judging by the reaction of Grace's brothers, who tripped over each other to be introduced to her.

Unlike the uniform she usually wore, the softness and drape of this dress highlighted Maggie's slender waist and the soft curves of her hips. The color brought out the warmth in her eyes, and her features seemed softer when her hair was curled and styled to fall over one shoulder.

Right then he wanted to win his bet with Hardie more than anything else he'd ever wanted. He cleared his throat to help himself think straighter. He needed to pull himself together before he approached her.

"You scrub up well," he said when Maggie wandered over after speaking with Grace's brothers. It was the understatement of his life, but words mysteriously vanished from his mind. Still, he basked in the glow that she radiated.

She beamed at his compliment. "Congratulations on the commission."

Oh yes, tonight was definitely the night to win his bet with Hardie.

Sir Henry Deroy joined them when the bell was rung for dinner. He didn't walk so much as stride into the room, with the dignity and bearing of a military man used to commanding attention. Alec almost saluted through sheer muscle memory, such was the man's presence.

He seemed to have the same effect on his sons.

When they sat down to dinner, Maggie was at one end of the long dining table, between Peter and Sir Henry. Alec was all the way down at the other end, next to Grace's mother and the girl Olive, who took quite a shine to him. At least from here he could enjoy the view—the curl of her hair as it tumbled down her shoulders, kissing her neck as it went—even if he did find it maddening to watch her laugh and smile without being able to get near her.

"She's very pretty, isn't she?" Olive leaned over to him so Lady Deroy didn't hear her.

"Yes . . . uh, who?"

He looked down at the girl, small and scrawny but dressed in plenty of pink frills for the occasion. He narrowed his eyes at her. "You don't miss a trick, do you?"

She grinned, then shrugged. "It's not that hard. You can't stop staring at her."

Food came at just the right time.

It didn't take much to improve on the slops that they ate with dutiful stoicism in the mess hall, but in comparison the food on the table in front of them was sublime, like something out of his dreams. He didn't know how it could arrive in such delicious quantities here when the whole country was subject to the same strict rationing, but he wasn't complaining.

There was chicken *and* ham as well as potatoes that were properly roasted in drippings, not like the gummy mash served at the station. The brussels sprouts looked crispy and creamy, the carrots smelled sweet, and the gravy looked better than anything his mother could make.

Lady Deroy brought up several bottles of claret from their cellars and made sure their glasses were always full. When they moved onto their pudding, served with real brandied custard—made from eggs, not powder, he was sure of it—one of Grace's brothers spoke up.

"Mother, Alice is a marvel. Please can we take her with us back to Debden?" Peter said. "There's no food like this anywhere else in the country."

"She's been working on this since October," Grace said. "Timed the harvest of everything exactly to make sure there would be enough for a feast. She even arranged for us to register with a pig club so we could get the ham."

"Please tell your cook she's done such a wonderful job, Lady Deroy." Alec smiled at his hostess. "I don't think I could eat any more if I tried. But," he added, "if there does turn out to be more, I'll definitely try."

Conversation moved to the foods they missed this Christmas. The lack of food seemed to make the memory of it more important.

"Roast goose." Grace sighed. "Alice does it so well."

"Chook with mum's gravy," Bill said. "Not that this wasn't splendid, Lady Deroy."

"Fish and chips," Olive called out from beside him, confused when everyone chuckled.

"Gingerbread." Maggie sighed too. "Decorated properly with icing in every color imaginable. That was my mother's favorite."

Why was he so far away? If he was at her end of the table, he could take her hand and give it a sympathetic squeeze. Maybe Grace saw the way Maggie's tears threatened too, because she skillfully turned the conversation toward foods that she and her brothers ate on family holidays in Greece and Spain before the war.

"Do you remember what we ate in Mykonos?"

"Octopus and ouzo!" Edward burst out. It was one of the only things Alec heard him say all evening, but the memory of the meal lit his eyes.

Alec listened with rapt attention to stories of things that he could never imagine eating. Olives. Aubergine, whatever that was.

"It is simply wonderful to have my family together," Lady Deroy said. She didn't add, "When many families are broken beyond repair," but the look that passed over her face made it clear that she thought it.

He noticed how Maggie kept her eyes on her dinner plate as their hostess spoke.

"How close to the end of it do you think we are, Dad?" Edward asked.

They'd all had enough wine, so the formalities could be dropped.

"The developments in Russia and Africa are encouraging," he answered. Deroy, whose actions in the last war had earned him a high rank and influence in the War Office, was no doubt privy to what Churchill and his cabinet were thinking. He might even know what was coming next for them at Bomber Command.

"What do you think our next move will be, sir?" Alec asked.

"Not my place to say. But I think that it's about momentum now. Peter and his boys held them off. But you chaps in Bomber Command"—he acknowledged Alec, Bill, and Edward, who had only recently graduated from training—"will no doubt play a big part in that. So all of you will need to look lively and stay on your toes for the next little while."

His words were so grave that Alec felt sorry for dampening the mirth about the table.

"But not tonight!" Grace sang out the moment the mood of the party looked like it was on a downward trajectory. "Tonight we dance!"

———∞———

They retired to the drawing room, where the yellow wallpaper glowed gold in the light from the blazing log in the fire. Pine branches and homespun decorations—Grace said she'd made them with Olive earlier in the week—gave the sumptuous room a homey feel.

"You're such a gem for doing this, Grace," Maggie whispered as they entered. "Thank you."

"I think Alec would like to talk to you. He hasn't taken his eyes off you all evening, you know," Grace said softly.

Maggie knew it was true. Whenever she glanced his way, he met her eye with a heartfelt smile that made her giddy. Although that could have been the wine.

She made a beeline for the open space on the settee next to him. Then as she sat down, she worried that the wine from dinner made her act in an obvious way. But they'd barely spoken all evening, and he did keep looking at her.

Peter adjusted the wireless so it bubbled over with music and mirth from the BBC while they waited to hear the King's Christmas address.

"Does your family listen to the King's speech on Christmas Day?" Maggie asked.

"It's already tomorrow in Australia, so I suppose they'll be listening in the future," Alec joked.

In between Christmas carols, the broadcast featured interviews with people from far-flung places in the Commonwealth. Canada, Rhodesia, New Zealand. She studied Alec's face as he and Bill leaned in, eager to hear the whispered portrait of home.

The more she knew him, the less he looked like Clark Gable. Not that he wasn't handsome anymore. In fact, the opposite was true. Knowing him, being able to see all the emotions filter over his face as he listened, real and tangible in front of her, was more beguiling than a face on the silver screen could ever be.

She watched his jaw tighten and his face become focused on the brandy in his glass as a lifeguard from Brisbane was interviewed on the wireless about how busy he was expecting to be on Christmas Day.

What a bizarre thing to spend Christmas Day at the seashore in the sunshine!

"Is that near where you are from?" she asked once "Oh Come All Ye Faithful" began to play.

He cleared his throat. "Oh, about five hundred miles away. But much closer than here."

"It sounds wonderful. I'd like to see it someday."

"I'd like to show you."

Certain she was blushing at the thought of being swept away to a beach in Australia, the King's message couldn't have come at a better moment. The monarch began, clear through the static. No one moved.

"It is at Christmas more than at any other time that we are conscious of the dark shadow of war. Our Christmas festival today must lack many of the happy, familiar features that it has had from our childhood. We miss the actual presence of some of those nearest and dearest, without whom our family gatherings cannot be complete . . ."

Once again she willed away tears at the too-relevant words, as though the King in his palace understood her situation. Alec must have noticed, because he reached into his pocket and handed her his handkerchief with a sympathetic half smile.

"Thank you." She couldn't hear how the King praised the comradeship with the United States of America or ran through a list of heartening allied victories because all she could focus on was how lovely it would be to snuggle into his side.

"In the Pacific we watch with thrilled attention the counterstrokes of our Australian and American comrades . . ."

Alec and Bill grinned and puffed out their chests. Maggie imagined the rowdy cheers that would ripple around the mess hall at the station as Canada, New Zealand, and South Africa were mentioned by the monarch before he concluded with talk of brotherhood, victory, and a hope of justice and peace.

"Finally some music for dancing!" Grace turned up the volume after the solemnities ended and the Glenn Miller Orchestra started playing their upbeat version of "Jingle Bells."

"Dance with me, Teddy!" she said to her little brother. "Let's shake dinner down into our legs."

Replete as he must be, Edward didn't dare refuse his sister. He led her to the corner of the room that had been hastily cleared of furniture to act as a dance floor. Maggie thought that Alec was about to lean across the space between them and ask her to dance, but Peter pipped him at the post.

"How about it, Maggie?" Peter grinned, holding out his hand.

He ignored Alec's scowl and leaned in when she hesitated. "Come on! It's Christmas. You wouldn't refuse a fellow at Christmas, would you?"

Whether it was Ralph Archer, Alec Thomas, or Peter Deroy, she just couldn't refuse a pilot. Not when they were charming, attentive, and lighthearted like this. She returned Peter's grin. "Only because it's Christmas." She took his hand and let herself be led away.

Olive was quick to take her place. She offered her hand to Alec, with the kind of assertiveness and expectation that Lady Deroy would find horrifying if she was in a less merry mood.

"I'd be delighted." He took it and joined Maggie and Peter on the dance floor.

Maggie gave a full-throated laugh at the couple. Alec took this as his cue, hamming up his dancing in a pantomime that delighted Olive but also thoroughly distracted Maggie from anything Peter tried to say.

When Olive demanded a dance from Peter too, Alec held out his hand to Maggie. She took it without hesitation, happy to be pulled close as Bing Crosby crooned about wanting a white Christmas.

His dancing was more serious and sedate now. With the speed of the song so slow, they didn't need to do much more than hold each other and sway, but occasionally he spun her out and pulled her back into him. When he did, his grin was so rakish she suspected that he'd twirled her out simply to enjoy the view. She didn't mind one bit.

"You know, I've never actually had a white Christmas," Alec admitted when he spun her back in, breath tickling her ear. "I have no idea what this bloke is singing about."

She giggled, then caught her breath as she saw that look steal over his face again. That "I'm going to kiss you" look. Her heartbeat kicked up.

He wouldn't, would he? Not with all these people in the room.

Teddy Deroy tapped Alec on the shoulder, cutting in before she could find out how bold he really was.

CHAPTER THIRTEEN

St Mary the Virgin's Church, Bottesford
27 December 1942, 10:40 a.m.

*D*ear Maggie,

It sounds like you will have a rather fantastic Christmas with your friends. Swanning it up at a fancy house and eating roast chicken sounds like <u>such</u> important war work! You probably won't miss us—or Mother—at all.

Oscar came for dinner last week. Father made us celebrate Christmas, despite having ignored it until now. Mrs. Bickham had to pull a celebration together at the last minute. He put on quite the show, pretending that nothing was wrong. I was so furious. How dare he be charming for Oscar, when I can barely get a full sentence out of him!

The worst part was that his showing up reinvigorated Father's matchmaking. The only words I heard from him that day were praises of Oscar. "Such a skilled theological brain." And "such a talent, and a lovely man. His wife will be a lucky woman."

Oscar sat across the dinner table from me, staring at me with his *beady, knowing eyes. I'm afraid he bore the brunt of my anger. I spooned out the mock goose with so much force, it splashed all over him. I must remember it's more like mashed potato than actual goose.*

"Was it really that bad?" Maggie asked Oscar as he tidied the pews after a quieter-than-usual Sunday service. She'd just finished reading him Rosie's letter.

"I thought I wore the potato quiet well." His dry remark bought a reluctant smile to her face. "Although I reject the characterization of my eyes. They may be knowing, but beady? I feel like that's a bit harsh."

"Be serious, Oscar. I need to understand what's really going on. What did you see when you were there?"

He set down hymnals and turned to give her his full attention. "I saw a house of people who are reeling from grief, Maggie. I won't betray his confidence. All I will say is, your father needs to work through things in his own way."

"What do you mean by betray his confidence? Did he tell you something?"

Oscar raised his eyebrow, indicating he would say no more. She knew that expression well from when she'd tried to extract gossip about parishioners from her father.

Maggie sighed at Oscar's impervious discretion. She glanced down at the letter in her hand, skimming over Rosie's full account of the week. Apart from the dinner with Oscar, Rosie had included a heartbreaking account of trying to talk to Father in his study. He'd barely looked at her. Once during the week he'd called Rosie by their mother's name.

"I hear you week after week preaching to men who could be dead the very next day, talking about how God's love defies and defeats the grave. That they needn't fear death if they accept His salvation. And I know you learned that at his side. When I hear about his despair, his hopelessness, I worry for him, for his soul."

"Maggie." Oscar's eyes, amplified as they were in his glasses, hurt with her, filled with pity and compassion. "Your mother was a brilliant woman. They were happily married, more than many others. Right now I think he feels like part of him has died too. He is struggling, but he is looking for answers in the right place. God will honor that."

"It's all very well for you to say that he should spend his days hunting through Scripture for answers, but he is shutting us out." Maggie hadn't had a letter from him since she had returned to work. "If he never comes out of his study, he risks Rosie doing something drastic. You don't know her like I do."

Oscar went back to his work of collecting the pew bibles. Maggie followed collecting the green hymnals as she had done for her father when she was a girl. "You might want to open up to her a little about what you do all day. She obviously thinks you are living the high life here, while she is locked indoors."

"That's not fair. I signed the Official Secrets Act, you know."

"I'm sure you can talk about things in broad brush strokes. Focus less on the fun things for her sake. How was your Christmas anyway? I heard you had dinner with Grace and her family."

"Yes. It was lovely. I met both her brothers for the first time."

"So was anyone else there?"

She suddenly took a deep interest in the hymnals, trying to sound casual. "Just a few others from the airfield."

"Any pilots among them?"

She met his eyes. Rosie was right. They were both beady and knowing. "Just one. Alec. You met him the other day at church."

"Ah, yes. The one who said church was not his natural environment."

She nodded.

"Well, tell him from me that if he's at all interested in you, he better start getting comfortable in a pew."

She grinned, partly at the idea of Oscar playing the big brother and partly at the idea of Alec being interested in her.

"I don't want another Ralph Archer on my hands."

"It's all right." She matched his fond smile. "Neither do I."

RAF Bottesford
29 December 1942, 7:09 p.m.

"You coming, Thomas?" Hardie leaned his arm on the car window as he rolled by. Grave, and several others squeezed into the car with him. "We're going into Nottingham."

The weather still hadn't cleared, and WingCo was generously granting leave passes to get the men out of his hair.

"I'll pass. Don't get yourselves into any trouble."

"Relax, Alec. We're just after a bit of fun."

He knew what kind of fun they were looking for: The kind that resulted in carved notches on their bedposts and broken hearts all across Lincolnshire. They'd head to a dance hall, scope out the room, and zero in on the women most likely to head into the shadows with them.

"Do what you like. But remember, the clock's ticking, Thomas," Hardie said as he accelerated away.

Maybe he shouldn't judge too harshly. He'd done the same thing himself before this winter, when it lost all appeal to him. Now, after seeing Maggie in civvies, she was the only woman he could think about.

Christmas at Grace's house had been the highlight of the season, despite the fact that Grace's brothers ruined any chance of locking lips with Maggie. Bill had teased him mercilessly all the way back to the aerodrome after they'd said their farewells.

"'You scrub up well, Maggie!'" Bill had mimicked him in the car. "And you didn't stop staring at her all night."

Alec cringed at the memory of being such an oaf. He'd never tried so hard to impress a woman yet failed so miserably. What was worse, he had begun to lose the argument within himself that this was simply about winning money from Hardie.

"Maggie," he called as he caught sight of her at the bicycle rack. She'd finished her shift in the control tower. Her hair was pinned up, and she was wearing military blue, not that beautiful peacock color, but the memory of her at Christmas lingered. "I hope you don't mind—I was at the post room and saw that this had arrived for you. I thought I'd bring it over."

"What?" She looked at him as though he were insane. "You came all the way out here in this weather to give me this?"

He leaned his bicycle against his leg and handed her a package. It was the size of a small bundle of books but much lighter, wrapped in brown paper and secured with an economical amount of twine. He suspected from the return address that it was from her family, so he wanted to make a special delivery.

"From my sister," she confirmed.

He matched her smile. "Well, are you going to open it?"

"Now? It's freezing out here!"

"Well, Christmas has been and gone, so there's no need to wait."

She bit her lip. He'd been thinking a lot about those lips recently. Perhaps this would be the night he'd kiss them.

"All right. Let's see what it is."

He held her gloves while she removed the wrapping. Her eagerness didn't stop her from being careful to preserve the paper and twine for future use. She tucked the wrappings under her arm while her hands examined the tin they concealed.

It looked like the biscuit tin that his mother kept on the highest shelf of the kitchen when he was a child. That one held any number of treats that a young boy would risk life and limb scaling pantry shelves to access. This one looked like it had been in use for many years. Mostly blue and white, an embossed picture on the lid showed a wide-eyed child entering a sweet shop. A man with rosy cheeks and a friendly grin stood behind the counter, presumably ready to make the child's long-awaited dreams come true.

Maggie held the tin to her ear and gave it a shake. She raised her eyebrows at the sound of something bouncing around inside.

He could spend a long time getting lost in the blue of those eyes, if only she'd let him.

Pull it together, Thomas.

Sweet and fragrant, the warming smell of spice hit his nose when she opened the tin. Her breath caught in her throat when she saw the contents. "Gingerbread." She swallowed hard.

He remembered what she'd said at Christmas. "Your mother's favorite?"

"Well almost. They aren't decorated in quite the same way. See?"

Several gingerbread men decorated with tiny currants smiled at him. Someone thought to line the tin with a frugal piece of floral fabric to keep the little men safe during their trip through the Royal Mail, but several were missing arms. Another was decapitated. Still, the cook managed to make them look friendly even with sparse decorations.

"Would you like one?" she offered. "Mrs. Bickham's gingerbread is the best in all of Warwickshire."

They both took one and went to take a bite. There was a pause before they burst into laughter at how hard the biscuits were.

"Maggie, are you sure Mrs. Bickham isn't working for Gerry? I think she has a secret plan to crack all our teeth!"

Maggie laughed as she searched out the stamps on the packaging paper. As usual, the laughter lit up her face. "Oh dear, this was posted weeks ago! No wonder!"

She obviously didn't need to eat the gingerbread to appreciate the gift. She looked down, concentrating on the tin.

"Fancy a drink at the pub?"

"Thanks, but no. It's early, but I think I'll turn in," she said, her voice tight. She avoided looking at him, but even in the dim light he could see that her eyes brimmed with tears.

"I'm sorry." She sniffed, angling her face away. "I'm such a wreck. I seem to always be on the verge of tears."

Cursing himself for not having a handkerchief on hand, he reached out to touch her arm, using a considerable amount of willpower to avoid wrapping both his arms around her. Not for the sake of a bet but because he hated to see her cry. The worse part of him considered kissing her right there for the sake of distraction. The best part of him refrained. He stooped a little, trying to catch her eye so that she would know he didn't mind how much she cried.

"Can I ride with you back to the dorm?" They'd be frozen solid if they stood out here much longer.

She nodded, turning toward the bicycle rack just as light snow started to fall. She rode ahead of him, her biscuit tin stashed in the basket at the front of her bicycle. For the whole ride, he strategized how he could stop her from bolting at the end, as was her habit. But he drew a blank. When they parked their bicycles in the common area, she gave a tight smile and hurried away to the WAAF quarters. He had no other choice but to wander back to the mess and see who was interested in a game of cards.

With most of the men granted leave passes, the pickings were slim. Jonty, the only one of his crew not out on the town, steadfastly refused to wager but agreed to play cards if no money was involved. Reluctantly, Alec agreed and dealt the cards for a game of gin rummy.

"How are things going with my guardian angel?" Jonty asked.

Jonty disapproved of gambling at the best of times. He had threatened to give the game away and tell Maggie about the bet several times now. But so far, thankfully, he'd kept mum about it. To her, at least. He saved his sermons for his crew mates.

Alec spoke more openly without Hardie around. "You'll be happy to know that if things continue as they are, Hardie will be five pounds richer on New Year's Day."

One corner of Jonty's mouth, though usually lopsided, tipped up into a smile. "I'm glad to hear it. She deserves better."

Alec looked down at his hand. Three tens, a pair of queens, and a nice run of clubs. Not a bad start. If only Jonty wanted to put money on it. They sorted the cards into their melds, discarding and re-sorting them as they drew better ones.

"I am trying, you know. I spend most of my free time in the Map Room or in the pub trying to chat her up. I've even been to church, for crying out loud."

"All for the sake of five pounds?"

Alec glanced up at Jonty, whose eyes were firmly on his cards. So why did Alec's skin itch as though the man opposite was giving him a penetrating stare?

"All right. It's not just that. I like her. There. You happy?"

"Very."

Their play continued. Alec tried to concentrate, adding up the score of his hand several times, suddenly glad there was no money riding on it. His admission had distracted him more than his opponent. Jonty knocked the table with his knuckles, indicating he was about to declare his hand.

"It's just whenever I think I might be getting somewhere with her, she runs away. Literally, in some cases."

"Well, I suppose"—Jonty laid out his cards in their melds—"the only way to change that is to be someone worth running to."

CHAPTER FOURTEEN

The Blue Pig, Grantham
31 December 1942, 6:15 p.m.

They were in a pub because of Hardie's ridiculous idea that it wasn't proper protocol to turn up before interval. According to him, it was customary to keep the ladies waiting while the gentlemen took their Dutch courage.

"That's all very well when there's not a million Yanks around," Bill countered. He didn't have a sweetheart like Fisher, but Bill had more principles than some of the others. He just wanted a fighting chance. "You might not have noticed, Hardie, but women are outnumbered five to one at the moment. They do the picking and choosing, not us."

"All the more reason to take our courage at the pub first." Hardie shrugged.

Alec noticed Bill's eye roll and shared his impatience. He would prefer to meet Maggie outside the dance hall, especially since she suggested it. However, he'd ridden into Grantham with these blokes in the station's transport lorry, which stopped at the pub, so he was stuck here for the moment.

The thought of finally winning that bet at the stroke of midnight cheered him up, since he'd received a telegram from his mother this afternoon. His sister—his baby sister, who had been a skinny girl when he'd left Australia—had gone and got herself engaged. Not to a decent local chap. No, she was engaged to an American. A US Navy petty officer he'd heard about for the first time in a letter before Christmas!

Quite frankly, he was in the mood to hold any GI he saw tonight accountable for the seduction of his little sister. Not that it was actually a seduction. The telegram assured him the young man behaved entirely properly. But that did nothing to remove the scowl from his face.

"Leaving things to the eleventh hour, Thomas?" Hardie said as he sidled up beside Alec at the bar.

Just what he needed. "Leave it, Hardie."

"Not having any luck? And you were so confident in the beginning!"

Alec gritted his teeth, deepening his scowl, but the effect was lost as the bartender brought over their beers. Hardie used that as an opportunity to goad him.

"I will say that you two seem thick as thieves whenever I see you. Play your cards right tonight, and you'll get more than a kiss."

"I said, leave it." Alec hands tightened around the five glasses he was delicately balancing between his fingers, which almost resulted in catastrophe. He gave Hardie a severe glare over the round of drinks. At least Hardie knew to shut up whenever he got that look from his skipper.

"I have an announcement," Fisher said.

While Alec was at the bar, Fisher's girlfriend—the farm girl with the mischievous grins and tight blond curls—joined them.

She stood next to him now, beaming like the morning sun.

"I'm getting married."

Fisher held up her left hand for them to see the ring wrapped around her fourth finger. A thin band that resembled a flattened bicycle spoke.

"My brother made it when he realized we had no ring," Lucy said.

Fisher glowed like the sun breaking over the horizon as he looked down at her. Alec had never seen a man so smitten.

"When's the happy day?" Jonty asked.

"Valentine's Day," Lucy said. "No sense in waiting while there's a war on."

"Hear that, Thomas?" Hardie leaned over and murmured to Alec. "No sense in waiting."

Grantham Public Dance Hall
31 December 1942, 7:00 p.m.

Maggie loved visiting Grantham. Bottesford was a sweet village, but Grantham had a cinema, a teahouse, a nightclub, and a public dance hall—all her favorite amusements. However, it wasn't those things that made the town an enemy target. The factory on Springfield Road did that. It made spitfire cannons, the very ones to hold back the Nazis during the Battle of Britain.

Even in cloud-obscured moonlight, Maggie saw evidence of bomb damage all around her as she tumbled out of the car. Flanked by her friends, she glanced at the sandbags and reinforced windows. The streets damaged in the most recent air raid still weren't repaired. But the local spirit must be resilient, because the public dance hall thrummed with the energy of a New Year's Eve party.

Muffled music welcomed them from the hall within as they safely navigated the double doors that stopped light escaping the building during the blackout. The tune beckoned to her, causing her hips to sway involuntarily as it mingled with the merry chatter of her friends.

"I heard there will be a full orchestra!" Katie enthused. "And an exhibition dance."

"As long as I don't have to dance with one of you lot," Amy said.

"I don't mind who I dance with," Maggie said. "As long as I get to dance."

"Well, don't monopolize Alec Thomas." Agnes sniggered. "Other people might like to dance with him too."

She glanced at Katie, who was already making eyes at a man next to her in the coat-check line.

"I doubt I'll even be able to find him amid all these people," Maggie replied, trying not to look disappointed Alec wasn't there to greet her outside the dance hall. The attendant took her coat and gave her a blue ticket in exchange, which she tucked safely into the pocket she'd sewn into the seam of her skirt.

The skin prickling across the back of her neck made her glance to the door, expecting to see Alec walking in with that broad grin on his face and too many compliments to really be serious. He wasn't there, and the prickle turned to a shiver.

"You all right?" Amy asked. "You look like you've seen a ghost."

"It's strange, but . . ." She shook her head, unable to put her finger on what was bothering her. "We better go in."

She glanced around one more time, scanning the foyer for Alec. When she didn't see him, she followed her friends toward the happy music.

CHAPTER FIFTEEN

He didn't always work the dance hall. It was risky with so many people about. However, on New Year's Eve it was usually worth it. People were less attentive in their excitement. He hadn't yet decided what tack he would take. He could use a classic distraction to get the attendant out of the booth. But sometimes it was better to target a single mark.

From his position across the foyer, he observed the clientele as they checked their coats, for a good half hour, looking for women arriving in mink and fur. Each time a woman checked her expensive coat, he watched where she stored her ticket. Did she give the ticket to a sweetheart to keep in his pocket or slip it into her purse? After that it was a simple matter of picking the pocket or swiping the handbag. He waited until the staff in the cloakroom changed, then came back, presented the ticket, and collected the goods.

When a group of excited WAAF girls walked in, he stepped back into the shadow of his alcove. That girl again. He'd seen her around the aerodrome several times. Hardworking and usually too serious. But now she was glowing and laughing like the others here. He noticed how closely she'd paid attention to her hair and make-up. The sensibly tied plaits were gone in favor of a fashionable style, and her features were accentuated in the best way by mascara and lipstick. His breath quickened when she turned his way, but he controlled it. He couldn't afford to make mistakes here.

She slipped her cloakroom ticket into the pocket of her skirt. She would be such an easy target, but he'd already searched through most of her belongings, so he knew she was unlikely to have anything of value in her military-issue coat pockets.

Tonight, he had a bigger score in mind.

After she and her group of friends dissolved into the crowd of the dance hall, he caught sight of a tall, elegant woman with courtly energy about her movements, especially her long fingers. She wore a striking emerald coat with a black mink stole. He could see the appreciation in the cloakroom attendant's eyes as she handled both items.

Perfect.

He'd check the pockets of the emerald coat for money and trinkets, but the real prize would be the stole. Her dress, the same striking color as the coat, drew as much female attention as it did male. But not his. He kept his eye on those elegant fingers opening the clasp of a small matching purse.

Many eyes would be on her tonight—a complicating factor, but not unworkable. He'd just keep watching for an opportunity to slip that purse away from her, just for a minute while he hunted for the ticket, claimed the stole, and left the party before anyone was any the wiser.

CHAPTER SIXTEEN

The excitement of walking into a dance hall never failed to take Maggie's breath away. The faces of her friends, alight with energy, told her they all felt the same way.

The large room, which would look more like a warehouse or factory if it weren't for lights hanging from the high ceiling, was a sea of air force blue with dots of olive from the USAAF or the other British services, and splashes of civilian color. The lights provided a magical shimmering effect on the dancers below.

The joyful sound coming from the stage at the far end of the hall fueled the room. A proper big band played Glen Miller music. She swayed to the happy rhythms of "Chattanooga Choo Choo" as the dancers bobbed happily in time. There was still plenty of room to move on the floor. At midnight it would be a happy crush of people—the way a dance floor should be on New Year's Eve.

She couldn't help but scan for faces she knew. Well, one face at least, with Hollywood features and a devilish smirk atop a blue RAAF uniform. After almost bursting into tears in front of him an embarrassing number of times, she came tonight determined to show him she could be happy. She might even flirt a little. It was New Year's Eve, after all.

She glanced at the refreshments stand set up on one side of the entrance, remembering as she did the briefing Amy Snee had given the younger, newer WAAFs before they'd left the aerodrome: "Don't drink the punch if you can't handle your liquor. It's bound to be spiked on New Year's Eve. And be careful of the Yanks. They can get a bit handsy."

Amy was on the money—about the alcohol anyway. Not the Americans. Maggie had always thought their politeness was impeccable. She'd never met one she didn't automatically warm to. Still, tea was the safest beverage for the night. She sighed.

"Can't find someone?" Grace leaned in to tease her.

Maggie denied she was looking for anyone in particular. "I'm just happy. I love New Year's Eve. That's all."

Grace saw straight through her denial. "I'm sure he'll be here. If he wants to find you, he will. And if he doesn't, well, there are plenty of other willing partners."

Grace gestured to the eager-looking single men. Next to her, Agnes and several others were giving out their most encouraging smiles as they cast their glad eyes about the room, beckoning over any attention they could.

It worked.

A group of US airmen approached them. They looked fine in their olive-green jackets and smart khaki pants. When they spoke, all the girls went giggly at their accents.

"Care to dance, miss?"

A sandy-colored man with unusual green eyes, taller than her but no older, was holding out his hand to her earnestly. "My name's Caleb."

Fascinated by the drawl in his vowels, Maggie smiled broadly. Grace was already being led to the floor by one of his friends, so she took his hand.

"I'm Maggie," she told him as they glided onto the dance floor.

He arrived seconds too late to swoop in and take Maggie's hand from the boy leading her onto the dance floor. The spark of joy he felt when he recognized her dissolved into gloom as he watched her disappear into the swelling sea of dancers.

He scowled at the way she grinned at her partner. Another reason to hate the Yanks. First his sister, now Maggie.

Fisher peeled off with his fiancé. Alec wouldn't see either of them much for the rest of the evening. The others quickly found partners of their own.

"Dance with me, Alec," said an eager voice next to him.

He hadn't seen Katie approach. If he had, he might have tried avoiding her. It was his fault for kissing her that one time. Now she just wouldn't let it go. But her pretty smile, accentuated by her red lipstick, broke his glower. Dancing was better than standing on the sidelines looking like a thundercloud about to storm.

He tried to follow the same path Maggie and her partner had taken, pushing away a pang of guilt for seeking out Maggie when he should be giving his attention to Katie. But he'd arrived with the hope of holding Maggie close and ringing the new year in with a kiss. Not just for the sake of the bet with Hardie either, but because since Christmas he'd barely been able to think about anything else.

By the time the interval arrived, he still hadn't seen her. The room emptied considerably during the break as couples sought out dark corners, waiting for the music to call them back to the floor. He avoided Katie's eye, in case she was thinking she'd like to repeat their night under the mistletoe.

Couples performing an exhibition dance swanned onto the floor as the second part of the evening kicked off. Usually he liked these. Not the staid waltzes that went first, but the demonstrations of jive and rhumba that followed. They gave a chap ideas to practice. Tonight six couples whirled fast and free across the floor while the audience looked on in awe from the perimeter.

He saw her through the movement of the dancers way over on the other side of the room. She sat on the ground, watching the exhibition with Grace and Jonty. They were surrounded by USAAF airmen, which brought another scowl back to his face. Why did they have to be everywhere?

Laughter sparkled in her eyes while she watched the dance, pointing out moves and swapping comments with Grace. Even from this distance, Alec couldn't help but appreciate again the way her smile lit up her entire face, which was already glowing from the exertion of her partner's energetic moves. It made his heart rate quicken a beat, wiping away any thought of US servicemen in Sydney and what they might or might not be doing with his sister.

She finished one glass of punch while he watched, and the American handed her another, which went down just as fast.

He frowned. She was usually so temperate. Did she know just how alcoholic it was? Three or four separate mischief makers had probably emptied their hip flasks into the bowl by this time in the evening. And the Yanks had access to imported bourbon. They'd been known to bring bottles, especially for the purpose of spiking girls' drinks.

He'd sprung to the defense of his little sister once, when a bully tried to pick on her on the way home from school. The same feeling compelled him now, only a hundred times stronger.

To get the jump on everyone else, he started planning how to get to her across the dance floor when the exhibition dance ended. Should he wait until the dancers gave their bows and then make a run across the floor when it was all done? Or should he try pushing his way around the circle now?

He turned to give an excuse to Katie. But when he looked back, the dance had ended and other couples were drifting back to the floor. He made a beeline across the circle, trying to get a fix on her. But when he got to the other side, he couldn't see her anywhere.

Caleb was chatty while they danced, and she enjoyed his accent. He was from Texas, he told her, and flew fighters with the Eighth Army Air Force. He was a pilot.

Of course he was. She was a moth to a particular type of flame.

He told her the details of where he was based, but she was too busy trying not to look like she was looking for Alec to take the information in. He finally captured her attention by being an excellent dancer. Better than Jonty. Better even than Alec. She enjoyed being led around the floor so much, the set before interval flew by. The Texan version of the confident, debonair pilot turned out to be just as charming as the British and Australian versions.

By interval, she was parched. Caleb brought her a drink, and she emptied the glass, then drank a second straightaway. The room swam around her while she downed a third, and she remembered she should be drinking tea. She needed air. She wasn't going to get any in this room, crammed as it was with people shouldering her in.

She found the emergency door that, in the case of an air raid, would let the crowd inside dissipate quickly to find shelter in the cold night outside. Without saying a word to Grace, she headed for it.

In the chill of the midwinter air without her coat, she quickly came to her senses. The sliver of moon struggled to illuminate the alleyway, and what she could see seemed menaced by shadows. She leaned against the wall to steady herself, taking deep breaths.

She could just make out a couple kissing in the shadows next to the wall of the building opposite. Her heart sank when she realized exactly what usually happened in the alleys outside dance halls and how silly it was to use the side exit instead of walking out to the public foyer.

Fear prickled through her. The kind of fear that she would have been aware of earlier if she hadn't had the punch.

"Hullo, luv."

The voice from her right made her spin around.

A man, much taller and broader than her, blocked her way to

the main roadway. Her skin crawled at the lecherous tone. Even though she couldn't see his face, she knew she needed to get back to her friends. Now.

The door leading back into the hall had closed behind her, so walking around to the front of the building was the only way to get back to the safety of other people.

The man loomed across her path.

"Don't go, sweetheart." He moved in closer as she took a step backward.

"I'd really like to get back to my friends now." She tried to sound airily unaware of the precariousness of the situation, but her voice came out flat. She sidestepped so she could make her way down the alley and back to the front entrance.

He stepped out to block her.

She made another step.

So did he.

"Let me through." She hoped to distract the kissing couple. She spent enough time with airmen to know the exact tone she needed to adopt to get things done. The "I take less nonsense than your mother" tone. She tried to adopt it now, but her voice faltered.

Before she had time to react, he yanked her arm and pinned her against the wall with his large body. Maggie didn't think anyone who might catch a glimpse of them would be able to see her small frame struggling behind his. An onlooker would probably think they were another couple who had paired off for some privacy.

She went to shout something—anything—to stop what she thought was about to happen from actually happening.

Maybe if she called out, someone might hear and help. But when she tried to shout, she couldn't make a sound from her throat. Fear paralyzed her vocal chords, just the way it did in her worst nightmares.

He pressed into her, and she couldn't move.

He kissed her, rough and greedy on her rigid lips. The coarse skin of his chin dragged across her cheek. She strained to keep even the smallest distance from him. His smell, alcohol mixed with sweat and tobacco, made her retch. Somehow, that helped her regain her voice.

"Get off me!"

It was no more than a whisper, but the words themselves woke up her body to make it move. She struggled with everything she had. She went to drive her knee into his groin, but before she could make contact, he flew backward, yanked off her by one shoulder. A familiar assailant wearing olive green and khaki landed a ferocious punch on his cheek.

The shock of the punch made her attacker's defenses too slow to avoid an uppercut that felled him completely.

She sank against the wall, her legs like jelly. Without warning, her stomach churned. She turned to the side, vomiting in the alley.

In front of her things seemed to be happening fast and slow at the same time. At the first whiff of a fight, a small crowd gathered, mostly servicemen ready for a brawl. The throng caught the attention of some officials, who were keen to stop anything before it started.

Grace appeared by her side.

"Come on." She put her arm around Maggie's shoulders and pulled her inside, toward the restrooms.

With Grace's protective arms around her, Maggie realized she was trembling.

CHAPTER SEVENTEEN

It took her a good hour in the women's bathroom to compose herself, with Grace's help. Amy even joined them when she heard something was wrong. They both insisted she splash her face with water and take deep breaths to stop herself from shaking. Amy offered Maggie a cigarette, but she declined.

"I just needed some air," Maggie mumbled.

"Of course, darling," Grace said, like she was soothing a child.

"Didn't you realize the punch would be spiked?" Amy asked.

Maggie nodded. "I forgot. I was so thirsty after the dancing."

She inspected her reflection in the mirror above the sink. Only a few hours ago, she'd been at another mirror pinning her hair. A sorry, pathetic sight looked back at her now. A silly girl with blotchy cheeks and hair askew.

"I can't go back out there and face people."

"Nonsense! You are made of sterner stuff than this, Maggie Morrison." Grace handed her a lipstick crayon, Amy's signature red, to draw Maggie's smudged lips back on.

"You can't let it get to you," Amy added. "Trust me. The best thing to do is march out with your head high."

Amy had an alarming practicality, under the circumstances.

"Alec is waiting for us out the front."

"Alec?" Maggie sniffed.

"Didn't you see?" Grace said. "He and Jonty looked like they were ready to take down the whole Eighth Army Air Force."

Grace explained Alec had come looking for Maggie after interval. He'd hurried after her when he realized she went into the rear alleyway with Caleb close behind her. Whatever he saw when he got out there made him think Caleb attacked Maggie.

"Alec was like a man possessed the way he pummeled that poor boy," Amy added, clearly impressed.

What a mess. Maggie sighed. "There's nothing for it. We can't stay in here all night."

With one woman on either side, she left the restroom. Perhaps they got stares, but she didn't look up. She just focused on the fastest path through the foyer to the coat stand, where the attendant gave her a sympathetic look.

"You all right, luv?" she said.

Maggie tried her best to nod and smile.

Expelled from the dance hall, Alec, Caleb, and several others slumped miserably on the low wall outside, clearly divided along international lines. Both men jumped to their feet when they saw her.

She approached Caleb first, without looking toward Alec.

Alec had certainly let him have it. Caleb's left eye sported a darkening bruise, and he'd already cleaned up a bloody nose, if the stains down the front of his uniform were anything to go by.

"Are you okay, ma'am?"

His fat lip reminded her of a sweet bull terrier puppy fussing over his master.

"I am, thanks to you."

She glanced up to see Alec looking on sternly from where he stood a few meters away.

"I'm sorry about my friend. He got the wrong end of the stick, I'm afraid. It was sweet of you to stay."

"The boys and I are going to head back to the airfield now, but I wanted to make sure you were okay before I left."

"You're very kind." She felt awful that he had to end his night this way. It wasn't even midnight yet. Standing on her toes, she reached to kiss him on the cheek. "Thank you."

"If that's the thanks I get, you can count on me any time you need rescuing, ma'am."

Alec ran an agitated hand through his hair. He'd fought against his every instinct not to march up and pull her into his arms when she appeared. But she lingered with the Yank.

His heart sank when she kissed him goodbye.

Banished out here by burly dance-hall staff, he'd spent the last hour wondering if Maggie was hurt, his mind playing out terrible possibilities of what might be happening in the ladies' bathroom. Massaging his hand, he paced back and forth with a scowl so thick, no one would dare approach him.

When he'd thought the American was attacking her, he got in a few good whacks before landing a punch that knocked the Yank for six. He didn't realize until it was too late he was beating up Maggie's rescuer, not her attacker. In the ruckus, her real assailant had scarpered away.

Not his finest hour.

Flanked by her girlfriends, Maggie wouldn't meet his eye when she approached him.

"Are you all right, Mags?"

It was hard to tell in the dark, but she looked like she'd rearmed herself with brighter, bolder lipstick.

"Thank you," she said, "for thinking you were rescuing me, but I don't think you're going to be allowed back into the dance hall for a while."

His smile had more to do with relief than anything else. He bent his head to try and catch those eyes cast stubbornly downward.

"I should be thanking you. Gave me just the excuse I was looking for to punch a Yank."

Those cute red lips turned up at the corners.

"Why would you want to do that, Alec?" Amy lit a cigarette to ward off the cold and blew her smoke into the air. "Aren't you happy that they are here to help us out?"

"I don't like that while they are helping us out they are also helping themselves wherever they go. My sister's just become engaged to some US Navy bloke who only showed up in Sydney a few months ago. Got a telegram today."

"Alec," Grace said, "tell me you didn't come out tonight spoiling for a fight to make yourself feel better!"

He grinned. "Of course not. I thought a dance with Corporal Morrison would make me feel better. That was just icing on the cake."

Now Maggie looked up, and her smile melted him.

"I don't want to think about it anymore," she said. "It's not twelve yet, and there's plenty of time for –"

An air raid siren rang out through the winter night, cutting short her words.

Alec said what they were all thinking. "Looks like the year is going out with a bang."

―――∞―――

Public Bomb Shelter Number One, Grantham
31 December 1942; 11:05 p.m.

Cold water seeped into her shoes the moment she stepped into the half-flooded communal shelter. The air around her smelled of residual fear from the hundreds of bodies crammed in here at some point over the last four years. Given the reputation these brick shelters had for collapsing, it wasn't an ideal place to seek protection, but better than nothing.

"Trust Gerry to ruin a perfectly good evening," Grace grumbled, looking like a spoiled child as she flung herself down on the bench seat next to Bill. Urgency swelled through the air, but not panic. Everyone was too practiced at this by now, conditioned to listen for bombs or for the all-clear siren. There was nothing else for it but to wait.

They crowded in close to make room for others, illuminated by a single, flickering bulb on the ceiling. Although the shelter could fit twenty people, it filled fast, and strangers pressed up against each other in the dark. A man close to Maggie made a lewd joke about it. Bile rose in her throat, and she willed herself not to vomit again.

"Shut your mouth or I'll shut it for you," Alec said to the man with enough menace in his tone to silence the stranger. Perhaps the other man had seen at the dance hall how Alec could follow through on that threat, because the bloke didn't say another thing.

"Here. Sit down, Mags." Alec guided her to the bench and sat beside her. His dark looks deterred anyone else from bothering her. The urge to be sick subsided in the safety of Alec's closeness. She pressed her back against the brick wall to wait it out.

How long would this raid be? She never knew if it would be over and done with in half an hour or last all night. Every ear in the shelter strained to listen for the sounds of destruction above.

"What do you think they're up to?" Grace asked Bill. "There's so much cloud about, they can't possibly think they'll hit anything."

"You never know with Gerry," Bill replied. "Maybe they've developed something new, something we don't have yet, that allows them to see through clouds."

"That's the way it goes," Alec chimed in from Maggie's other side. "We work out something new and surprise them with it. Then they work out what we're doing and fight against it. They do the same to us. We're neck and neck, scrambling for an advantage."

Maggie looked down at her hands and saw that they were shaking.

"Are you all right?" Alec asked softly.

"I'm fine." She wasn't. She felt foolish to be trembling like a frightened schoolgirl.

"You don't sound very convincing."

She clasped her hands together, wishing she had her knitting to stop—or at least conceal—her quaking hands and racing mind. She tried to laugh it off. "We've all been through air raids—and much worse besides. I can't think why I'm trembling."

"Can't you?" he asked, with a new gentleness to his voice. "It's okay, Maggie. It's just a delayed reaction to . . . what happened before."

Her breathing became fast and shallow. Her hands desperately tried to find something to do—fidgeting, grabbing at her uniform, twisting each other in the hope that she could calm herself down.

"Hey." He took one of her hands and squeezed it. Not grabby, like he wanted something from her, but like he was trying to give her his own strength. It sent a current of warmth through her that stopped her from hyperventilating. It stopped her breathing altogether.

Despite the fact they were surrounded by people, the way he turned his body toward her and held her hand in his cocooned her away from everyone else. She leaned into his warmth and to see his face better in the dark. She studied every detail. The small creases next to his eyes. The depth of the almost-dimple in his right cheek when he grinned. Tonight provided plenty of new features for her to study. A graze on his cheek from his run-in with Caleb. A cut on his lip beginning to swell.

With him so close, she only needed to speak in a low murmur to be heard. She wished she could be like Amy Snee, who was flirting with an airmen a few meters away. Then Maggie wouldn't be a shaking leaf, and she'd be able to say something clever.

"Tell me about your sister. The one who just got engaged," she managed to say. Definitely not one of Amy's opening lines, judging from the surprised laugh Alec let out. But he squeezed her hand.

"Well, she's my little sister, you see. And naturally I always thought I would meet the bloke she was going to marry. Give my approval, so to speak. Maybe introduce her to one of my friends. I never dreamed I'd be over the other side of the world when she announced her engagement."

"Is it just your sister at home?"

"And my mother. My dad's not around anymore. I don't miss him, in case you're wondering."

Even in the low light, she saw the dark look that passed over his face. "Do you miss it? Your home, I mean."

"I miss the blue of the sky." He gave the answer immediately, like he'd thought about it a lot already. "It's so bright. There's nothing like it here, even in summer. England has all the green a man can want, but the sky isn't the same."

"What did you do before the war?"

"I worked for a law firm, thinking about university."

"Will you go back to it?"

"Not sure. Sorry. I wasn't aware we were playing twenty questions."

Her little laugh probably sounded like a giggle to the people around her. "Sorry. I didn't mean to ask so many."

The intensity of the questioning allowed her to quell her breathing. Her heart still raced, but for a different reason now.

She swallowed as he glanced down at her lips. She knew that if the Luftwaffe had scheduled their operation just two hours earlier, before Caleb, before the alley, she would have closed the distance between their faces with her lips on his. Instead, she dropped her gaze to their hands, to his bruised knuckles.

He took the hint and shifted back, so her senses weren't completely filled by him. Which she appreciated and loathed at the same time.

"I don't mind the questions. Really. But do I get twenty in return?" he asked.

"All right."

He screwed up his face in mock concentration. "How many sisters?"

"Just one."

"Have you always lived in the same house?"

"Since I was ten. We lived in Coventry before that."
"Why the WAAF? Why not one of the other services?"
"I thought the blue would suit me more."
"Wise choice. It looks very good on you." He watched her reaction. "Do you always blush when you get a compliment?"
"Only when I'm hiding from German bombs in darkened shelters."

They laughed together. The questions allowed easy banter. He asked her silly things to make her laugh. She asked him questions about his home and childhood, about the past and the future. Twenty for her, twenty for him, alternating between deeply personal and completely frivolous.

"What's your first memory?" she asked.
"Being dunked by a wave at the beach."
"Can you play a musical instrument?" he asked.
"My mother taught me piano."

As the questions wore on, their fingers played a game of their own. She traced his bruised knuckles with her thumb, and their fingers laced between each other in one long, conjoined caress. His touch thrilled up her arm like an electric current, so addictive. She didn't spare a thought for Grace, Bill, or anyone else nearby, likely hearing and seeing everything. Much better than knitting as a way to occupy her hands.

"Do you ever think that this is what you do? That there are people huddled together just like we are under your plane when you fly?" she whispered.

The smooth tracing of his hand on hers stopped, although he didn't let go completely. Horror at her words passed across his face and resolved in a wounded expression—as though she'd punched him.

"Never. How could I do it if I did?"

He turned away from her so that his back was pressed against the wall, his shoulder against hers, her hand in his.

"Sorry," she whispered.

What was she sorry for? For reminding him of the work he'd be doing when the sky cleared? Or for driving him away and stopping his electric caress? Both.

He squeezed her hand gently, letting her know it was okay. She leaned her head on his shoulder, enjoying the comfort of their arms touching shoulder to fingertip. Hoping he did too.

He should be thankful for the way her question ruined the mood. Her words were the bucket of cold water he needed to stop himself from acting like a selfish beast.

He wasn't trying to make good on his bet with Hardie after what she went through tonight. Still, it almost happened anyway. They were both enjoying the repartee, he was sure, with their faces so close he could easily lift his hand, cup her soft cheek, and then lean just that little bit farther to touch his lips against hers the way he'd thought about doing so many times.

Her last question instantly dissolved the momentum, like an aircraft engine stalling midflight. He wouldn't let it ruin the feeling of her hand in his or the comfort he took when she leaned her head on his shoulder.

What had she asked him? Did he think about the people in German bomb shelters when he flew over occupied territory? Did he wonder if his bombs forced people to huddle in cramped bunkers or interrupted romantic liaisons? Did he think about the fear inspired by the mechanical groan made by thousands of bombers flying overhead?

Never.

They were cities dotted on a map. Targets. Never once did he try to give faces or names or emotions to the people under his aircraft. He'd never be able to live with himself if he did.

And he still had to do it eight more times.

Bowles had told him the weather was looking up and they'd be in the air again soon. He let slip a major offensive was on the cards in the new year. Maybe that was what this German raid was about: the Nazis trying to get ahead of the game.

But they hadn't heard any explosions yet. A good thing surely. Unless, as Bill surmised before, it meant the Nazis developed some kind of new soundless weapon. Perhaps they'd silently gassed the world outside this shelter. Or maybe it was just a false alarm. The air raid on Grantham in October killed thirty people, so the town was naturally on edge. The observers who sounded the alarm might be trigger happy.

Now that he wasn't so caught up in Maggie, he could take in the various scenes around him. Next to them, Grace and Bill were laughing companionably. Amy was consolidating her reputation in the shadows with one of the airmen, if the giggles were anything to go by. Strangers were playing cards as best they could on the wire bench. Quarrels between lovers proceeded in vicious whispers. Slow and lonely sips from hip flasks warded off the cold as well as the fear.

Jonty announced New Year at midnight, and a cheer rippled through the crowd. Not as hearty as if they were warm inside a dance hall, but well intentioned.

Another year passed, another one to discover. Maybe this would be the year the war ended. Someone began singing "Auld Lang Syne" in a clear baritone, and one by one they all joined in. At the end of the song, the music continued. A cornet played the slow dance tunes that normally ended the night at the dance hall. A medley of older songs that he recognized, and newer ones he'd only heard a few times on the wireless, filled the shelter.

He wanted to lean over and kiss Maggie to welcome the year in, but neither of them moved.

"Happy New Year, Alec." She spoke so quietly he barely heard her over the music.

"Happy New Year, Maggie."

And despite it all, it was. He'd lost the bet, but the kiss would come.

They stayed like that, with Maggie's head on his shoulder, her hand in his, until the all-clear sounded.

CHAPTER EIGHTEEN

WAAF Mess, RAF Bottesford
1 January 1943, 5:30 p.m.

"Are you really going to fly planes, Maggie?"

"It's not that I wouldn't mind being able to shoot Nazis out of the sky, but no. We do all the other jobs so that the boys can be in the air."

"Will you get to meet Mr Churchill?"

"I don't think so. Not on my first day, at least."

"I'll be lonely without you, Maggie."

Maggie remembered the conversation as clearly as if it were yesterday. They'd been huddled in the dark, squeezed in under the robust Victorian oak dining table their mother had inherited on her wedding day, listening to the low thrum of planes overhead and the boom and tremble of bombs being dropped on Coventry, they later discovered. It had been the same story each night for three weeks.

Two years ago, when Maggie had left home to join the WAAF, Rosie had still held tea parties with dolls and tried to dress their cat, Pickles, in baby clothes. In Maggie's most recent visit home,

Rosie had seemed so changed. She bore her grief with poise, but it wasn't mourning that brought about the change. It was time. Time that Maggie had missed while she was away, when Rosie grew into a very attractive young woman.

Their age difference was just so much that envy flowed too easily between them. Although the details had changed over the years, the theme was constant. Maggie had resented the way her sister seemed to receive a lighter touch of discipline, and Rosie had yearned to be old enough to do the same things as Maggie.

Maggie glanced down at her half-written letter on the desk. Amid the quiet chatter of women returning to the airfield after their leave, she'd penned a pages-long description of the Christmas celebrations at the airfield, including the pantomime that both WingCo and Queen Bee had dressed up for. Perhaps she had made it sound too fun.

Did she dare go into detail about New Year's Eve? Oscar had told her to focus less on frivolous things in her correspondence. Rosie would not appreciate her description of a night on the town if she wasn't allowed to leave the house. Maybe Maggie should focus on the grimmer aspects of her evening. The almost-attack by the man in the alley or cowering in the public air-raid shelter. Let those serve as cautionary tales in case her sister got it in her head to do something stupid. But how could she write about the air-raid shelter without saying something about Alec?

A smile tweaked at her lips. She bit back a contented sigh as she recalled the dance of her fingers in his and the gentle thrill of being so close to him. That "I'm going to kiss you" look had stolen over his face several times, until she'd put her foot in it with her question about his work. Now she wished she'd closed the distance between them herself. But how could she write about that to a little sister already stewing in jealousy and grief?

"Don't you look like the cat that got the cream." Katie Baines plonked herself down on the seat opposite Maggie and leaned her elbows on the table between them, a dangerous glint in her eye. "I heard about you and Alec."

"I don't know what you mean." Maggie feigned indifference and packed up her writing supplies. Katie was the last person she wanted to speak to about Alec.

"Must be such a shock to learn that he was just cozying up to you for the sake of the bet."

"What?" Maggie's eyes locked on Katie's, unwilling to show how deeply the words had stung but knowing it was all over her face.

"Haven't you heard yet? The Sweetheart Sweepstakes, they called it."

Katie watched for her reaction. Maggie shook her head.

The dangerous glint in Katie's eye faded. "The men were tallying up points on us."

Maggie's stomach turned over. It had all been a game to him.

"Don't worry. You wouldn't have helped anyone score highly if all you did was kiss. Amy, on the other hand—"

"We didn't kiss." Maggie's words were barely whisper.

Katie rolled her eyes. "Don't be so high and mighty, Maggie. We all got stung."

She pushed to her feet, leaving Maggie staring at the blank pieces of writing paper in front of her. The only words she could think of to fill them with were accusations of her own foolishness.

Alec was Ralph all over again.

———∞———

Above RAF Bottesford
2 January 1943, 10:25 p.m.

The new year brought with it a welcome change in the weather, which meant Alec could finally fly useful operations instead of constant training. Their first operation was a nighttime mission to lay mines in the sea off the coast of France.

The job was simple: fly in low over an inlet or bay and drop mines. They floated to the surface on parachutes, then gently slipped into the drink. The genius of them was they didn't explode immediately. They waited to be triggered by enemy ships or submarines before exploding and doing their damage. Or better, kept the Germans busy trying to sweep for them, so they couldn't wreak havoc somewhere else.

No fires below, little flak from antiaircraft guns, and only the occasional fighter to fend off—this was the perfect way to ease the squadron's newer recruits into combat.

Alec and Bill worked closely to get the plane in position, and aiming was a cakewalk for Hardie. But Alec remembered the conversation that followed more than anything else about the night.

He should have noticed the cold tone in Maggie's voice when she gave him permission to land. But she was always strictly professional over the radio, so he didn't think twice about it. The rush of a successful operation, the first in two full months, seized him as he jumped from the side door of the aircraft and felt the ground under his feet.

In the cold January air, under the still-warm engines of the hulking aircraft, he saw her for the first time since they'd left the air-raid shelter on New Year's Eve. He'd been ready to meet her with a grin. Until he saw the fury in every one of her steps.

Purposeful and determined, her stride told him from afar he was in for it. When she came close enough, he could see her eyes were on fire with rage.

"You are despicable, Alec Thomas! If I were Scarlett O'Hara, I would slap right you across the face right here."

He didn't doubt it, not when he saw her fierce expression.

"I've been speaking to the others about the gambling that goes on among the airmen," she said by way of explanation.

"Gambling?" He cringed, knowing what would come next.

"Yes, specifically the bets made around New Year's Eve. What was it called again? Oh, that's right: the Sweetheart Sweepstakes. Cute."

Her tone made it clear that she thought it was anything but. This was not going to turn out well for him.

"Look, Mags, it's not what it looks like."

"Really? Because it looks like you made a bet with Hardie about whether you could get into my knickers before New Year's

Eve ended? And don't call me Mags."

"Just kiss you—I wasn't part of anything else!" He had to clarify that so she knew he wasn't a total scoundrel.

That was where he should have apologized. He knew that now. Perhaps if he'd showed more remorse right at that point, things would have turned out differently. But he was feeling the triumph of a successful operation and enjoying the attention of those eyes, golden in their fury. But no matter how many times he'd replayed the conversation differently in his mind since then, in reality he'd said the wrong thing.

"It was harmless fun. You didn't even kiss me, remember, so I lost soundly."

"Good," she scoffed.

"No it's not! I lost five pounds."

"That's an awful lot of money to bet on a kiss. How irresponsible!"

Then he made it worse. He leaned in, so close that the condensation clouds of her breath warmed his face. "Yes, but it would have been a good kiss, I'm sure of it."

That almost earned him a real slap.

"Well, now you'll never know, will you!" She stalked away, so he had to run to chase after her.

"C'mon, Maggie. Please let me make it up to you. Can I take you to the cinema? They are replaying *Gone with the Wind* at six . . ."

She turned toward him. The look of disgust she directed at him told him he'd been a fool.

"Never come near me again," she said.

"Maggie, I'm sorry!" He called after her, but it was too late.

Jonty gave him a friendly slap on the shoulder, and Hardie smirked as they walked past him toward the mess.

———∞———

"What did you think she was going to do when she found out?" Bill said a few days later as they shined their shoes by the coal heater, resting their tins of black polish on the stove to warm them.

"I wasn't thinking that far ahead."

"Like always." Bill shook his head, smearing the thick paste on his shoe before working the polish into the leather with a rag.

"What's that supposed to mean?"

"It's what you always do. You never think about the future—you just do the most expedient thing in the moment."

Alec raised his eyebrows at Bill's sudden philosophical turn. "I don't know whether you've noticed, mate, but there's a war on. There might not be a future for any of us." He spat on his shoe, using more energy than normal to add his saliva to the polish, thinning it out. But he couldn't shake Bill's assessment of his character.

"Remember when we met?" Bill asked.

"Sure. Initial training in Bradfield Park." How many years ago was it? Two? Three? Right at the beginning of air force training, before the rounds of transferring through different Empire Air Training Schools to learn and upgrade skills. Alec's movements became faster as he buffed the shoe to make it shine.

"You told me you were just there for the free flying lessons."

Alec laughed. "It was true. What can I say? I'm opportunistic, and Hitler presented me with an opportunity."

"See? Most expedient thing in the moment."

He felt like Bill was spoiling for the kind of philosophical argument Alec usually avoided, so he stayed quiet.

"Now, that's not always a bad thing," Bill continued, on a roll. "In fact, I think it makes you a great pilot, and it's certainly got us out of some scrapes in the air, but sometime or another you have to think beyond the here and now. Think about the bigger picture, not just the odds of surviving the moment."

"Mate, are you getting religious on me? Or offering me advice to get Maggie back on side?" Better to shut this conversation down than let Bill push deeper into his psyche.

"Well, she's a vicar's daughter." Bill chuckled. "Maybe both."

Alec smirked. He held his shoe between his knees and one end of the rag in each hand for the final frantic polish of the toe. He appreciated the joke, but it hit too close to home. Since chasing Maggie, he'd thought more about the future than ever before. About what he might do after this tour and who he might be with when he did it. God help him, he'd accepted the promotion to impress her, and after Christmas he'd done a few calculations about whether or not he could support a wife on his new salary. He didn't commit anything to paper, mind you, but even thinking about such things was a new development for him.

All in vain. Maggie wasn't going to have a bar of him now.

CHAPTER NINETEEN

RAF Bottesford
7 January 1943, 8:00 a.m.

"Oi, Mr Stockton!"

The new head kitchen WAAF called after him from the kitchen door as he left after his delivery. Her voice wasn't friendly.

He stopped and swung around, smile in place, as she strode out of the cookhouse. He'd put in a lot of effort with the last head cook. She was lonely and, he suspected, unused to the attention of men. It didn't take much to turn on some charm and distract her so that she forgot to count the eggs in the delivery or question a missing bunch of produce.

But this new one, with ginger hair and a face that was more freckle than skin, was more astute. She hadn't once been tricked. She wouldn't simply sign the form with a giggle the way the last one did. This one made him stand there while she counted everything, immune to any kind of friendliness he feigned.

Today she was distracted by something happening with one of

her charges in the kitchen. He used that commotion to slip away with the signed form while she was occupied.

No such luck.

"Stockton! There are two dozen eggs missing this morning!"

With her red hair and angry eyes, she was scarier than his mother in full flight. That was saying something.

"I'm catering for three thousand men and women. I don't have time to chase up missing orders. Deliver what you are required to, or I will take this to the wing commander. I'm fairly sure he'd view your shortchanging us as sedition."

"I'm sure it's a mistake, ma'am." He had to be polite, deferential even. The fact he had a naturally quiet voice helped him sound contrite, even though he felt nothing but contempt.

"It's happened too many times to be a mistake, Stockton. Don't let it happen again." She stalked back to the kitchen.

This one was wily.

He wondered where her sleeping quarters were. Maybe he could search through her things and find a weak spot to use against her. Failing that, he could plant something incriminating among her belongings and call it in to the WAAF police.

He liked that idea.

What he didn't like was the kerfuffle she raised with her loud voice. It drew too much attention to him. He'd have to get Bessie, the land girl, to do the deliveries for the next few days. They only had one land girl on the farm at the moment. His mother had applied for another two to help with this year's planting. Plump and smiley, Bessie liked the opportunity to chat up airmen, so she'd be happy to do it.

Normally, on mornings like this he would hunt around the station for trinkets. But since the cook had shouted at him, people might remember his face. He'd lose the friendly anonymity he'd strived hard to cultivate. He didn't want to risk it today.

But sometimes he didn't have to. Sometimes he didn't have to find things to steal, because they found him. Today three radio plugs—or connectors or something he didn't know the use of but that looked small and solid—sat on the seat of a transport lorry. The vehicle caught his eye because the door hung open.

Maybe the plugs were forgotten. He glanced around for anyone who might be coming to claim them.

No one stood nearby.

It was easy to swipe them into his pocket without being seen. He might not know what they were, but they would be useful to someone, and that was all he needed.

CHAPTER TWENTY

Above RAF Bottesford
23 January 1943, 2:25 p.m.

Almost every time he flew, her voice filled his radio communications headset, giving him permission to take off with the rest of the squadron and welcoming him back to the airfield. But he never detected a flicker of feeling in it. Just flat, professional instructions.

"Clear for takeoff, M Mother," she said today, using their aircraft's common name to give them permission to take off for their night flying test.

Despite the serial number made up of five numbers and letters written on its side, they identified each Lancaster in the squadron by a letter of the alphabet and the corresponding term from the phonetic alphabet. Most of the crews adopted a single aircraft as their own, even though there was nothing official to say they always had to fly the same one. The seven of them were part of the machine for the long hours in the air and inevitably formed a bond with their kite—one that they couldn't explain and that their girlfriends would definitely scoff at.

Theirs was called M Mother.

They'd heard rumors they would soon be forced to rename her Mike, to match the phonetic alphabet the USAAF used.

"It doesn't sit right," Hardie had said. "Kites are female, after all."

"I don't think the brass mind what we call her, as long as everyone agrees," Alec had noted. "We'll just keep M Mother. As long as the ground crew and control tower agree, it should be fine."

"Or," Jonty had said, "we rename her altogether. Give her a *lucky* name to keep Gerry at bay."

Alec had known from the glint in Jonty's eyes exactly which name he had in mind.

They'd cleared the change with the ground crew and most of the other radio staff. Alec had tried like the blazes to approach Maggie about it personally. Out of professional courtesy, not as an excuse to seek her out. But she wouldn't let him anywhere near her.

He tried to send Jonty in to patch things up with her. Jonty confirmed she was avoiding all of them, so they hadn't gotten around to breaking the news to her that they'd renamed the kite. Maggie still used M Mother when giving him permission to take off. It was probably time she found out. If she didn't want to talk to him, he would respect her wishes and leave her alone. But he would get her attention. Then perhaps he could make up for the damage he'd done.

―――∞―

Control Tower, RAF Bottesford
23 January 1943, 2:30 p.m.

A busy day working in the control room occupied her mind. She had to concentrate on the movements of the aircraft. The night shift had a different rhythm. Frantic at the beginning and end, with a long lull in the middle. But during the day, there was no time to think about anything besides the job.

No time to dwell on the behavior of certain Australian pilots.

Except when their voices over the radio made her stomach do a weird kind of loop-de-loop, making her work hard at keeping a professional tone.

She hadn't spoken to Alec since the morning she'd ambushed him on the tarmac. At the time, she was outraged and hurt at the idea of the bet. Now, she wondered if New Year's Eve was just a part of an elaborate deception.

Grace, who had seen Maggie through two broken hearts at the hands of pilots in the space of as many months, said Maggie should give him a chance to explain himself.

"At least stop avoiding him so that we can go back to the pub," Grace urged. "For all our sakes."

"I'm not avoiding him. I talk to him almost every day via the radio." She knew exactly what the look Grace gave her meant.

An unidentified plane appeared on the horizon. Maggie grabbed her binoculars to get a closer look. Definitely friendly, the aircraft was a low-flying Avro Lancaster. She checked the delivery schedule, running her finger down the list until it landed on the right serial number. *Captain Elizabeth Bates, ATA* was printed next to it.

Pilots from the Air Transport Auxiliary crisscrossed the country delivering aircraft from factories and repair stations to operational airfields. The Air Ministry wouldn't let women fly in combat, but the ATA didn't have any such restrictions. They allowed female pilots alongside male ones and gave them glamorous ink-blue versions of the WAAF uniform.

Maggie thought "Attagirls" only flew the smaller planes, but this was definitely a Lancaster. She watched over the runway as the new aircraft landed with precision and taxied toward the dispersal pans that kept the aircrafts separated from one another in case of an enemy attack. She hoped she'd get to meet the pilot herself over lunch in the WAAF mess.

"Bedrock. This is M Maggie. Requesting permission to land."

The sound of Alec's voice saying her name startled her. She shifted in her chair and glanced sideways at Agnes, hoping she hadn't heard Alec misuse the phonetic alphabet. The trouble she would be in if anyone higher up the chain of command heard him using her name instead of the aircraft's proper one! Misusing the radio was a serious offense, and it was always the WAAF operators who were reprimanded, never the pilots.

She cleared her throat in annoyance.

"Thank you M *Mother*," she emphasized. "You are cleared for landing. Runway six."

She allocated him one of the shorter runways to land on. It would make him sweat, but he was good enough to make it.

Next to her, Agnes didn't seem to notice anything unusual. Perhaps there was no harm done.

WAAF Mess, RAF Bottesford
23 January 1943, 3:15 p.m.

"I suppose they do their best," Amy said apologetically, looking at the tray of food in front of her.

Maggie couldn't tell whether Amy was making excuses or comforting herself. The watery mashed potatoes and gray peas on her plate accompanied a thin slice of what Maggie assumed was corned beef but looked more like shoe leather a dog had already chewed.

One by one every WAAF in the mess did the same thing: stared at her tray, sighed, then picked up her fork and dutifully ate.

"At least the tea here is drinkable," Maggie said. "Remember during training? They served something with the milk already mixed in. It was orange." She shuddered.

Maggie and Amy looked quite prim in their blue skirts, compared to the others sitting at the long tables. Mechanics wore greasy coveralls, and some others wore trousers so they could do more energetic jobs.

"So you and Alec Thomas? What's happening there?" Amy asked over her tea, watching Maggie closely.

Maggie nearly choked on the beef. She avoided Amy's eyes,

wishing she didn't blush. "Nothing. I haven't spoken to him since New Year's Eve."

"That's not what Agnes says."

Agnes had heard, she must have. Maggie knew she was going to be in so much trouble. "What do you mean?" She tried to sound light and not strangled with fear.

"She says he's been sniffing around trying to find out what your roster is."

"Really?" This was news.

"Take it as a compliment, Maggie. Alec Thomas could put his boots under the bed of any girl at this station, but he seems fixated on you. I say make the most of it."

Maggie was sure she was bright red from the heat she felt in her face. "Hilarious," she said flatly.

"It's not a joke. You haven't been at the pub to see how Katie has been throwing herself at him for the last month. But he only seems interested in talking about you. I say make hay while the sun shines."

She wanted to ask more, but she also didn't want Amy Snee to think she cared two hoots about who Alec talked to at the pub.

"Alec Thomas is nothing but trouble. Katie can have him."

Officers' Mess, RAF Bottesford
23 January 1943, 4:00 p.m.

A woman jumping down from a Lanc cockpit was not something he saw every day. And this was a particularly striking woman. Very tall, with dark hair so frazzled it looked like she'd stuck her finger in a power socket when she took off her head gear. He had to look twice to make sure his eyes weren't playing tricks on him.

He wasn't the only one to notice her. She attracted stares from every other man on the airfield. And whistles. Next to him, Bill watched her slack-jawed until Alec gave him an elbow. But for her part, she moved and interacted with the ground crews with complete ease, obviously accustomed to this kind of greeting. A crew transport drove up to meet her. She and the rest of her all-female crew jumped into the vehicle with practiced ease.

She strode into the officers' mess just as he sat down to his flying meal of bacon and eggs, introducing herself to the dozen or so men who immediately crowded to her table. Her height (she was at least a head taller than Hardie) acted as a beacon. He noticed Bill among them, seemingly unable to contain his fascination with the woman.

"I've visited every factory, maintenance depot, and airfield in the country," she said.

They let her tell about how she delivered kites for the ATA. The happy timbre of her voice attracted more and more men over to hear her. That was quite a power she had.

"Do you fly all the kites?" Alec asked, succumbing to her powers and joining the throng listening to her. He liked her relaxed smile and happy way of bantering with the boys, but thought more about offering Bill an assist.

"Absolutely," she answered with firm pride, taking out a cigarette. At least three men stumbled over each other to light a match for her. Bill got there first. Good for him.

"They wouldn't let us fly the combat machines at first, but I've flown everything now. Spitfires, Hurricanes, Lancs. You name it, I've flown it."

"You don't struggle with the mathematics?" asked a voice Alec couldn't see from where he sat.

He recognized the look of barely concealed disdain in her eyes as she drew on her cigarette.

"No. I also don't struggle when I have to fly low below cloud so I can find my way by land formations, without navigation equipment or radio communications. But that's not something you need to do, now is it?" No one dared respond, and Alec saw Bill's admiration deepened, if his expression was anything to go by.

She moved the conversation on, asking questions about how

the Lancs handled in combat, about their strategies for evading night fighters, and about what it was like to fly through flak. She even asked who had flown all the way to Berlin, a mark of honor among them.

"Three times. We consider every flight our personal 'up yours' to Goering," Bill replied, mocking the Nazi air force chief's claim that no enemy planes would fly over Reich territory.

"I like your style." She chuckled.

Bill beamed. Alec shook his head at his smitten friend. Bill had it bad.

She encouraged their stories about escapes in the sky. Halfway through the telling of one of his best tales about a narrow escape from a Messerschmidt—one where Alec made sure he gave all the credit to his navigator for getting them home safely—Maggie threw open the doors of the mess and stormed up to where he sat.

He sensed trouble.

Again.

More so when he saw the double take she did at the woman sitting opposite him, listening intently to his every word.

"Can I speak with you outside?" she asked, pointedly. "Now."

He grimaced. Next to him, Bill, who'd told him to expect some kind of trouble if he hadn't told Maggie about the name change first, smiled into his tea.

"Good luck, mate."

"Not a word from you." Maggie glowered at Bill.

Thrilled at finally getting her attention, Alec stood and obediently followed her out of the mess.

The moment they emerged into the chill, she spun on him. "What do you think you are doing?"

"I don't know what you mean." He affected innocence.

"Don't try that. I heard you and so did half the control room and all the WAAFs in the monitoring station. You may think you are being smart or clever, but you don't have to bear the consequences. I could be demoted for your improper use of the radio!"

"Come on, Maggie. It won't come to that!"

"It has for others before! I could lose my job because of your stupidity."

"No, I mean it won't come to that because there was nothing improper about the use of the radio. Everyone else agreed to rename the kite after you."

"I didn't agree!" She looked like she was about to unleash the wrath of the gods upon him. "And since I am the one in the control tower, I would have thought that mine was a fairly important opinion to seek out!"

"How could I ask you when you've been avoiding me for a whole month? I've been trying to catch you at the end of a shift for days now."

She shook her head, brow furrowed in a deep, disbelieving glare.

"Look, it was Jonty's idea. You were already his guardian angel, and you're my girl. This just makes you the good luck charm for the whole of 467."

"Oh, let's be clear—I am most definitely *not* your girl, Alec Thomas!"

He tried not to let the words cut him, although he knew they were intended that way.

"If you even think that I would—"

"Birdie! How wonderful to see you!" Grace's joyful cry cut off Maggie's insult, distracting Maggie before she could get it out.

Grace had pulled up in an RAF car as the ATA pilot emerged from the mess, and Grace now waved madly from the driver's seat.

"Grace Deroy! It's been ages!" Birdie called out in reply.

Grace jumped out of the vehicle and moved to embrace her friend.

But Maggie didn't stay to find out more. She was already storming back across the airfield, leaving Alec in her wake.

———∞———

The Bottesford Arms
23 January 1943, 7:15 p.m.

She might be at the pub, but she wasn't in the mood for chit-chat. She'd only agreed to come with Grace and Birdie because she was sure Alec was flying tonight. Grace had cajoled her, determined Maggie would like Birdie if she got to know her.

"Birdie Bates is an old school chum of mine. You'll love her. She has such spirit! She and I—and, would you believe it, Amy Snee—used to be on the debating team at school. Trumped the boys on more than one occasion! She and I were inseparable once, but I couldn't convince her to join the WAAF once she found out we wouldn't actually be flying. She's mad for it and absolutely obsessed with Amelia Earhart. Always has been."

When Grace was determined for something to happen, it invariably did. But that didn't mean Maggie had to be happy about it. On top of the business with Alec, Rosie's last letter played on Maggie's mood. The tone of everything Rosie sent grew increasingly irate. Now that she was regularly working overnights in the control tower, Maggie had less time and energy to write back. When she did, she followed Oscar's advice and mentioned her work, carefully considering which details she could include without divulging official secrets. But it didn't help. Rosie's grumblings had become strident complaints. She was clearly champing at the bit to experience the world. Injustice at being the sister required to keep house while Maggie enjoyed adventures in the WAAF underpinned Rosie's every sentence.

Maggie sat silently while Grace and Birdie chatted about past times. Birdie eventually drew Maggie in with her stories about zipping across the country for the ATA.

"Birdie Bates! I'd heard you were here. How are you?" Amy approached with a greeting that held a little too much enthusiasm to be genuine. "It's been such a long time."

"Amy! I didn't know you were here too." Birdie returned the embrace Amy offered.

"Oh yes! Grace and I work side by side now."

"Hardly." Grace sounded extra polite in her disagreement. "I work in the Map Room, while Amy bats her eyelids at the airmen to get information about what they've seen over Europe."

"Intelligence officer?" Birdie asked, ignoring Grace's snark.

"Intelligent? Can we honestly give her that title?"

Maggie's jaw dropped. Grace didn't like Amy, but Grace was usually a personification of effortless politeness. She'd never heard Grace be so churlish. Maggie glanced down to see if Grace had somehow drunk too much, but she seemed sober.

"Oh, leave off, Grace," Amy snapped. "It's good to see you, Birdie. Let's catch up when Her Haughty Highness isn't around."

Amy obviously returned Grace's feelings. Grace glared unrepentantly at Amy's back as she left. One hundred questions about what had just happened burned on Maggie's lips.

"So you haven't forgiven her then." Birdie looked to Grace for an explanation.

"Enough to work with her." Grace gave a tight-lipped smile and tilted her head toward Maggie. Birdie changed the subject in whip-smart fashion.

"So what is going on with you and that pilot?" Birdie asked.

"Absolutely nothing," Maggie said. "He's just another one of those pilots who thinks he is God's gift to women!"

"He seems keen on you. He followed you out of the mess today like an attentive little puppy dog. And he's a dish."

Maggie sniffed. "Handsome. Arrogant. Self-absorbed. The list goes on."

"Oooh, that sounds like a good story. Do tell!"

Maggie gave a potted history of Alec Thomas to Birdie, who looked confused at the end of it all.

"So all the men around him are competing about how many women they can sleep with, and you're angry at him because he *didn't* even kiss you?"

Grace gave Maggie an "I told you that you were being daft" look. Maggie got the creeping feeling she was being ganged up on.

"I'm angry at him because he pursued me for a bet, and that's a deplorable thing to do." She tried to sound sure of herself.

"Maggie, a few months ago you were weeping into your tea about Ralph. What *he* did was deplorable. But despite all his considerable charm and bluster, all Alec did was play handsy with you, for goodness' sake!"

"But the bet . . ."

"But he wasn't part of that! Bill says Alec made a single wager with Jimmy about whether he could get you, just you, to kiss him by the end of the year."

"Men can be so stupid sometimes." Birdie vocalized Maggie's thoughts.

"And you can say what you like," Grace continued, "but that man did not rush headlong into the alleyway behind the dance hall for the sake of a bet."

"Grace, he as much as admitted he arrived that evening spoiling for a fight."

"Yes, but I was in that air-raid shelter on New Year's Eve, remember? He could easily have won his bet. All he needed to do was work his defense of your honor into his spiel, and you would have thrown yourself at him! And he didn't!"

Perhaps Grace had a point. Until she'd found out about the bet, she'd spent New Year's Day in a day-dreamy haze, imagining what it would have been like to lean that little bit closer and close the gap between their lips.

"You think I should let it go?"

"I think you should stop pretending he is in any way the same as Ralph. He's spent the best part of the month trying to make it up to you, ignoring every other girl on this station in the process."

"For what it's worth, I don't you think should let it slide. But I think you should quit playing the victim." Birdie shot her a mischievous grin. "To quote Bomber Harris—he sowed the wind. Let him reap the whirlwind!"

Maggie didn't want to ruin the moment by telling Birdie, like the good vicar's daughter she was, that Arthur Harris, head of Bomber Command, had actually appropriated the Bible in his pep talk about the role of heavy bombing to defeat the Nazis. But for the first time in a month, Maggie smiled when she thought about Alec Thomas and his crew, wondering just how much of a whirlwind she could get away with.

CHAPTER TWENTY-ONE

Control Tower, RAF Bottesford
26 January 1943, 6:40 p.m.

The frigid air in the control room chilled Maggie to her bones. This room was little more than a concrete box on the side of the three runways crisscrossing in a triangular pattern on the airfield, but it was the heartbeat of the station during any operation. The air always felt taut with focus as the people around her worked on their specific jobs to control the movements of aircraft during takeoff and landing.

With no heat, Maggie wore her coat and wrapped a scarf tightly around her neck. She had to remove the blue knitted beanie her mother had made her, to fit the radio headset over her head. Her woolen gloves came off when she needed her hands to operate the radio properly.

Maggie waited for her order. Even with all the planes on the runway lined up and ready to fly, the operation could be aborted at the last minute. Several times before, she was the one to radio that news to pilots and had heard their distinct sighs of relief and frustration through her headset.

Not tonight.

The order came from the operation commander, Flight Lieutenant Grant, next to her. "On your call, Corporal Morrison."

One by one she gave them permission to take off.

"S Sugar. This is Bedrock. Cleared for takeoff on green."

The pilot would be watching for the signal light at the end of the runway to flick from red to green. Once it did, she'd watch the aircraft roar along the runway and up into the winter sky. A crowd often gathered to wave the men off from the side of the runway, but Maggie oversaw it all from her window in the control room.

The trick was to get every aircraft into the air as quickly as possible. Some aerodromes boasted about getting one off the ground every thirty seconds. But Maggie erred on the side of safety and caution. She wouldn't let two aircraft smash each other into smithereens during takeoff just because her commanding officer wanted to shave seconds off the station's takeoff rate.

"M Maggie. This is Bedrock. Cleared for takeoff on green."

She managed to use her own name over the airwaves without rolling her eyes. Everyone else at the station had agreed to it, after all.

"Roger that, Bedrock. See you on the other side."

She wrinkled her nose at Alec's confidence. Shouldn't he be more subdued, under the circumstances? Of course, she didn't wish him ill. She just wanted him to be more serious, considering his aircraft was loaded with thousands of pounds of explosives.

In a flurry of activity, she saw all the aircraft into the air, off on their way to an industrial target in Belgium.

"What are you planning?" Nancy, the WAAF telephonist, next to her asked. "I see a scheme on your face."

She wasn't wrong. Maggie filled her in on her plan to take Alec Thomas down a peg or two if everything went smoothly with the operation tonight.

While Maggie communicated with the aircraft, Nancy spoke with the outside world. She made and received calls during the night, relaying orders from group headquarters in Grantham or reporting on downed aircraft. She would be a helpful ally to make sure Maggie's operation went smoothly.

"I like your style, Maggie."

Nancy knew Maggie's heartbreak intimately. A natural camaraderie had developed during the long overnight hours of their shift, so Maggie had shared almost as many details with her as she had with Grace.

"Cards?" Nancy held out the deck she brought to occupy herself during the quiet middle of the shift.

"No, I think I'll read tonight."

Maggie glanced at RAF Flight Lieutenant Grant on her other side. She barely saw him outside this room, but during the night they often shared solemn chatter about the course of the war and when it might end. Plenty of laughter and a thermos of tea helped get them through.

Maggie made some mental calculations. Four and a half, maybe five hours in the air, all going well. Nothing compared to the time it took to fly to Berlin or Turin or the South of France. They'd be out and back before she even started to feel drowsy.

Perfect conditions.

A blackboard on the wall behind her listed all the aircraft in operation. Ordered by the pilot's name, it recorded the time an aircraft flew out and the time it landed again, every minute meticulously calculated. Several WAAF officers tracked and scribed events as they happened. Every single one dreaded having to write *DID NOT RETURN* next to a pilot's name.

With just her book to occupy her, the hours felt longer than they were. Maggie glanced at her wristwatch when she heard the telephone ring.

"Hullo. This is Bedrock." Nancy answered the call.

"Roger that, Coastal Command."

Nancy grinned at Maggie. "All twelve have just been spotted over the channel."

Maggie sighed out an excited breath. This might just work.

The first pilot's voice crackling over the radio would shoot electricity through the control room. The team would abandon their games and books and scramble like fighter pilots to get to their positions, suddenly wide eyed and alert.

But she needed to be ahead of the game. She laid down her book and listened intently for Alec's voice in her headset.

The sortie wasn't a complicated one, just some factory or another that the Nazis had commandeered in Belgium. After getting the bombs away and holding steady for twenty seconds to confirm the hit with an aiming point photograph, the relief of knowing that all he had left to do was land the kite safely felt palpable. Just one more thing and he had beaten the odds again.

Hearing the WAAF radio operator at the end of an operation was music to any pilot's ear, confirmation that you were nearly home. Of course, one radio operator's voice in particular gave him more of a thrill than the others. He relished using her name when it was her shift, imagining the way her eyes would roll under the band that held together her radio headphones.

She was talking to him again. Sort of. She wasn't throwing herself at him, like Katie was doing. But she seemed less frosty lately, like the ice in her eyes was thawing.

Tonight he felt particularly chipper. Not even the niggling cough he'd developed could dampen his spirits at the thought of the week ahead. In order to keep up morale, each man received six days off after every six weeks of flying—to give them something to look forward to, something to live for.

Some of the boys were going to Scotland, but Alec didn't want to stray too far from Lincolnshire. He planned to ask Maggie to the cinema. And to dinner. If his luck held, he would do that several times over the six days. And tonight he was feeling lucky.

Before takeoff, he'd wagered with some of the others he could beat Bob Burgess—"First-Back Bob" they called him—back to the aerodrome. Tonight Alec raced for the title and five pounds to fund his time with Maggie.

He enlisted his crew's help by promising them a cut of the money. Bill helped, making his calculations account for every possible factor that might slow them down.

"Hello, Bedrock, this is M Maggie, requesting permission to land."

Alec radioed in, sure that they were first home. In the long pause that followed, he imagined Maggie fuming. A jubilant grin spread across his frozen face.

"Negative, M Maggie. Rise to eighteen thousand feet."

He searched the heavens. Bob would be here soon, but right now they flew alone in the sky. Perhaps a plane in distress needed a priority landing.

As he climbed higher and circled the aerodrome, he watched several of his squadron land safely, including Bob Burgess.

The penny dropped.

He couldn't rule out the possibility that Maggie knew of an aircraft in distress, but his gut told him this was punishment for the stunt over the radio the other day. Maggie didn't just hold his landing—she sent him to the maximum possible height. Somehow he knew she would make him wait for several, if not all, the other aircraft to land before he would be allowed to.

"She responded well to us naming the kite after her, then?" Fisher said next to him.

Alec radioed back to Jonty. "Rear Gunner, did you happen to mention to our guardian angel that we had a bet going?"

Jonty took a few moments to respond. "Not *directly*, Skipper."

Not directly, but she clearly had gotten wind of it.

Served himself right. Now he'd lost the wager and landed on her off-side again as well. He wouldn't hear the end of this from the others.

He risked returning to the radio.

"Bedrock, this is M Maggie. You've proved your point, but the fuel won't last all night. Permission to land?" He tried to sound contrite.

"Permission granted, M Maggie. Runway three."

Safely on the ground, he dealt with the wrath of his crew—all of whom felt cheated—before going through the usual postop rigmarole.

Maggie waited for him when he stepped out of the mess after his breakfast. Rugged up tightly in her overcoat and thick blue scarf, she looked like a cute Eskimo.

He braced for a slap, but thankfully, the little bit of her face he could see didn't look angry. In fact, she looked pleased with herself

"Gambling just doesn't pay for you, does it?" she said.

"I don't know what you mean." He tried to sound innocent, but the last word came out as a cough. Walking in the cold night air after the warmth of the briefing room made his lungs seize up, and it took a minute to shake the coughing fit.

"Are you unwell?"

"It's nothing. Just the change in air temperature."

She grinned, and even better, she lingered.

Out here.

Alone.

Just to talk with him.

He enjoyed the magic in that—the spell of which he promptly broke by coughing again.

"Are we even now? I'd really like to be friends." More than friends, but they had to start somewhere.

She nodded. "No more bets. About me anyway. I'm not a game, and neither are any of the others here."

"I know. I'm sorry, Mags."

Her smile warmed him from within in a way no rum-laced tea ever could.

"I have six days off now."

"Oh," she said. "Are you going anywhere?"

She sounded wary. She must have known that it was common for the airmen to take their six-day leave in London. Getting into trouble.

"Well, I hope I am going to the cinema, and out to dinner, and dancing. With you—if you'll come with me."

She bit her lip, but it didn't conceal her smile. "You're the optimistic sort, aren't you? Why don't you just come for a drink with me at the pub when I get a leave pass?"

The happy banter they'd found on New Year's Eve had returned, making his heart do a little flip.

"Are you asking me out?"

"Technically, you asked me out first."

"Touché. But if it means I get to spend an evening with you, Maggie Morrison, count me in."

Later that night, he wrote in his logbook with the red ink he used for operations, putting a red *26* in a circle next to the entry.

Four more ops now.

Bill's words from a few weeks ago, about him always doing the expedient thing, ran through Alec's mind. Bill accused him of only thinking of the moment, not having a plan. Bill was right, but something inside Alec had shifted since New Year's Eve.

He used to just want to survive this tour and go home. He was now thinking he actually wanted someone to survive this tour for.

Bottesford Common
31 January 1943, 2:15 p.m.

Maggie could confidently say she had never thought about rugby before in her life. She didn't have brothers to help her learn the rules by osmosis, like Grace had. She'd never stepped out with a bloke who made her serve tea on the sidelines of his matches, like Amy did. Wholly uninterested, her parents hadn't taken her to see matches, like some of the other girls here.

She only had Alec, who'd tried to explain the rules to her when they'd been in the pub, using a handful of spoons, three beer glasses, a cigarette packet, and a matchbook. It flummoxed her then, and it made no more sense to see the game in person.

The local Bottesford boys, annoyed at the Australians for becoming an ever-present feature in their pub, challenged the squadron to a football game. After a confused round of discussions about what each man meant by word football, everyone agreed rugby was the game that would settle their dispute. Even though night operations were in full swing, Wing Commander Palmer agreed to a Saturday game to give the airmen a way to blow off steam.

At first Maggie didn't give two hoots who won. But the athleticism of one player snared her attention. When he walked onto the common in his sport kit, she couldn't tear her eyes away from the outlines of the muscles in his forearms and calves. When he caught her looking and gave her a wink, she snapped her head away to hide the blush she felt blooming across her cheeks. But she suddenly wished she understood the explanation he'd given about the game so she could understand what on earth was going on.

After the drizzle from the first half rallied itself into rain for the second, she huddled under an umbrella with newly engaged Lucy Mathis.

"You must have divided loyalties," Maggie said to Lucy. "Aren't your brothers out there?"

A cheer went up from the small crowd. On the field, someone seemed to have scored, but she couldn't tell which team. Mud covered the players from head to toe.

Lucy grinned. "I'm barracking for Chris, of course, but I secretly hope the local boys win."

On the other side of her, Grace scowled at Lucy. Despite technically being a local girl herself, Grace cheered for the men from Bomber Command. She disliked Lucy's equivocation.

Maggie laughed aloud at Grace's utter seriousness toward the game, although she smothered her outburst for Grace's sake. When Grace wasn't shouting praise for her team or insults for their opponents, she vocalized her hopes and disappointments through little groans and gasps.

Jonty, sharing an umbrella with Katie, desperately wanted to be part of the action, but the station doctor wouldn't allow it due to the delicate nature of his burned skin. His body moved vicariously as he watched the ball, as though it were going through the motions of play. Katie kept shooting him annoyed glances when the umbrella shifted.

Maggie's heart rate kicked up a notch whenever Alec moved near the ball. Despite the slippery brown mud coating him like every other player, she could still pick him out. She cheered when he made a break with the ball—although she wasn't yelling anything in keeping with the play, judging from the look Grace gave her. She caught her breath when a local player twice his size tackled Alec to the ground in front of her. He came up from the ruck with a bleeding nose and scowl but ran back into the thick of the game.

"Go Alec!" Katie shouted, obviously tracking Alec's every move too.

The jealousy creeping into the corner of her mind surprised Maggie. She wasn't shy, but she couldn't—and wouldn't—compete with Katie's enthusiasm and determination to grab Alec's attention. Katie rushed to him with a drink during a break in play, toying with a damp curl that fell loose at her ear while he drank.

It served Maggie right for ignoring him for a month. If he did start something with Katie just as Maggie was beginning to like him again, it would be her own fault.

He took the cup from Katie and swished the water around in his mouth to wash away the blood before spitting it on the ground. Maggie hid her smile. He wasn't exactly flirting back.

"Worked out what's going on yet?" he called out to her just as the game was about to restart, ignoring Katie's injured look.

"Are you the spoon or the beer glass?" She winked at him to prove she could flirt just as well as Katie.

The smile he shot back before he ran onto the field again warmed her down to her frozen toes.

With five minutes to go in the game, the evenly matched teams sat neck and neck on the scoreboard. Not even the driving rain could distract the crowd from the tension.

Next to her, Grace grew hoarse chastising the team's sloppy and useless plays, but Maggie didn't know how any of them could keep hold of the ball.

Eventually Bill was able to break free from the messy squabble of players fumbling over the ball. He made a run up the field toward the goal, fast and agile despite the mud, leaving his opponents sloshing in his wake.

"Run! Run! Run!" Grace screamed.

"Go Bill!" Maggie, Jonty, and Katie called out in unison. Maggie hadn't thought she could ever feel such exhilaration while watching a sport.

Encountering little defense, Bill headed for the center of the goalposts and deposited the ball over the try line as his team ran to him, clapping, cheering, and throwing themselves on top of him in congratulation.

When the referee rang the bell to indicate the end of the game, the Bomber Command boys hoisted Bill onto their shoulders and marched off the field as a loud bunch of muddy bodies glowing with happiness. Laughter rang out, and their beaming smiles ran from ear to ear.

Maggie didn't want to join the happy throng like Grace and Lucy. She held back, clapping and cheering them as they walked by, freezing this vibrant picture in her mind, like a photograph.

The Bottesford Arms
31 January 1943, 6:15 p.m.

The prize for winning was a round of drinks shouted by the losing team.

"Three cheers for Bill. Hip hip hooray!"

Half the pub joined in the cheer, while the other half mumbled into their beer glasses.

What a game! He hadn't played rugby like that since . . . he couldn't remember when. His school days probably, and even then he'd played on a rock-hard dust bowl rather than in a complete bog. Seeing Bill run the length of the field like a man possessed wasn't something he would forget anytime soon.

To warm up, the players stood in prime positions around the fire, amused by the debriefing Grace gave them. She obviously knew rugby and happily relived the final moments of the game. The man of the match himself gave an electrifying recount of his run across the field to score the winning try.

After deconstructing the game and reveling in the glory of its final moments, Alec's mind wandered to a different part of the pub. Maggie sat at a booth, quietly chatting to Amy and one of Katie's friends. He wished she'd come over and join them here.

Grace leaned in when she saw him looking over. "Maggie doesn't like the open flame," she explained. "Not since Jonty."

Of course. Maggie had pulled Jonty free from the burning wreck. How could he not have noticed that in all the times they'd been in here, she never sat near the fireplace?

"Her scars are harder to see than his," Grace said. "She hides it well, but fire still makes her anxious."

Maggie looked up, and their eyes met. He took it as an invitation.

"You still have mud in your ears," she chided him when he sat next to her.

The cooler air where she sat couldn't dampen his spirits, not when she smiled at him like that. He ignored the desire to unpin her damp hair so it fell over her shoulders again, the way it had at Christmas.

"Come on, Agnes. Let's find another table," Amy said with a knowing look, hauling Agnes away to another conversation.

They needn't have gone. He and Maggie were simply friends now, nothing more. Every time he saw her, he wanted there to be more, but he couldn't risk rushing. He didn't want to jeopardize the hard-won peace between them.

"I may never get the mud out of my ears. Not after one of the Mathis boys pushed my face into it, thinking I was Fisher." He laughed.

They talked about the game. He sensed she tried to understand the intricacies of rugby, even if she couldn't care about it the way Grace obviously did.

When that line of conversation died, he asked the question that had first formed the night they met. "I've been wondering something . . ."

"Shoot."

"What did the last bloke do to give you such a dim view of pilots?"

She held his gaze like a challenge. "Let's just say that the Sweetheart Sweepstakes was right up his alley."

"Ah, I see."

He wasn't sure he did. But he was certain he'd been an idiot to agree to Hardie's bet, and now he needed to nurse this fragile connection carefully.

Very carefully indeed.

CHAPTER TWENTY-TWO

Above the North Sea
4 February 1943, 2:23 a.m.

The operation over Dusseldorf went smoothly. The clear sky made for perfect conditions. The takeoff was on time, the flak was light, and Hardie was right on target. They would be warming themselves from the inside out in the mess hall before long.

Although Alec tried to keep his mind on the flying, pleasant distractions kept creeping in. After three long evenings talking together in the pub, the elusive Corporal Morrison agreed to go to the cinema with him.

Hardie, Graves, and Boyd, who spent their leave debauching their way up to Scotland, gave him no end of strife when they discovered all they'd done was talk. Alec even surprised himself by not trying to push things. But no matter how uncomfortable and unfamiliar the feeling, he wanted to do this right. What was it that Jonty had said at Christmas? That he should be someone worth running to?

Her hesitation gave him a chance to puzzle out all the contraditions in her character. A vicar's daughter who was anything but homely. The level-headed voice they relied on in the control room who got nervy when he tried to make her sit nearer to the fireplace at the pub. Someone who was simultaneously obsessed with silver-screen romances but unwilling to rush into a real-life one. He cursed the last bloke for whatever he had done to make her so cautious. But at the same time every little step she took toward Alec was sweeter victory than winning every penny from Hardie's pocket.

He'd asked her to see *Casablanca* with him in Grantham, expecting her to shoot back one of her withering looks and declare that she had already seen it. But she'd given him that confident, full-faced smile, the one that melted him.

Maybe he was concentrating on that instead of being alert to the sky around him, because he didn't notice the night fighter appear. Jonty's voice crackling through his headphones tore him out of his happy thoughts about Maggie.

"Rear Gunner to Skipper—night fighter at four o'clock."

Alec began evasive flying like they'd practiced, his heart thundering in his ears.

"Gerry is persistent tonight," Bill said. No doubt he'd spent the last five minutes bracing himself against the midair inertia caused by Alec's flying. "Where is he now?"

"I didn't see him go down," Hardie said.

"Don't relax, boys. He's still out there somewhere," Alec said.

They flew steadily now, each man peering through the windows in order to spot the enemy.

Boyd's position at the top of the aircraft meant he caught first sight. "Above! Above!" he called as he fired, but not before they felt the night fighter's bullets strafing through the metal shell of the plane and hitting the viewing window above Bill's seat.

"Crikey! The astrodome's gone," Jonty called as Alec dipped to avoid the fire.

The Messerschmidt pursued them with relentless efficiency.

"He's good," Alec said.

The guns hammered, adding their heavy *ack-ack* over the engines' rumble.

"I think I got him," Jonty said through the intercom.

"Yep," Hardie confirmed. "I can see him going down."

Alec glanced at the instrumentation. "Skipper to Navigator—I'm going to need you to give me a bearing."

The comms crackled. "Bill, a bearing?"

Above the crackle, a gurgle in his headset sent a chill down Alec's spine.

"Oh God!"

Dread pooled in Alec's stomach at his radio operator's exclamation.

"What's wrong?" Jonty asked. He couldn't see anything from his position at the rear.

"Chris, find out what's wrong," Alec ordered Fisher, who disappeared behind him.

After a few minutes, Fisher sank onto his fold-out seat beside Alec. There was enough moonlight for Alec to see dark stains down the front of his flight suit.

Blood. Alec's flesh tingled inside the layers he wore.

Fisher shook his head. They didn't have to exchange words for Alec to understand.

He took a deep breath. "Chaps, Bill's been hit."

Fisher nodded solemnly. "He's dead."

For a moment static over the comms and the monotonous thrum of the engines filled the emptiness in the air above the channel.

"Flight Engineer, help me work out where the hell we are and how we get home from here. Wireless Operator, radio Bedrock as soon as we are in range."

When Alec finally found his bearings, they still had another dreadful hour to fly with the body of their friend next to them, his blood smeared where he'd fallen from his seat to the floor.

———∞———

Control Tower, RAF Bottesford
4 February 1943, 3:14 a.m.

Alec's voice, devoid of its usual composure, shot into her ears through the radio.

"Bedrock, Bedrock. This is Maggie. We have a man down. Repeat. We have a man down. Request priority landing. Over."

Everyone else accepted her name as the identifying moniker for Alec's aircraft, so she didn't give it a second thought anymore. But hearing Alec say it tonight sent a cold rivulet down her spine.

She longed to ask for details but stayed succinct and professional. Next to her, Nancy telephoned for the ambulance.

"Bedrock to Maggie. You are cleared to land on the main runway. An ambulance will meet you. Over."

"Too late for that, Bedrock. Navigator took a hit. Bill is dead."

Even with the static over the radio line, she could hear the crack in Alec's voice, and her heart ached. For him. For Bill. For all the others who hadn't come home yet. Lieutenant Grant took control of the radio from her and asked Alec questions, while Maggie took note of the time of landing for her records.

With two other aircraft yet to return, she couldn't leave her post or even turn her mind to what might be happening down on the airfield, where the ambulance scrambled, ready to meet the aircraft taxiing toward it. She stayed in place, listening intently for call signs or distress calls until the end of her shift.

As she left, Nancy wrote *DID NOT RETURN* next to two names on the control room blackboard. Maggie wouldn't know more until the morning, when the intelligence officers would compile the debriefing reports. She rode her bicycle back to the mess with heavy, tired legs, hoping that she could speak to Alec before he turned in.

When she peered into the mess hall, she could tell the outcome of an operation by the sheer number of bodies present. She looked for Alec but couldn't see his face among the stricken expressions greeting her. The room felt so empty. Losing two Lancasters meant fourteen men were missing tonight.

Then there was Bill. Her lip trembled. She bit down on it so she couldn't be accused of being a weepy WAAF hanging about looking for a man. She'd spent all last night chatting companionably with him and Alec. Now he was gone. Recalling the emotion in Alec's voice over the radio kept her looking in the window, hoping he would appear. For the first time in her life, she wished for a roomful of raucous men bragging about their prowess instead of the slumped shoulders and ashen faces.

She watched Wing Commander Palmer, who'd flown tonight as well, bring a bottle of rum into the room, adding an extra tipple to every man's empty teacup as a toast to the fallen. She turned away, aware the ritual wasn't for her.

Her mind buzzed with unanswered questions, so she couldn't sleep. After trying uselessly for hours, she drifted off sometime around dawn. When she woke, she splashed water across her face and looked around for her compact. With so little sleep, she could do with a bit of powder to cover the dark circles that ringed her eyes.

The compact was probably the most expensive item she owned, and she protected it fiercely. Sterling silver, with a simple floral pattern decorating the cover, her mother had given it to her to celebrate her eighteenth birthday just a few days before Maggie had enlisted. Engraved with the words *Both brave and beautiful*, the tiny message decorated the only part of the cover that had a smooth enough surface, next to the clasp.

Usually she kept it in the drawer of the small nightstand, but she sometimes left it on her desk. Today, it wasn't in either place. Odd. She was sure she'd used it yesterday. It wasn't even worth one of the others borrowing it—the powder was almost gone.

She decided her vanity could wait until she found out more about the night before. Her plans to see a matinee with Alec would be on hold, so she headed to the Map Room. Grace could usually find out details—through official channels as well as nonofficial ones—and would no doubt have news for her.

Grace sat at her desk with several sheets of monogrammed writing paper in front of her. She wrote with an elegant gold pen with her initials engraved on it. Several completed letters, sealed in envelopes and neatly addressed, sat stacked in front of her.

She looked up as Maggie entered, Grace's eyes puffy eyes and nose red tipped. "Oh, Maggie, I'm sorry. I lost track of time."

"Whatever are you doing, Grace?" Maggie picked up one of the letters. The address was in Grace's elegant hand: *Mrs. Edward Belton, 43a Station Street, Portsmouth.*

"I write to the families," Grace said. "Every airman who doesn't come home has a family. A mother, sometimes a wife. Some of them even leave letters on their pillows before they fly that are only to be sent if they don't come home. I can't bear the thought of just sending that letter on its own. So I write the family a note to offer my condolences to go with it. It's silly, I know, but I suppose I can't escape the manners my mother taught me."

"It's not silly at all, Grace," Maggie said, moved by Grace's giant heart. She glanced down at the pile. There must be over a dozen letters. It looked like Grace was writing to the whole RAF.

"One of the Lancasters crashed somewhere over occupied France, so there's a chance some of them survived. But it's cold comfort for the families to think their men might be German prisoners."

"What do you write to them?"

"Just the kindest thing I can think to say. That I knew them, or if I didn't, that I think the work they were doing was very brave." She shook her head at Maggie's sympathetic look. "I do it all the time, and I'm not usually such a wreck, but I've been trying to write this one for hours. Bill was such a darling."

Grace looked like she would say more if she could do it without crying.

"Are there any others? I could help." Maggie drew a chair closer to Grace's desk.

Grace hesitated, but she let Maggie take a few sheets of her paper and gave her another pen. Together, they made short work of the half-dozen letters Grace had yet to do.

Maggie's hand hovered over one particular letter, to Mrs. Thomson in Perth, Australia. Such a similar name to Alec's. Did Alec leave a letter on his pillow for his family at home? Her heart broke at the thought of having to write a note like this to Mrs. Thomas in Sydney. What would she say?

Dear Mrs. Thomas, I'm not sure if your son ever mentioned me, but despite his ridiculous inclination to wager on anything that moved—including me—I actually found him to be very kind, and I fell in love with him.

She shifted uncomfortably in her chair, at her own admission and also the terrible thought of referring to Alec in past tense.

"Are you all right?" Grace asked.

Maggie cleared her throat. "Yes." But she couldn't concentrate on her letter through her ache to see him. "Shall we go to the pub tonight?"

Grace nodded. "Ops are canceled, and I think there's a bit of a memorial for Bill."

―――∞―――

The Bottesford Arms
4 February 1943, 6:15 p.m.

"There's so much water in this beer, it is barely having any effect." Alec glumly swirled the remainder of his beer around in the bottom of the glass he hunched over.

"I'd hope not, because that's your third." Maggie's glass sat untouched in front of her.

"Sorry for being such a drag, Mags," he mumbled. "Sorry we didn't make it to the pictures either."

The evening turned into an informal memorial for Bill. The local boys, who only a few days before were grumbling about him outplaying them, nodded gruffly along with the men from the aerodrome as they offered toasts and shared memories.

Maggie learned more about Bill in those few hours than in the time she'd known him in person. His everyday habits, his superstitions, and his terrible snoring all featured in the impromptu eulogies from his friends. The men concealed their tears well behind their beer glasses. She dabbed at hers as they ran down her face.

"I'd known Bill longer than I've known anybody else here." Alec stood on unsteady legs to begin his speech. As skipper, his job was to sum everything up and give the final toast. He slurred his words slightly after so many toasts.

"It's funny how things work out. I never spoke to him much back home, but here we spent every day together. He probably knew me better than I know myself. He was a brain, that's for sure—even though he said his job was basically 'doing calculus inside a refrigerator.'"

Several others, including Grace, said the words at the same time as Alec, repeating the catchphrase that Bill used when flirting.

He swallowed, cutting his speech short. "To Bill." Alec raised his glass. "We'll miss him."

Now they sat alone at the window seat. Heaviness filled the space between them. Despite aching to see him all afternoon, Maggie couldn't work out what to say now. He was determined to drown his sorrows. She didn't know how to help him or if he even wanted her to try. But she knew she couldn't leave him alone while he was hurting. In fact, she wanted the opposite. To wrap her arms around him and hold him until his pain went away.

"You're not a drag, Alec."

She put her hand over his on the glass. Her touch made him look up, revealing despair and questions in his eyes.

"Just when you think that you're one of the lucky ones . . ."

He couldn't finish his sentence.

He drained his glass instead.

He stumbled out of the warm and comforting pub with the other airmen who congregated there. They'd drunk the afternoon and evening away in solidarity with their dead mate.

The cold air hit him, making him cough. But cool air wasn't nearly enough to sober him up after the amount he'd put away.

They would go on, they decided drunkenly as the evening wound up.

For Bill.

Because that was what he would expect them to do. Follow the course that was set.

His hand still felt warm from the press of Maggie's against it, even though she'd left hours ago.

She was a comfort today, even if it wasn't the kind of comfort he'd been imagining enjoying with her at the cinema.

"Over here." Hardie waved him over to the lorry that would drive them back to the aerodrome.

Alec's feet moved first, then the rest of his body, which felt heavy and hard to maneuver. Tomorrow's hangover would be a whopper.

He leaned against the truck with one hand stretched out, concentrating on stopping the world around him from moving when he wasn't. It was harder than it should have been.

A blond woman appeared in front of him, but he was too slow to figure out where she came from.

Did he know her? He struggled to focus. She looked very pretty, swimming in front of his face as she was. But she wasn't Maggie. He might be drunk, but he was still sure he would recognize Maggie's eyes anywhere.

She should be Maggie.

The girl said his name, but he couldn't think of hers through the fog and jumble of the beer. He probably knew it, but it just wouldn't come to him.

She kissed him. His hands slid to her waist to steady himself as she pulled down his head.

The kiss felt good on his tingly lips. But something was wrong about it. Either because of the kissing or the beer, the cogs in his brain turned too slowly.

She should have been Maggie. And she wasn't.

He mumbled something when the kiss broke up.

The girl in front of him looked horrified, he thought. It was difficult to tell with his vision so blurry—but nothing registered until he was in the back of the truck bumping back to the aerodrome.

———∞———

Sergeants' Mess, RAF Bottesford
5 February 1943, 7:15 a.m.

The hangover was a brute. At least he wasn't due to fly today and could stay in bed nursing it.

Most of them would be worse for wear this morning. Although looking around the room, it appeared not all of them even made it home.

He stumbled to breakfast.

The mess hall held several sorry-looking men trying to line their stomachs. They sat in silence, with the BBC on in the background. Focusing on the words helped, even though Alec's mind kept wandering.

According to the newsman, the Soviets were socking it to the Germans in Stalingrad and the Allies were having success against Rommel in Tunisia. This was good news. Perhaps it was even the turning of the tide for the war. Maybe there would be no more nights like last night. No more reasons to drink like that. No more dead best mates.

". . . the surrender of the Sixth German Army in Stalingrad is a significant blow for the Nazi regime, whose dominance was previously feared to be untouchable."

Some of the men had nicknamed Maggie "Untouchable," although they didn't dare say it in front of him anymore. Alec's head throbbed when Hardie sank down next to him on the hard messhall bench. Hardie's energetic movements and cheerful whistle were more than Alec could handle right now.

"I've got to hand it to you," Hardie said after he'd finished his meal, "I don't usually like to take another man's seconds, but in your case it seems to be worthwhile."

Alec looked at the plate in front of him, confused. Seconds? He glanced up at Hardie.

"Oh, I see. That bad, is it?"

Nothing good could come from Hardie's sinister grin.

"How much do you remember?"

All through breakfast, something played with Alec's mind, a memory trying to break through but eluding him each time he tried to recall it.

"You don't remember snogging Katie by the transport lorry?"

Hardie watched on as the memory came back. The man enjoyed Alec's pain like the snake he was. His wicked grin grew as Alec allowed horror to spread across his face. He put his elbows on the table and leaned his face into his palms. The memory broke through like a punch in the gut.

"Your loss is my gain, mate." Hardie smirked as he carried away his mess kit, leaving Alec to wonder how he would ever make this up to Maggie.

CHAPTER TWENTY-THREE

WAAF Mess, RAF Bottesford
8 February 1943, 7:25 a.m.

With fifteen minutes to spare before she had to leave the mess, Maggie lingered in her thoughts. Apart from the heavy losses hanging over the aerodrome, she had two letters to read through—one from Father and one from Rosie. They both made her thoughts whirl in different directions.

Her father's short note contained a few philosophical ramblings, but she couldn't quite work out if they were positive. She pushed the note into her pocket so she could take it to Oscar, who would hopefully have some advice for her. Rosie's letter had a more optimistic tone than her previous ones, no doubt because she was being allowed out of the house with her friend Clara. She mentioned two shopping trips and an excursion to Warwick. Happy her sister's life was back to normal, Maggie was already drafting a reply, telling her sister for the first time about Alec.

Agnes broke Maggie's reverie when she leaned in close, and

spoke in a hushed voice. "Can I speak with you privately for a minute? It's about Katie." Worry was written across the girl's face.

"Of course. In here, or should we go outside?"

Agnes shook her head. "Not in here."

They rose from the table, washed their meal kits, and found a quiet place outside to talk without being interrupted.

Agnes bit her lip, obviously unsure how to start. "Katie's not *well*." The way Agnes emphasized the final word and the privacy she'd insisted on told Maggie the very reason Katie was feeling under the weather.

Maggie sighed. "Where is she?"

"She won't get out of bed. I don't think she can. She was throwing up all yesterday."

Maggie insisted on being taken straight to her. She knew that Katie wasn't asleep when she walked into the WAAF quarters by the way she was lying on her side.

When Maggie sat gently on her cot, Katie let out a groan and opened her eyes to slits. "Not you," she moaned before rolling over.

"Is there something I should know, Katie?"

She tried to be delicate, the way her father was when he spoke with troubled parishioners.

"I don't want to talk to you," Katie mumbled.

"I know you don't, Katie, but Agnes is worried about you. We all are. And we need to work out what's next."

Katie reluctantly sat up in her bed, but she wouldn't look Maggie in the eye. Instead she toyed with a loose stitch in the gray military-issue blanket. She looked miserable and green, as though she hadn't slept much in the last week.

"How far along?"

Katie still didn't look up. "I can't be very far. But my mother got this way with each of hers. I'm the oldest of eight."

"Was it someone from the aerodrome?"

Katie nodded. "But I won't tell you who. He'll be in so much trouble."

Maggie doubted it. In situations like these, the men rarely bore the consequences of their actions. "Does he know?"

Katie shook her head. "Not yet."

"Well, best that happens sooner rather than later, don't you think?"

Katie's eyes widened, and she shook her head vigorously, then groaned and slipped back down under the covers.

"I'll find someone to cover your shift for today so you can rest, then tonight we'll talk about what comes next."

On her way out, Maggie passed Agnes. "How much do you know about the circumstances?"

"Not much." Agnes bit the inside of her cheek the way Rosie used to do when she was fibbing, leaving Maggie to wonder why Katie and Agnes weren't being forthcoming with her.

"I don't think you are going to like what I have found out." That evening Grace slipped into Maggie's room and shut the door behind her.

Maggie looked at her quizzically from where she sat on her bed, trying to read her Bible for the first time in ages, searching for something to help her to help Katie. She had seen other girls in this situation, but something about Katie's pained expression told her this one was different. She'd asked Grace to gather some intelligence from the other WAAFs.

Grace leaned her back against the door, pressing her head into it as her eyes stared at the ceiling pensively.

"Out with it then," Maggie said.

"I think the father might be Alec."

The words felt like a punch to her stomach. Her eyes fell to the book in front of her. "Why do you say that?"

Grace took the few steps across the small room and sat on her bed, just as Maggie had done with Katie earlier in the day.

"Well"—Grace clearly was trying to be delicate—"you said that she was reluctant to mention a name to you—which would make sense if it were him. Katie's been practically throwing herself at him for months." Grace paused, as if choosing her next words. "But there's another thing. After the get-together for Bill, he kissed her. At least four of the girls agree they saw them."

Why did Maggie feel shame when he was the one who'd done something wrong? But then, it wasn't like with Ralph, was it? They didn't have any kind of understanding. They were just friends. He could kiss whomever he liked, because there was nothing between them. She tried to think that thought repeatedly so it became true.

"I suppose everyone just thought that he was sweet on you," Grace said.

Not so sweet. She couldn't stop the picture in her mind of Katie in Alec's embrace. Her brain played the scene over and over, like a passionate kiss at the end of a film.

They sat in miserable silence while every kind of emotion ran through Maggie's mind. Anger at Alec for leading her on. Jealousy, because if he wanted to kiss someone, why hadn't he tried to kiss her? Disbelief. In the last week, with their late nights in the pub, she'd begun to think, to hope, they could be more than friends.

How could he?

Finally she said, "There's nothing for it. We have to approach him."

She didn't let herself cry until Grace left.

CHAPTER TWENTY-FOUR

Barrowby Farm, Lincolnshire
8 February 1943, 9:30 a.m.

A watch, two cigarette cases, and another ladies' makeup compact. Not a bad haul, all things considered.

He leaned into the heavy barn door to push it open, then slipped through. He needed to get to the station and run an errand for his mother. No need to shut it behind him, since he just wanted to add these items to his stash.

He approached the large oak chest in the far corner of the barn, simply but sturdily designed, concealed behind a stack of hay. He didn't bother with any kind of lock on the latch. No one but him ever came into this place.

After a prolific winter, the chest overflowed with pilfered goods, and he had to store some larger items separately. Yesterday he'd carefully balled a fur coat, wrapped it in fabric, and set it to one side, making sure that it looked like another piece of agricultural flotsam left in a barn.

The volume of items here was incriminating. He'd have to

move some of it soon but was still deciding the best way to get rid of it all.

"Clive!" his mother called through the open barn door.

Blast! He hastily shut the lid of the chest and emerged from behind the haystack. "Coming, Mum."

His mother looked more tired than usual. She helped with the manual labor on the farm, but her work became much more intense after his father's accident. The products and quotas enforced by the government made farm work even harder than before the war. Her hair, which a few years ago was shot through with just a few silver strands, was now mostly gray, and the lines around her kind eyes were deep furrows when she smiled.

Which she wasn't doing now.

"Get going, boy! We don't have any time to waste with your daydreams and tinkering. You're already late to collect the new land girl."

He obediently followed his mother out of the barn, closing the door behind him this time. "Take Bessie with you."

He scowled. Bessie's over-cheeriness grated on his nerves. As they made their way along the lane to the railway station, she tried to engage him in conversation as hard as he avoided talking to her.

In the sky above them, the bombers from the airfield did their circuits and bumps, practicing their takeoff and landing maneuvers. After their sluggish start, the airfield was preparing for something big. He'd noticed security tightening every morning when he did his deliveries, and the sound of Lancaster engines practicing above the farm felt constant.

Bessie had obviously given up on conversation as he stalked towards the station, but that didn't mean she was quiet. She prattled happily to herself, voicing every one of the vacuous thoughts that popped into her mind.

"I hope this new girl is the chatty sort. It will be so nice to have some company as I go about my work, since there's precious little conversation to be had otherwise."

When they reached the station, the train had already left and the passengers dispersed. A young girl with dark curls sat alone on the platform, which prompted suspicious looks from the ancient stationmaster. Clive grunted when he saw her dress, stockings, and high heels. She looked like she was ready for a day of high-street shopping. Judging from her wide eyes and delicate features, she must only be just eighteen. He doubted any of those eighteen years had been spent in the country.

Since he was likely to snarl rather than speak, he held back while Bessie made the introductions. They didn't need something to look at on the farm—they desperately needed someone to work.

"Rosalind Morrison? I'm Bessie Mills. Sorry we're late! It's a bit of a trudge from the farm, I'm afraid, and we aren't allowed to cheat and use the tractor."

Bessie held out her hand as she said her name, grinning in her lopsided way. Bessie's clunky Land Army uniform, brown and bottle green, contrasted with the new girl's elegant figure as she stood to shake Bessie's hand. Clive suppressed a groan.

"Call me Rosie."

Bessie looked her up and down, admiring her clothes. "I hope you don't mind too much if they get dirty. The mud around here is beastly!"

He snorted as he reached for the new girl's case and yanked it up.

"This is Clive Stockton. His family owns the farm we'll be working on."

He grunted and tipped his hat but strode off down the lane without saying a word. He should let her carry the suitcase, to get her used to heavy farm work, but he preferred to have an excuse to walk ahead of them and avoid talking.

Bessie babbled nonstop, reciting details he already knew. She was from Bristol. She wasn't keen on being conscripted into the services, so she'd volunteered for the Land Army. This was her second posting, and the work was back breaking. Old news, but whenever he glanced back, the new girl had a wide-eyed, fascinated expression. Just how young was she? He wished Bessie would shut up and let the new recruit get a word in.

"There is plenty of fun to be had once the work is done," Bessie said. "The pub is full of airmen every evening, which makes things interesting."

"We're very close to the airfield, aren't we?" The young girl picked her way along the lane in her impracticable shoes.

"You can hear them all the time. Especially at night. But you get used to the noise."

"What's Barrowby Farm like?" Rosie asked.

"The Stocktons, who own it, are fine. The father lost an arm in an accident last year. Crushed by a tractor. Now his wife is in charge. She's the firm but fair kind." She paused, lowering her voice, but the wind was blowing in the right direction, so Clive still heard every word. "Clive haunts the place. There is a rumor going around that Mr. Mathis, from next door, once came by and threatened him with a shotgun because he'd been snooping around his daughter's room. So lock up your things well." She continued at her normal volume. "You don't say much, do you? How old are you?"

"Eighteen. In fact, it was my birthday last week."

Bessie wouldn't have noticed the slight hesitation. She didn't listen closely enough. Not like him.

"Lovely! Well play your cards right, and the drinks will be on me."

Bessie barely took a breath before launching into another long speech that took them all the way back to the farm gate.

CHAPTER TWENTY-FIVE

RAF Bottesford
9 February 1943, 5:30 a.m.

"Katie Baines is pregnant." Maggie met him as he left the mess hall after his post-operation breakfast. If he'd been less tired, he might have been more alert to the way her eyes blazed.

"All right." He drew the syllables out as he scrambled to understand why Maggie had come out in the dark to tell him this.

"Apparently by some cad who told her that if they did it standing up, that was impossible. Was it you?" She spat the question.

"No! Maggie, of course not! No!" The denials kept coming, but she couldn't believe them.

"Then why does everyone say you were kissing her at the pub last week?"

What could he say that didn't make the situation worse? To make sure she knew this wasn't a case of history repeating itself?

"Well, she kissed me."

No. It didn't sound any better out in the open than it did in his head. Why couldn't they be having this conversation after he'd had a full night's sleep instead of now, when his body and brain were confused with adrenaline and fatigue? Not to mention the cold he was trying to shake.

"That's not how half of the WAAF at Bottesford tell the story. Believe me, I've heard descriptions in great detail."

Hurt and rage blazed from her eyes. But he couldn't give her the full denial that would make her trust him.

"I was drunk."

It was a poor defense but the only one he had. Besides, it was the truth. He could barely remember what happened and relied on the accounts of others to fill in the blanks.

"That excuses it, does it?" The look of disgust she gave him cut him to the core.

"Maggie, I promise there is nothing else! There has never been anything else between Katie and I. Nothing."

Apart from that one time under the mistletoe. But she knew about that. And she knew he had been steadfastly ignoring Katie for months now, didn't she?

"Maggie." He moved closer so he could take her hand, but she snatched it away. Hurt and confusion swirled across her face like storm clouds in a thunderous sky. "I promise this wasn't me."

At least she waited for an explanation. It had to be a good sign that she hadn't stormed off yet.

"I did kiss her . . . well, sort of. It wasn't . . . that makes it sound . . ." He shook his head to clear it. "I know what it looks like. But I promise you with everything inside me that nothing else happened."

"Well, who was it then?" she demanded.

Weariness hit him suddenly. It wouldn't do to laugh right now. But he felt like it. What else could he do? Life had become a ridiculous seesaw between the downright terrifying and the completely banal.

A few hours earlier, he'd flown over the heart of the Third Reich under heavy flak that had mangled an engine. He and Fisher managed to stabilize the kite, but the new navigator was so green, they'd flown back to Bottesford via Timbuktu. It was hard enough getting into the air tonight without Bill. More than once he'd thought he was going to cark it with one op to go.

Now he was having the kind of tiff that no doubt played out trillions of times the world over since Adam and Eve first quarreled. The contrast between terror and banality gave him whiplash.

He rubbed his hand over his face so she wouldn't see any of that emotion. "I'll try to find out. But before I can find out for sure, I need some sleep."

Sleep would be good. He wasn't feeling well.

She nodded, but she dropped her eyes to the ground.

"I wouldn't do this to you, Maggie. I promise. You're my girl," he added softly.

Her eyes shot up and pierced him with their indignant rage. "I most certainly am not! Like I've always said, I'm not interested in fickle, good-for-nothing pilots who two-time a girl as soon as the going gets tough."

She stalked away, leaving him miserably alone in the drizzle. He plodded toward his sleeping quarters, still stinging from her words, when with one almighty clang the fire alarm jolted him out of his heavy thoughts. Airmen poured out from the buildings around him, tired and confused but suddenly activated.

Odd for the bell to go off at this time in the morning, without any explosion or smoke or sign of distress.

Jonty appeared at his side. "What is it, do you think?"

"I don't know," Alec replied. "Everyone was present and accounted for as far as I know."

"Could it be the bomb stores?"

"Dear God I hope not." He truly meant it as a prayer. With the sheer tonnage of explosives kept on an RAF station like this, even a small fire could set off an explosion that could blow them all to kingdom come.

But they didn't hear an explosion. There wasn't even any smoke.

Martin Macpherson burst upon them. He looked at Alec with incredulity. "It wasn't flak," he gasped, leaning over with his hands on his knees while he caught his breath

"What do you mean, Macpherson?" Alec asked.

Macpherson responded through heavy, panting breaths. "It wasn't flak that cut out your engine. It was a bomb. A bloody incendiary bomb!"

Alec was stunned. He tried to comprehend Martin's words.

"You landed with a live bomb bouncing around in your fuel tank! Burned through the engine from above but didn't go off. One of ours, looks like. I don't know who is looking out for you, Thomas, but I'd be down on my knees thanking the Lord Almighty if I were you!"

Jonty, face as white as fresh fallen snow, suffered from one of the rare moments when he was utterly lost for words.

Alec was too. He fished in his pockets for a cigarette and tried to hide the way his hands shook as he struck the match to it. Jonty, who didn't smoke, bummed a cigarette and lit it with Alec's.

"I'll have to remember to go back and adjust my log," Alec said, voice shaking. "I just wrote 'tank three hit by flak.' This is much more exciting."

"It's a story for the grandchildren!" Jonty joked.

"Well, with this kind of luck, you both might just hold out long enough to have them." Martin shook his head.

Alec huffed out an involuntary laugh, and then another. Wonder tingled through him at the realization of the danger they'd been in for the entire four-hour flight home.

Jonty grinned and laughed as well.

The panic set in later, when Alec's head hit his pillow and he felt blood thundering through it.

A live bomb! An incendiary bomb, no less! In the fuel tank. Probably a friendly that he had flown under in the confusion of the raid.

Who survived that kind of thing? Inside his fuel tank, and they were all still here!

Freakish.

Any of the moments in the sky between Germany and Lincolnshire could have been his last. One wrong move during landing could have obliterated them all. But against all odds, here he was, lying awake in his bed. It was no less random than Bill taking a stray bullet to the head from a rogue night fighter.

Martin's words from earlier in the evening rang in his ears. They'd been a jest, but something about them felt more true than ever.

He should be thanking his Maker. But he couldn't think how to begin. Surely as an adult he didn't have to kneel down by the side of his bed with his head bowed and eyes closed, his palms pressed together, like he did as a child, did he?

The one person who would probably tell him if he asked wasn't speaking to him right now. Which made him feel lonelier than he had ever felt in the sky above Europe.

CHAPTER TWENTY-SIX

RAF Bottesford
11 February 1943, 11:30 a.m.

Even though she was well past school, Maggie occasionally dreamed she was back inside its confines. More like a nightmare, the kind you wake from relieved to find it wasn't real. But whenever Queen Bee summoned Maggie to her office, she felt like she was inside one of those dreams.

Like an all-too-knowing head teacher, Carver eventually got wind of everything that went on among the WAAFs in her charge. She'd called Maggie and Grace in to report on Katie Baines.

They disclosed everything they knew about the situation. The girls at the station had closed ranks, confided in one another. It was clear that the Sweetheart Sweepstakes had done considerable damage among them. Queen Bee listened with deep creases cut across her forehead.

"Alec Thomas, you say? Isn't he the one you've been stepping out with, Corporal Morrison?"

How could she possibly know that?

"Stepping out is a gross overstatement, ma'am. But we don't think it is him. We think that the father is James Hardie, one of the gunners on his crew. He was sort of the ringleader when it came to the sweepstakes."

True to his word, Alec divulged that Jimmy Hardie was a likely candidate. Regretting he'd drunk so much that night, he'd come to the Map Room to let her and Grace know what he'd found out, apologizing to Maggie at least a dozen times. Not that she looked up from her knitting when he did.

For the last few months each time Alec had rejected Katie's attentions, Hardie had swooped in to comfort her. Katie had confessed too, utterly ashamed. She knew Hardie wouldn't do the right thing by her, but she'd thought Alec might if she could make him think he was the father. Her plan failed spectacularly. Katie was now too sick to do her work.

"Does she want to keep it?"

Maggie's jaw dropped open at the thought there was even an alternative to consider.

"We haven't asked her directly, ma'am," Grace said.

"Well find out, would you? I don't pretend to like it, but there are ways to deal with this." She dismissed them.

"She can't really be suggesting abortion, can she? How awful!" Maggie said when she and Grace were out of the Queen Bee's office.

Grace looked at her sadly. "I don't think it's the first time Queen Bee has dealt with something like this. 'Needs must' during the war and all that."

"Grace, we can't—"

"I know. We'll think of something."

Their heavy steps took them past the post room, where they met Alec as he was stepping out into the cold.

"Here, Maggie," he said, holding out two letters with her name on them.

One from Mrs. Bickham, by the looks of things. She couldn't see the one underneath.

"I was going to bring them to you in the Map Room."

"I'm perfectly capable of collecting my own post." She snatched the letters from him and spun. "See you later, Grace."

After a rocky start, Rob Staunton, the new navigator, seemed to settle in well. At first, Alec had thought him too young, a little too eager to see action. But once in the air, he was sharp and focused. Alec resolved not to judge him too harshly. It wasn't the kid's fault Bill had copped it.

Alec wanted them all to put in extra hours of practice to better function as a well-oiled machine again.

Wing Commander Palmer agreed to remove them from the operational flying roster for a week to focus on drills. Staunton needed them, but so did Alec. After Bill and the bomb in the fuel tank, his mind felt messed up and his insides shook every time he sat in the cockpit. The next op was number thirty for him. But what if his luck ran out this time?

The additional practice also served to distract him from his inability to sleep, his developing cough, and the words Maggie had spat at him when she'd confronted him about Katie: "I'm not your girl."

By any objective measure, that was true—she wasn't his girl. They'd only danced a few times and hadn't so much as kissed—even on New Year's Eve, when conditions had been perfect. They'd barely even been alone together! Right now, the only words she spoke to him were cold and over the radio, with goodness knows how many other people listening in. But in all that nothingness he was sure there was something. He just had to find a way to convince her of that.

Those thoughts, and the headache that plagued him since this morning, kept him distracted as he rode back to the dormitories on the crew transport after another round of drills. The sound of Hardie sniggering with Staunton pulled him from his thoughts. A particular kind of snigger Hardie only used when talking about the women on the station.

"Don't go giving Staunton ideas, Hardie," Alec ordered. "He's just a kid."

He didn't want another Sweetheart Sweepstakes debacle on top of everything else he was dealing with.

"Who are you, Thomas? His father?" Hardie retorted.

Alec's jaw tightened. Usually Bill would calm things down when Alec and Hardie clashed. But Bill wasn't here.

Alec could have pulled rank, but he ignored Hardie. Now wasn't the time. He'd speak to Hardie later about not leading Staunton astray.

The snickering continued as the crew transport, more like a low trailer pulled by a tractor driven by a WAAF, bounced along the track.

He couldn't help but hear Hardie giving Staunton pointers on the best places to take a girl for *uninterrupted* time alone. Names of places every man on the station knew. But coming from Hardie's mouth after what he'd done to Katie . . . they made Alec's blood boil.

He balled his hand into a fist on his leg, trying to hold in his agitation.

When the transport rolled to a stop, Alec moved like lightning, launching himself out of the trailer, grabbing Hardie by his shirt, and hauling him out of the transport. Before Hardie had a chance to recover, Alec's fist met his jaw in a vicious right hook.

The blow sent a jolt of satisfying pain up Alec's arm. Hardie staggered back, hand to his face. "What was that for?"

"Katie Baines, you spineless piece of—"

"Why? You didn't want her. All you bang on about is your frigid radio operator."

At the mention of Maggie, Alec flew at him. Hardie was ready this time, but he still wasn't fast enough to get away from the barrage of punches. In a fight with anyone else, Hardie might enjoy some support from the fellow members of his crew. But no one challenged Alec's righteous anger here. Jonty shouted encouragement to his skipper from the sidelines, sounding as if he wanted to join in with punches of his own.

A crowd gathered around them, drawn by the sound of shouts and punches. But within minutes it was all over. Hardie curled on the ground, a black eye already forming, and Alec stood over him with bloodied fists.

"Do right by Katie, you bastard," Alec spat before thundering off to calm down.

Outside St. Mary the Virgin's Church, Bottesford
12 February 1943, 3:30 p.m.

Maggie tramped along the muddy roads and bridle paths into the village, hoping the long walk would clear her mind. The village's usual morning bustle of deliveries to the pub and grocer had already faded when she arrived. She enjoyed this quiet time alone to untangle all the thoughts crowded in her mind like a mess of yarn that needed attention.

Queen Bee's terrible suggestion to Katie's dilemma pressed like a weight into Maggie's chest. Adding to her worries, Katie hadn't moved out of bed for days, although Maggie couldn't tell how much of that was physical sickness and how much was plain old misery.

Then there was Alec, whose face had a wounded puppy expression on it every time she saw it. She pretended not to care when he spoke with Grace, although she strained to listen to their every word. Grace always chastised Maggie afterward. "You need to talk with him."

Why was that always Grace's advice?

She tried to pray as she wandered. The words didn't come as easily as she wanted them to. She rested in the thought that the Lord could see everything, even the tangled mess inside her. "Please, help me know what to do," she murmured.

"Maggie!"

If she didn't recognize the voice, she might have thought that she was having some kind of spiritual visitation.

Oscar Williams approached her, riding his bicycle through the puddles on the lane. Mud from his ride splashed up his ankles, and even his thick glasses wore smudges.

She smiled broadly, taking comfort in God's immediate answer to her prayer.

"You look windswept! How long have you been out here?" he asked.

"Not too long. I needed to clear my mind."

He looked at her the way he always did, as though he saw straight through her attempt at a brave front.

"Want to tell me about it?"

She nodded, realizing in that moment that she really did.

"The church isn't very far. We can walk there together," he said.

He pushed his bike up the little hill to the chapel so they could travel at the same pace. "I've known you long enough to know when something is the matter. So spill it."

That was all it took for the words to tumble out of her.

About Katie.

About Alec.

But also about the worry about her family that simmered underneath the distractions of the day to day. She showed him the last letter from her father, still in her pocket.

"Well, I can give you some hope there. I've been to see him again, several times now. I'm sure he would want me to shield you from the details. But I believe, by God's grace, he is coming out of the wilderness he's been wandering in."

Her eyes welled up. If it were any other man, even Alec, she might have turned her head away. But she didn't need to hide from Oscar.

"What about Rosie? Did you get to speak with her?"

"I believe he's trying to repair what he has broken there."

She nodded, that concurred with the letters she had been receiving where Rosie spoke about her outings with Clara, and even the possibility she would be allowed to go away with Clara's family for a week once the weather got warmer.

"What about the other things I mentioned? Do you have any advice for what I should do with a faithless airman?"

"I'm not sure *I* am the one you should be asking, Maggie," he said. "But since you have . . . I don't approve of what he's done, and your father would throttle me if I didn't tell you that a man who gets drunk and kisses someone else is a scoundrel and you should stay right away from him!"

Her lips curled up at the fatherly voice.

"But right now we aren't talking about him, are we? I think you know what you need to do. It's time to live out everything you've been taught since you were a child."

"Blind forgiveness, you mean?" She knew she sounded as petulant as Rosie.

He shook his head. "Real grace isn't blind. Maggie—you know that. It sees all the messiness and forgives it anyway."

"He doesn't deserve it."

"None of us do. That's the point—it's undeserved. I'm not excusing his behavior at all—there's still an uncomfortable conversation ahead of you—but you have to look at the way God treats us and follow that example."

He sounded so like the father she'd known before her mother died that it made her choke up again.

"But forgiveness doesn't necessarily mean letting him back into your heart, Maggie."

"He never really had my heart."

He raised an eyebrow at her. She wasn't convinced by her own words either. She narrowed her eyes at him. "Who knew a local vicar would be such a good agony aunt?"

"Don't tell it too widely. I'd rather deal with my parishioners' spiritual problems than their romantic ones."

"I'm so glad I ran into you. I should try to get back before the light goes, but I'll remember what you said," she said.

Her walk back to the village had a lighter step.

———∞———

After having spent all the afternoon walking, she called in at the pub to get some water before returning to the aerodrome. To her surprise, Jonty lingered at the bar.

"Despite what you might think about Scotsmen and whisky, I'm actually a teetotaler." He confirmed this by raising a glass of water to his lips.

She did the same thing with hers. "I'm on my way back to the airfield. Will you walk with me?"

They were out again on the quiet country paths when Jonty turned to her suddenly. "You know, I was driving that night, and I saw—more importantly, I heard—everything."

She knew exactly which night he meant. "I've already had the blow-by-blow account, Jonty. I really don't want to think any more about Alec Thomas and who he kisses."

A bald-faced lie. She wanted to know everything, and she thought Jonty could tell.

"That's the thing though, isn't it? You've just heard what the girls who saw them from the pub door saw. I was right there, sober as a judge. I probably remember things better than Alec himself."

Her curiosity won. "So what happened?"

"He was very drunk and paid no one any mind. She threw herself in his way and kissed him. I don't think he knew what was happening. But when she came up for air, he said your name. I think it killed the mood as far as she was concerned."

She huffed with indignation. "So he got incredibly drunk and used my name while unwittingly kissing someone else? You really know how to cheer a girl up, Jonty."

"But it wasn't just that he used your name. He monologued about how he couldn't kiss her because of how much he was in love with you. Didn't let up for a full five minutes. I don't think Katie was quite expecting that."

"It's still despicable," she said, with less conviction.

"It wasn't pretty, I can say that much. The drunken slurrings of a man obsessed with his girl."

"How many times do I have to tell people—I am not his girl."

"Och Maggie, trust me on this. You're his girl—you just don't know it yet."

The tense hand pressing on her heart since she'd first heard the news about Alec and Katie eased. But she changed the subject as soon as she felt herself soften toward him.

"Carver offered to get Katie an abortion."

The thought of an innocent life being taken made her sick to the stomach. From the look on his face, Jonty felt it too.

"Poor Katie." He frowned. "Hardie is a reprobate."

She couldn't agree more.

"Alec gave him a good beating though."

"Did he?" One corner of her mouth quirked.

"Och, that wasn't pretty either! Alec has a sister, see, so I think he channeled some big-brother energy into his punches—not to mention his frustration that you won't talk to him. Hardie's stocky but small. He didn't stand a chance. I was wondering whether we'd need to find a new bomb aimer at one point. But Alec seems to think Hardie's learned his lesson."

Maggie didn't know whether she should feel good or bad Alec had spent so much energy defending Katie's honor. "Is Alec all right?"

"He'd be better if you would talk to him. I understand if you can't forgive him, but talk to him."

CHAPTER TWENTY-SEVEN

St Mary the Virgin's Church
13 February 1943, 9:30 a.m.

He couldn't stop thinking about that incendiary.

Of all the nightmares to visit him since this blasted war began, none compared to the ones at the moment. The ones where he was flying with a perfect moon hanging unobscured in the sky, then suddenly a flash of white and he was dead.

The dream felt so real. He'd bolted upright with fear gripping his heart, breath caught in his throat, and sweat drenching the sheets. Then sleep eluded him. For several nights in a row now, he lay awake wondering what would happen if he died. What exactly would he say if he met his Maker?

If he knew how, he might pray, but he still had no idea.

He needed expert advice. The station chaplain was called away, and Maggie wasn't speaking to him, so there was only one other person he knew. He met the young vicar on the pathway in front of the church and did his best to suppress unkind thoughts about the froglike quality of his face.

"I'm just on my way out. Alec, isn't it?" the vicar called out to him. "I haven't seen you around here, have I?"

Alec forced himself to engage in chitchat. "Once or twice."

"Ah yes, a friend of Maggie's, I believe."

Not at the moment, but probably best not to mention that. "Yes. I, uh, heard one of your sermons, and I had a question about it."

His speech was all fits and starts, making him feel like an inarticulate child. The vicar raised his eyebrows and ushered Alec into the church building. White bunting and ribbon covered the otherwise imposing stone inside. Wedding decorations. Of course, Fisher was getting married here tomorrow. Alec glanced around, hoping he wouldn't see anyone he knew, then fixed his eyes on his own hands, spinning his pilot's cap in circles as he tried to voice his question.

Oscar waited for Alec to speak. Alec supposed, in this place, in this war, people came to a vicar with all sorts of concerns, from the ordinary to the existential. He shifted uncomfortably under the vicar's gaze as he tried to find the right words. "The thing is, I've never done it—never prayed, I mean. Not since I was told what to say as a kid."

Oscar nodded. "What's made you think you might try?"

Alec explained the dreams and his growing fear he would cark it just as randomly as Bill. The man's way of listening, soft eyes and inclined head, drew information out of Alec.

"I'm not a good person. I've done terrible things. All the sins! Even murder if you consider what I do every night in my kite. If God is so good, how can I even start to speak to Him?"

The vicar regarded him. "Are you familiar with Jonah?"

"You mean the story about the whale?" Alec scoffed at the Sunday school fable.

"It's easy to get distracted by the whale," Oscar said. "But the fish isn't the point of the story. The point of the story is God's love. He pursued Jonah to the depths of the ocean when Jonah tried to run." Oscar paused. "The trick is to understand that we are all that way, every single one of us. We are fleeing and He is chasing."

Alec's kept his face blank and expectant. He wasn't fleeing now. "Have you ever read any of the Bible?"

"The Christmas and Easter bits," Alec said. Not really an answer.

"I'm afraid there are no secrets to praying. No special words you need to utter. Just turn your heart to God and let it speak."

Before he left, Oscar prayed for him. It was strange, almost unreal, to be speaking with an invisible companion. But then he felt peace in a way he never expected to.

"Take this." Oscar handed him one of the black Bibles from the pew. "Read Jonah's prayer from inside the whale, and then let's talk after the wedding tomorrow."

"No time. Have to take Fisher out for one last hurrah before he's a married man ."

The admission slipped out before he remembered he was speaking to a man of the cloth.

Oscar nodded. Alec had the feeling that Oscar was sizing him up under those glasses and deciding whether or not to speak further. Finally he did.

"I've known Maggie for years, you know. I'm a very good friend of her family. In fact, just yesterday I was catching up with her about everything that's been going on."

Under Oscar's steady gaze, Alec understood exactly what it felt like to be on the receiving end of one of the talking-tos that he would give boys showing interest in his sister. He figured he must have featured heavily in Oscar's discussion with Maggie.

"You know, before you arrived on the scene, there was another airman just like you. Clever. Charming. Handsome. He took a shine to her just like you have. She was swept off her feet. But when push came to shove, there was no substance to him. So you might like to consider how pursuing an answer to your question about prayer might also open up a path back into Maggie's good graces."

Convenient advice from a clergyman.

But motivating.

Very motivating.

From Alec Thomas, Lincolnshire, England
To Mrs. Moira and Miss Elizabeth Thomas, Sydney, Australia
13 February 1943

Dear Mum and Lizzie,

I know I haven't written in a while so I figure I owe you a letter.

You'll probably think I haven't written because I am sour about Lizzie's engagement. Tell her it's not that. It's just that I've been in the sky much more since Christmas, which means there's much less spare time on the ground. Tell her I am happy for her, but only if he's worthy of her. If he's not, I'll be round to sort him out. Just as soon as I finish with Hitler.

A friend of mine is getting married tomorrow to a local girl. He's from Caloundra, and she's from Barrowby, but they are both from dairy farms. I guess cows are the same the world over, so they'll have that in common. I was at the church this afternoon, and everything looks good. I promise to pay attention to what the bride wears tomorrow and add it here. I know you'll want to know.

Maybe Fisher's wedding is making me feel sentimental, but I want to tell you that I've met someone too. Her name is Margaret, but she goes by Maggie. She's pretty special. You've always told me to be careful with a woman's heart, and I'm afraid I might have let you down. I'll spare you the details. They aren't the kind of thing you write in letters to your mum. But if I don't write again for a while, it's because I am busy making things up to her.

I hope I can introduce her to you both one day. At very least it would mean seeing my favorite women all together in the one room.

I will try to write again soon. I love you both.

Your loving son and brother,

Alec.

PS: The bride wore white.

CHAPTER TWENTY-EIGHT

"I, Christopher Allan Fisher, take you, Lucy Ann Mathis, to be my lawfully wedded wife . . ."

The timid voices of the bride and groom barely reached him at the back of the church. The words didn't feel real.

He'd been sweet on Lucy Mathis once, all those years ago when they were in school. Back then her hair fell down her back in picture-perfect ringlets, and her blue eyes glowed like jewels. She looked like one of the dolls in the windows of the toy store in Grantham. So much so that when he saw the doll, he wanted to take it for his own. It was the first time he could remember wanting something that wasn't his.

". . . to have and to hold, from this day forward . . ."

Lucy hated farm life. Like the doll in the window, she didn't belong among the mud and muck. That was what she'd told him when he'd asked to take her to the village dance when they were fifteen.

She was meant for something greater, she'd told him, and she would never kiss a farm boy.

They were neighbors, so she couldn't give up seeing him entirely. As she'd grown taller and plumper, her curls changed from their golden blond to a mousey brown. He knew for a fact she dyed them back to their original color. He wondered if the man in front of her knew.

". . . for better, for worse, for richer, for poorer, in sickness and in health . . ."

Lucy almost cried with delight when the RAF invaded Bottesford, especially when the latest batch of airmen arrived. Too international for his tastes, but she wasted no time in snaring herself an Australian. One who quickly promised to take her away from the English mud and back to his land of sunshine and oranges, just as soon as he'd defeated Hitler.

So here he was at their wedding, watching her promise her life away with unrestrained glee.

He sat farther back than he did on Sundays. Initially he'd been hoping to catch her eye as she walked in. To . . . what exactly? Sweep her away at the last minute?

He was a fool. Her eyes only saw the man waiting for her at the altar, looking adoringly back at her.

". . . to love and to cherish, till death us do part, according to God's holy law. This is my solemn vow and promise."

That was that.

He recognized all the people here. He'd known many of them all his life, like she had. The other half—the half in uniform—all gave him vague smiles, recalling his face from the aerodrome. That was, after all, what he'd been working for there: bland recognition.

Seeking out one face in particular among the uniforms became a habit recently. The dark-haired girl with the plain prettiness seemed all the more attractive now that Lucy was taken.

He saw her now. Just the back of her head, of course, but when she glanced sideways to grin at her friend, he saw her sweet profile and her eyes shining with joyful tears.

He wasn't the only one watching her.

A pilot in the same pew as her but several places to the left kept glancing her way, trying to catch her eye, the way he'd tried to catch Lucy's.

The girl steadfastly ignored the airman.

That she would ignore a handsome face like that, so determined to get her attention, gave him the encouragement he needed to try to talk to her.

CHAPTER TWENTY-NINE

St. Mary the Virgin's Church
14 February 1943, 9:30 a.m.

"Such a beautiful ceremony!"
"Don't they look so lovely together!"
"Congratulations to the happy couple!"

Maggie walked away from the merry comments floating around her friends. She needed to get back to the aerodrome for her shift, so she said her congratulations and slipped down the path out of the churchyard.

When she reached the gate, a young man, probably from a local farm, stepped out in front of her, causing her to jump back a few steps in fright.

"Oh, excuse me." She held a hand over her heart, which leapt at the scare. She tried to walk past him, but he wouldn't move out of her way. "I'm sorry. Do I know you?"

He had a vaguely familiar look. About her height with mousey hair and soft features hidden under a tweed cap. Definitely old enough to enlist, but with farming a reserved occupation, he probably hadn't been called up.

He took off his cap, looking bashful. "I'm a friend of the bride."

"Oh, right." She looked at her watch. She couldn't afford to be late for this shift but couldn't move on with him in her way.

"Will you be at the reception? I thought maybe we could dance?"

He took a step toward her. The skin on the back of her neck prickled the way it had done in the alley on New Year's Eve. She swallowed hard and willed herself not to freeze.

"Oh, sorry. I'm headed back to work now."

He looked disappointed but glanced up the path. She followed his gaze and saw Oscar, still garbed in the clerical robes he'd worn for the ceremony, on his way toward them. The farmhand dissolved away when Oscar approached.

"Off so soon?" Oscar asked.

"Yes. I do so love weddings, but I have a shift that I couldn't change." Actually she'd swapped into this shift especially so she could avoid the celebration after the ceremony. She didn't want to attend one anywhere near Alec.

Oscar smiled. "Did you talk to your airman?"

She shrugged. "Not yet. No time, you see. There's a war on, you know."

"Not the impression you gave me a few days ago."

"All right then. The truth is, I just don't know how I feel about it all."

Actually she was thoroughly sick of all the emotions swirling around her head at the moment.

He chuckled. "Well, I wish I could bottle this moment. I'd label it 'The one and only time that Margaret Morrison didn't know her own mind.' There's more to him than you give the man credit for. And he was trying to catch your eye the whole service."

She'd felt it, but she wasn't ready to yield to him just yet. Speaking of which, she was now in position to see Alec coming down the path the way the farmhand had seen Oscar.

"Must fly. See you again soon." She stood on tiptoes and reached up to kiss Oscar's cheek.

"What was that for?" he called as she swung her leg over the station bicycle she'd left at the church gate.

Oscar would know the answer as soon as Alec caught up with him.

Map Room, RAF Bottesford
16 February 1943, 4:30 p.m.

Maggie, who'd finished a day shift, sat quietly at Grace's desk in the Map Room, reading a copy of *Women's Illustrated*. If anyone asked her, she'd claim to be reading the latest advice for how to blend the perfect mix of tea and gravy for substitute stockings. Only that wasn't true. Mrs. Patricia Blakewell's column on "What to Do When Your Sweetheart's Untrue" captivated her attention.

At first, Maggie disapproved of Mrs. Blakewell's obsession with said sweetheart's morale and her recommendation for English wives to forgive the transgressions of unfaithful husbands in the forces. However, she was coming around to the gist of her argument: the war complicated everything, so everyone should try to look beyond their hurt.

Someone cleared a throat behind her.

She ignored it, as she did most of the sounds in the room when she was seated here, thinking it was an airman waiting for Grace to attend the counter separating her room from the hallway.

But then she heard it again, closer now. She looked up.

Alec stood in the center of the room, holding his cap in his hand in front of him. Never before had she seen a man embody the word contrite like Alec did here.

She glanced around in time to see Grace disappear out the Map Room door. Somehow she knew Grace would station herself in the hallway to stop anyone interrupting. But even so, they didn't have a long time to talk. Grace would need to be back at her station soon.

"I'm so sorry. For all of it. I'm the biggest kind of idiot. Please forgive me, Mags? I want to make things right between us."

She tried to stay aloof but found she couldn't. Looking drawn and pale, he wasn't even trying his grin on her. Good thing too—she wouldn't have trusted him if he did. No witty banter danced between them now, just an invisible thread of elastic so taut after all her pulling away, it was likely to give at any moment.

"I don't believe you when you say there is nothing between us. There is something. Something real—and I think you feel it too."

She didn't speak, forcing him to plough on.

"There's no excuse for what happened with Katie, but I want you to know that when I close my eyes at night—and even when I am awake and mean to be concentrating on other things—it's you I see. And it's been you ever since I met you. I'm sorry for being unworthy of you—betting with Hardie, drinking too much. But I . . . really like you, and I'm asking for you to forgive me."

No artifice. He'd come to her with a bare soul.

She still didn't speak. Instead, she fought an internal battle while trying to keep her face still.

His eyes dropped to the ground, dejected. "Anyway, I've put all that in a letter too. In case . . . you know. It's on my pillow with the one for my mum and sister. But I wanted to tell you face to face too."

Her heart decided to take Mrs. Blakewell's advice—and Oscar's, for that matter. What was it Oscar had said about seeing the messiness of life and forgiving anyway?

"You're right. You are a fool, Alec. But I forgive you."

Relief washed over his face, resolving itself in a wholehearted smile. "Right." He swallowed, gulping back his emotions. "So you'll come dancing tomorrow? We have to go to the Pelican Club because I'm banned from the dance hall, but all the others will be there."

The mention of the dance hall took her straight back to New Year's Eve, sitting intoxicatingly close to him in the dimly lit bomb shelter. The dance of their hands as they talked in their own bubble. She wanted that again.

The invisible strand of elastic between them strained so far now, it could release at any moment, sending her flying toward him. She stood, but before she could take a step, she heard Grace through the door.

"Oh yes, of course, Wing Commander. Right through here."

Grace projected her voice, no doubt to warn them she was about to burst in. With Palmer hot on her heels, Grace gave a relieved smile when she saw she hadn't ruined a private moment.

Maggie dipped her head to hide her reddening features. A second or two later and things might have been different.

"Thomas! What are you doing in here?" Palmer demanded, although Maggie thought WingCo had his suspicions.

"Corporal Morrison was just minding the Map Room for me while I used the ladies' room, sir," Grace improvised.

"Yes," Alec followed. "And when I found Corporal Morrison here, I simply had to apologize to her for not telling her that we had changed the call sign of our kite. You know we all call her M Maggie now, sir, due to my rear gunner's obsession with the name. But somewhere along the line, Corporal Morrison missed getting that news and was worried it would reflect badly on her since she is often the one in the control tower. Of course, I told her you were a reasonable man who would never jump to the wrong conclusion."

As smooth as butter.

"Very true. Very true," WingCo said. "You should feel complimented, Corporal Morrison, that such a fine aircraft, piloted by such fine men, has been named after you."

Alec's smile reminded her of the Cheshire cat from Alice in Wonderland.

"I'll be off now, sir, if you don't mind. Corporal Morrison, will I see you at the club?" Carefully angled so WingCo couldn't see, he winked.

It took every fiber of her being not to roll her eyes in front of the wing commander. She sighed in half exasperation, half happiness. "See you at the club, Pilot Officer Thomas."

Grace gave her a knowing smile after the men departed. "I want to hear everything!"

CHAPTER THIRTY

Sick Bay, RAF Bottesford
17 February 1943, 11:30 a.m.

Alec had never felt so sick in his life. Even though he was tired enough to sleep through an air-raid warning playing right in his ear, his cough kept him awake. When he did drift off, he woke up sweating and shivering. And that was before the dreams began.

He was definitely in no fit state to be out of bed, let alone romancing Maggie like she deserved. Reluctantly, he hauled himself off his cot, dressed, and shuffled to the doctor's office.

Dr. Martin took his temperature and listened to his chest just as Alec had an enormous coughing fit. The doctor looked at him gravely.

"I see that you've had bronchitis several times since enlisting," the doctor said, glancing down at the medical record he held open.

True. The infection was a recurring problem since he'd joined Bomber Command, even though he didn't suffer from it before the war. The cold night air and damp accommodations on the ground were likely to blame.

"Yes, sir."

"It's back again, with a vengeance this time. Some rest will help. Don't make any strenuous plans for your time off, or you will end up in hospital, no use to anyone. And give the cigarettes a miss until it passes."

Alec saved his cursing until he left the doctor's office, but even that seemed like an extraordinary effort. He threw himself back into bed to get a bit more fitful sleep, hoping against hope he'd be well enough to take Maggie out this evening.

Squadron Dormitories, RAF Bottesford
18 February 1943, 9:00 p.m.

"Alec! Are you in there?"

Maggie rapped on the door. Gently at first, then harder when she got no response. She glanced around, hoping no one could see her, dressed to the nines and furtively tapping on Alec's bedroom door. How the station would gossip!

She tapped again on the door and pressed her ear to it.

"Are you there?"

When she heard the groan on the other side, she didn't hesitate. She risked a formal reprimand and pushed it open.

Through the dim light of a kerosene lamp hung in the center of the room, she saw Alec's bed—she assumed, as it was the only one with someone in it—farthest from the doorway. She tiptoed across the dormitory, feeling like an intruder as the room's masculine scent engulfed her.

She knew something wasn't right when he hadn't met them at the club. He couldn't feign the kind of contrition she'd seen a few days ago. He wouldn't stand her up unless something terrible had happened.

"He hasn't been out of bed today," Jonty had explained as Agnes pulled him by the hand through the door of the Pelican Club, leaving Maggie alone outside.

She defied every rule in the WAAF handbook as she crept toward his bed. She said his name again.

"Maggie," he mumbled.

He didn't stand or sit, but she saw the form under the covers shivering.

"Yes, it's me. Are you all right?" she whispered, sitting on the bed, next to him.

Warmth radiated off him. She put her hand on his forehead and felt the heat rising from his clammy skin.

His fever was higher than anything Maggie had seen before. Sweat soaked his hair and pajamas as well as the bedclothes.

"Mum."

"No, Alec. It's Maggie. I was worried about you."

"Bill . . . No! Bill!"

He groaned again. A shiver rippled down her spine at the sound of it. What was he seeing in his fever dreams?

"Alec? Can you hear me? We need to get you to a doctor. I'm going to . . ."

The sentence died on her lips when he convulsed, eyes rolled back in his head and body rigid.

She now didn't care if the air chief commandant herself saw her in Alec's room. Maggie ran out of the dormitory, shouting to anyone who could hear that she needed help.

Grantham Hospital
21 February 1943, 2:10 p.m.

The plump, cheery nurse in a crisply pressed uniform with a bleached-white bib and well-starched cap guided Maggie to the open ward, where patients—mostly airmen—lay convalescing. At the observation desk, the sister on duty pointed out Alec on the far side of the ward.

"He's asleep at the moment, I'm afraid. I don't want to wake him."

Maggie glanced over at Alec's form, relieved to see his peaceful sleep. No sweating and shaking.

Once when she was no more than ten years old, her father had taken ill with pneumonia. She'd watched from the door as her mother tended to a body that looked like the shell of her father, not the real man. Decimated by illness and shaken with chills, he'd been forced to weakly accept his wife's ministration. They'd barred her from entering his room, but she remembered her doorway glimpses clearly even now and how her little heart had ached to see her ever-capable father so reduced.

She felt like that little girl again, seeing Alec's strong, fit body diminished by sickness. When she'd insisted on getting him medical attention in his barracks, she'd pushed back the same helplessness she'd felt as a child. Now that he slept peacefully, something else tinged her feelings. Without intending to, she pictured herself lying next to him, resting her head on his chest and blending into the rhythm of his heartbeat.

"Do you want me to tell him that you called by?" the nurse asked with a knowing look.

Maggie blushed, hoping the nurse hadn't been able to read her thoughts. "No. I'll come again another time."

She delayed going again for several days, letting pure confusion, as well as night shifts, keep her away until she could delay no longer.

"He's asking why you haven't come by, Maggie. I mean, it would be a shame for him to survive pneumonia only to die of a broken heart," Jonty teased.

The nurse must have remembered Maggie when she asked after Alec again, because she gave her a broad, beaming smile.

"He's awake, and I think he'll be happy to see you."

The sparsely furnished ward held five other beds apart from his. All the men were awake, but none had visitors. Two sat with a chess board between them. Others, like Alec, were reading.

The amiable conversation weaving its way around the room came to an abrupt halt when she entered the ward with the nurse.

"Look lively, chaps. We have a visitor," exclaimed a man with his leg in traction.

From the far side of the room, Alec called out, "Only the matron has come for you, McGill. The other one is Margaret Morrison, four-six-seven's very own good-luck charm. And I believe she's come for me."

His bravado told her he felt better.

She made her way to the far side of the ward, where he sat grinning broadly from his neatly tucked hospital bed. In gray-striped pajamas, he looked less debonair than in his uniform. But the broad lines of his chest and shoulders under the thin material distracted her in their own way.

"This is the perfect medicine," he said as she put down her heavy overcoat and sat tentatively on the edge of his bed. She hoped the men around her had enough manners to ignore the conversations of fellow patients with their sweethearts.

He put away his reading material—a Bible—by his bedside.

He noticed her gaze. "Yes. It's a Bible. I don't want you beating me over the head with it."

She burned to ask more but tried not to show it. "What part of it are you reading?"

"Jonah. I'm trying to work out if what your vicar friend says is true."

"Oh, have you come to any conclusions?"

"Not yet." He changed the subject before she could ask anything more. "I know that I am saying this a lot lately, but I don't actually remember that day. When they brought me in here, I mean. The doctor said my fever was so high, I probably never would. I didn't say anything stupid, did I?"

"I'm just glad you are speaking sensibly again."

"Why were you even there?"

"I was so angry at you for not showing up that I came to personally throttle you," she said, enjoying his smile. "But the fever got to you first. When you didn't make a single joke about the circumstances, I knew something was terribly wrong."

"You mean, I had you right there alone in my bedroom and I didn't try anything? I must have been at death's door!"

"See. I know you're better now."

"I had the most wonderful plans for my six days of leave."

"Oh yes?"

"Six days of stepping out as many times as I could with this gorgeous WAAF."

She played along. "Oh, anyone I know?"

He went to take her hand resting on the bed beside him, but she pulled it away, teasing him.

"Does this woman actually want to step out with you? Or are you bullying her into it?" She grinned. The lighthearted banter covered the thrum of her heart in her chest.

"Difficult to say. But I want to take her to the cinema. I hear she has a weakness for it." His eyes danced with hope.

"Ah, well. This WAAF is probably the sensible type. I'm sure she'll go with you, but you'll have to get better. She wouldn't want you coughing through the whole picture. It would ruin it completely for her."

"So my only chance with this girl is to make a full recovery?"

She shrugged. "I'm afraid so." Her stomach fluttered, and she, rather hurriedly, stood to leave.

"Don't go!" he pleaded. "It's so dreary here without you."

"I have to." She busied herself with buttoning her coat to avoid his eyes. "My pass is only until three."

He was busy rolling his eyes with mock disappointment, so he was entirely unprepared when she stepped forward and leaned down to place a single sweet kiss on his cheek, just to one side of his mouth.

"What was that for?"

The way he looked up at her when she straightened, full of wonder, made her belly do that fluttery thing again. "Incentive to get better."

She turned and sped out of the room, head down, unable to look at the other patients.

They had the good sense not to whistle and hoot until after she left the room.

CHAPTER THIRTY-ONE

RAF Bottesford
4 March 1943, 6:05 a.m.

Maggie Morrison.

He knew her name now and wanted to see her again so that he could use it.

Where was she? It wouldn't do to lose concentration just now. Not when he was likely to be prosecuted under special defense regulations if someone caught him lurking here.

He lingered by the WAAF mess after he dropped off the kitchen order, but didn't see her among the sea of uniforms. He'd heard the planes last night, so there was obviously some kind of operation. Perhaps she had a night shift? She might still be asleep. He slipped away to the dormitories to see if he could find her there.

He checked for signs of movement in the main dormitory, but the twenty beds sat empty, made with neat precision to pass a sergeant's inspection.

He listened at the door to the room that separated her from the rest of the dormitory. The sound of her soft breathing mesmerized him—like it was calling to him. He turned the handle and pushed the door open until it was slightly ajar.

A lump under the bedcovers was all he could see. An appealing, curvy lump. If he wanted a glimpse of that face, he needed to move closer. Slipping through the door, he crept to the bed and looked down on the sleeping form.

She looked peaceful, like she was enjoying happy dreams. The same way Lucy used to when he crept in to watch her. But Maggie didn't wear pretentious curlers the way Lucy did. Her small sink wasn't crowded with creams and concoctions like the farm girl's dressing table.

His eye caught on the one sign of disorder in the room, writing materials strewn across her small desk. Out of habit he moved closer. He didn't expect to find anything for his collection, but he might learn more about her.

He picked up a creased letter, written from Wales, that described a stay at the seaside in the voice of a frivolous young girl. Then he glanced down at Maggie's reply. She'd completed two pages of praise to some airman she worked with. Wasn't that always the way of things lately? Women were transfixed by the uniform.

He placed the letter back down and turned his attention back to her sleeping form. How could he show her what she meant to him?

"Maggie," he whispered, smiling down at her.

That was why he'd sneaked into here, after all—to use her name. He'd never been good at talking to girls when they were awake. Having to do it made his mouth go dry. He'd made a fool of himself outside the church at Lucy's wedding.

It was easier this way.

He caught his breath when she stirred, breathing out a sigh. His lips curled up when she didn't wake. He fantasized about seeing her face emerge from sleep with a broad smile just for him.

He mustn't touch her. That was what had made Lucy fly off the handle. He'd thought she would enjoy being admired, but she'd cried and screamed when she woke up to him stroking her hair.

She'd flung all sorts of names at him on his retreat from her room. Later, Lucy's father stood at his kitchen door with a shotgun, shouting at him to never go near her again.

He leaned in, wishing he could join her in those dreams she was enjoying.

Without warning the eyes in front of him flicked open. He saw the progression of emotions in her eyes, from basic awareness to unconcealed terror, before she let out a scream that would surely draw people in here.

In her passive sleeping form she was exquisite. Now she was terrifying. She wrenched the covers up to her neck and backed right up into the corner, screaming again and again, "Get out! Get out! Get out!"

He fled from the barracks, escaping the building unnoticed, then avoided the personnel heading toward it with the invisibleness he'd perfected over the past few months.

CHAPTER THIRTY-TWO

She sat in the wing commander's office, happy she wasn't being made to stand to attention. Her legs wouldn't hold right now.

If either Palmer or Carver, who were both there to listen to her story, pulled rank, they would tear strips off her for the disheveled presentation of her uniform. She hadn't even done her hair.

Seated next to her, Grace drew her chair close and laid a hand on her back, imparting her strength as Maggie recounted what had happened that morning. Maggie was sick to her stomach thinking about it. She'd already retched several times.

Queen Bee, in her gruff-but-to-the-point manner, enquired if Maggie had been interfered with in any way. Maggie shook her head, sure she hadn't been.

"But I don't think this is the first time he's been in my room." She wrung her hands, wishing she could find another way to keep calm. "Things have been going missing. And not just from my room—all of us have had things go missing. Nothing very valuable—hairbrushes, lipsticks. Trinkets really. Things we might misplace, only now I can't believe that all of us could be so careless all at once."

She might be shaken, but she didn't miss the look that the two senior officers exchanged.

"And you have no idea who this man was?" the wing commander asked.

"I have seen him before, I think. Maybe in the village. But he was at Flight Engineer Fisher's wedding. He said he was a friend of the bride."

Palmer sent a messenger to call Fisher, back at work after the briefest of honeymoons, into his office.

Maggie and Grace waited on the bench outside the room until Fisher arrived. Her hands felt so empty. She wished she'd thought to bring some knitting so she had something rhythmic and steadying to concentrate on.

Fisher arrived with Alec. The flight engineer cast her a worried look as he headed straight to Palmer's office.

At the sight of Alec, Maggie's stomach tightened. She avoided his eyes. She wanted to see him and also didn't want to see him at the same time.

Not after this.

Not *looking* like this.

As the door to WingCo's office clicked shut, he sat next to her on the bench, looking to Grace to fill in the details. His eyes flooded with concern as Grace retold the story.

"Mags," he murmured, laying his hand on her back in that way he did that made her feel stronger.

They sat in silence, straining to hear what was being said behind the wing commander's door.

———•∞•———

It was no use trying to listen through the door. It was built to guard official secrets. Besides, he was busy fighting the urge to pull Maggie into his chest and hold her there.

He often imagined her with her hair down, but not in this wild and fearful way. Her breathing was fast, and her hands were fighting each other in her lap, like they had been on New Year Eve.

He hadn't seen her since that day at the hospital. Her kiss had had its intended effect. The medical staff all commented on his new outlook on life. But instead of being able to dedicate six days to trying to get another kiss out of her, WingCo canceled all planned leave and threw the whole aerodrome into a heavy schedule of practice drills.

"Were you hurt?" He took one of her hands in his to still them. She relaxed into it and clearly tried to slow her breathing.

She shook her head. "No. Not hurt, just shaken. But with everything that has gone missing lately, I shudder to think how many times he might have been there without me knowing."

So did he. In fact, it made his blood simmer. But he kept his tone composed. "You think he's a thief?"

"It would make sense. All the things that have gone missing are easy to carry in a pocket or small bag. Have things been going missing in your dormitories too?"

He thought for a moment. Hadn't Jonty been yelling last week that he was missing the razor his mother gave him? And before that Graves had complained he couldn't find his good pen.

He supposed these could be coincidences, but put together with what Maggie was saying, it felt a lot more suspicious. He didn't like the idea of someone wandering in and helping themselves. And he really didn't like the idea of someone sneaking into Maggie's room while she slept.

"Do you think Chris is in trouble?" Grace asked no one in particular.

"For the thefts, I doubt it," Alec said. "But they'll need to make sure. It's clear we're preparing for something big. Canceled leave. New engines for the entire fleet. I suppose they have to make sure it's just petty theft they are dealing with and not espionage."

"What kind of a spy stops to stare at a woman in her sleep?" Grace asked as the wing commander's door opened.

Fisher emerged looking ashen and shut the door behind him. They all fixed their eyes on him. He looked straight at Maggie.

"Maggie, I'm so sorry. Clive Stockton is Lucy's neighbor. He did the same thing to her once."

Alec felt the shiver run down her spine under his hand.

"What are they going to do?" Grace demanded.

"I don't think they are going to do anything." Fisher shrugged apologetically. "Not yet anyway. Once they realized it was probably a local kid sneaking about and not an immediate threat to the ops they've been planning, they eased up a bit."

"Nice to know the powers that be take the welfare of the women here so seriously." Grace's voice dripped with sarcasm.

"Something big's happening. They're locking down the station and calling everyone in for a briefing at seventeen hundred," Alec said.

Chris nodded. "Don't worry, Maggie. I'll speak to Lucy and her father. We'll set him straight."

Maggie nodded weakly. Tears she had obviously been holding back came out with a single sob. Without warning, she turned and flung her arms around Alec's neck, burying herself into him. He froze for a millisecond, stunned at finding himself being the one she ran to rather than the man who repelled her. But then he didn't hold himself back. He pulled her into him, stroking her hair and forming words of comfort.

"I don't want to be alone."

He caressed the back of her neck at her hairline, making small circles in her loosened hair. "You don't have to be. I'm sure you can shift your bed into the main dorm so you have others around you. Or you can stay with Grace if you need to."

He felt her relax. Thank God he'd said the right thing because, circumstances aside, he never wanted to leave this embrace. She pulled away first.

Lucky, because he didn't have the willpower to end it.

CHAPTER THIRTY-THREE

Barrowby Farm
5 March 1943, 9:50 a.m.

He made one of the Land Girls do the delivery this morning. Not the new one, because she didn't seem up to the task.

Bessie happily obliged. She was always keen to get off the farm, hopeful she'd get to speak with some of the airmen, and didn't question his insistence.

"Security's certainly tight," she remarked when she returned, moaning about not getting a chance to see her friends.

Was that because of him?

He'd been foolish to go into Maggie's room, but the temptation had been so strong. He couldn't quell it without seeing her. Now he had to lie low and keep his head down until they moved on to other worries. He needed to find a way to shift these goods too. It wasn't safe to keep them here anymore.

The trophies in the oak chest in front of him didn't give him as much of a thrill now anyway. Except for the few he knew were Maggie's.

When would he see her face again? The happy sleeping face, not the screaming one. He wanted to enjoy her when she was smiling and laughing too. Then he could pretend she was smiling and laughing at him.

No. With him.

Or better, *for* him. Just for him.

Perhaps waiting in a darkened corner outside the pub was his best chance. Or maybe he could follow her to the cinema and get in position to view her face as she watched the picture. He'd seen several ticket stubs among her things, so he knew she was a regular attender.

"Hello? Clive? I've finished the pigpen."

The high-pitched voice of the new Land Girl made him shut the chest with a thwack and drew him out from his corner of the barn.

The light cast on her face reminded him of Maggie, just smaller and skinnier. She looked downright scrawny in the bulky Land Girl uniform his mother had handed her a few days ago. Perhaps it was the way she tied her dark hair back in braids this morning that pulled Maggie into his mind.

No, it wasn't just that.

She had the same delicate nose, the same sharp chin, and in this light similar bright flecks in her eyes.

"Clive?" She looked at him expectantly. "What are you doing?"

"You're not allowed in here." He grabbed her arm and hauled her out into the morning light. When she wrestled her arm free and took two steps away from him, her startled face bore an even stronger resemblance to Maggie's.

His lip curled up to see it. He loomed over her, drawing out more fear in her face. The more fear he saw, the more Maggie he saw.

Interesting.

"Clive! Stop chatting up that girl and get back to work," his mother shouted from the kitchen door.

"Stay out of there. There's nothing in there for you!"

He spat the words at the girl before stalking away, hoping she got the message.

CHAPTER THIRTY-FOUR

RAF Bottesford
5 March 1943, 5:05 p.m.

The briefing was scheduled to begin at 1700. Maggie arrived to standing room only. She was glad to be working tonight. It meant she didn't need to think about her sleeping arrangements just yet.

The operations room, which felt large when it was empty, could hardly fit all the RAF station personnel gathered for this special briefing. The maps of Europe lining the walls were barely visible due to all the bodies around the perimeter.

The activity of the last few weeks was a world away from the boredom of the gloomy midwinter months, when it was all theory and exercises. New engines for the fleet meant additional test flights. The control tower was busier than she'd ever known it, staffed with several extra people.

Apart from the eighty-four aircrew due to fly out tonight, the wing commander broke with protocol to allow some members of the ground crew, both RAF and WAAF, and all the staff who worked in the control tower to be part of the briefing.

"We're about to find out what all the effort is about," Grace whispered as she sneaked in next to Maggie. She'd been run off her feet in the Map Room for the past few days—although she couldn't tell Maggie exactly which maps she'd ferried around.

At the tables in the center of the room, airmen sat mulling over the extra instructions. Her eyes immediately sought out Alec, sitting with his crew at the front of the room. Concentration lined his brow as he focused on the papers he discussed with his new navigator.

Every mouth fell silent, and the room stood to attention as their superior officers entered. Group Captain Lewis, Palmer's commanding officer who oversaw several of the air stations in the area, joined them tonight. Amy Snee and another intelligence officer, as well as someone from the meteorological office, were also part of the briefing team.

Lewis spoke first, from in front of a large map of the western portion of Germany.

"Many of you will have flown over the Ruhr Valley before, so I don't need to tell you that it is the heart of the German industrial complex. We've always thought that if we can hurt them here, then their whole effort against us suffers. We'll be stepping up attacks on this region over the next few months, and we hope to cripple German steel production."

Palmer took over the briefing. "Tonight, the target is Essen. I know that for many of you, this is not your first go at this city. The main target is the Krupp's steelworks—but you'll see the secondary targets listed in your documentation. You won't be lonely up there. Over four hundred aircraft from our side are flying out tonight, so we should do some major damage.

"But we want to be precise about this. Pathfinders will mark the targets with red indicators. Note the very specific timing for the waves of attack. You'll have people coming in behind you, so hold steady for thirty seconds, then get the hell out of there."

WingCo took some questions from the aircrews before dismissing everyone.

"Happy Valley, here we come," called someone from the back.

The room responded with a solemn murmur as they all set about their work with an extra frisson of energy. Maggie wanted to catch Alec's eye and perhaps thank him for always being so kind to her, such a solid support. But even from this distance she could see the steely purpose in his eyes. He didn't need her distracting him from things that might otherwise bring him home safely.

It was always solemn in the locker room. Apprehensive. Every man in there knew he might be dressing for his own funeral.

Alec preferred to wear a thick roll-neck sweater under his flight suit rather than his dress jacket. Some chaps saw it differently, but he figured if he got shot down over enemy territory, he had a better chance of evading capture by posing as a farmer or fisherman if he had something other than a RAAF uniform jacket to work with.

He pulled on his silk socks, then his woolen ones, then shoved his feet into his lambswool-lined fly boots. Heavy things, but they kept away the frostbite. Then he shrugged into his Irvine jacket. His Mae West life jacket went over that, just in case they ended up having to ditch into the ocean. God willing he'd never have to use it.

They called in at the Nissan hut on the side of the airfield to get their parachutes before running the kite through its checks. All the chutes were fitted individually by the WAAFs, whose one job was to keep track of the condition of all the parachutes at the aerodrome. Each one had its own logbook so they could tell when it needed to be routinely opened and checked.

He'd gone steady with a parachute girl once. It didn't last, but while it did he'd gotten to slip into the parachute room where the silk was aired and dried, hanging in great billows from the ceiling. Two stoves constantly ablaze kept the large room at a steady, warm temperature year round. It'd been a cozy place to sneak away for some privacy.

Not that he had a second thought for the parachute girl anymore. They still hadn't been on a proper date, but he was pretty sure that Maggie was his girl now. That thought would keep him warm in the air above Germany tonight.

Jonty was still being fitted into his heated suit when the others were ready to leave. The gun turret in the rear of the Lancaster was the coldest part of the aircraft, so rear gunners wore a suit with electric coils that heated during the flight to keep them warm. His suit was tested before each operation by being plugged into a socket. Jonty's parachute and Mae West went over the top of the heat suit, so when he followed the others out onto the airfield, he looked three or four times his usual circumference.

"I don't mind as long as I can still use these," he often said, wiggling his two trigger fingers in the air.

Alec inspected the aircraft a final time with Fisher and signed the 700 form to say that everything was serviceable.

There was one last thing to do before they boarded.

Every crew he knew had some sort of superstitious ritual they ran through before they flew. Tommy Peters and his crew each kissed a white rabbit's foot that the gunner kept in his breast pocket. John Fletcher's crew each urinated off the portside wing. His crew each took a draw from the same cigarette before he stubbed it out in the dirt below the portside wing and clambered in.

He sure hoped the superstition held, because this was the last operation of his tour. It would be a shame not to come home in one piece.

Safety first. That was what was drilled into them in training. So even though every hatch, lever, and instrument was already checked and rechecked by the ground crews, Alec and the others went through the procedure of confirming they were all in working order.

With the help of the starting crew on the ground who called out the checks one by one, they confirmed the bomb doors and the undercarriage were in working order. Then following the direction of the ground crew's flashlight indicating which engine, Alec pressed the starter button to fire each of the rumbling Merlin beasts into life.

Starboard inner.
Portside inner.
Starboard outer.
Portside outer.

He flipped the slow running switch for each of them. Even so, once they were all active, it was an incomparable sound. God willing, the tremendous noise would thrum through them all until they landed safely again back on this airfield.

He ran through the final checks with Fisher, then taxied along the airfield to the runway, deftly controlling the plane by manipulating the engines as they moved along. On the runway, he checked that the gyro compass was working and the tail wheel was straight, then listened for the radio operator to give him permission to take off.

Maggie, his girl. But professional as always.

He couldn't say everything he wanted to say to her. Not now. Not like this. He took the comfort he needed from the fact that it was her voice in his ears.

"M Maggie. This is Bedrock. Clear for takeoff on green. Come back in one piece, would you?"

He smiled under his oxygen mask and flight helmet. "Roger that, Bedrock. See you on the other side."

The red light at the end of the runway turned green. He stood hard on the brakes, pushed the control column and throttles forward, and released the brakes. With their full-throated roar, the engines shot the plane along the runway lined with station personnel waving them off, a few more than usual, it seemed. The gunners waved back with grim faces, but Alec focused on getting the kite up safely.

Halfway down the runway, the tailwheel rose, and he used rudders to control the aircraft. Fisher, who sat on a fold-out seat next to him, helped him keep the throttles open so what was a giant, lumbering mechanical beast on the ground transformed into an elegant, fighting machine in the air.

Once airborne, Fisher raised the undercarriage while Alec listened for Staunton to give him the course.

Essen was already lit up when they reached it, blazing beneath them. The Pathfinders did their job perfectly, as usual, dropping red and green flares that burned in the air as they fell and gave bomb aimers a visual guide to their target. Waves of aircraft from other stations had already rained down their payloads when Hardie took control of the aircraft to aim the bombs. Timing was everything. For a direct hit, the bombs had to be released twenty seconds before they flew over the target.

"Steady. Steady. Steady. Bombs away," Hardie said while he lined up the target and added their five tons of explosives to the fiery mix below.

Alec held their course to take the aiming photograph with the specially fitted aerial camera. Then as flak from the antiaircraft guns flashed in the sky, he pulled the aircraft around and flew like a bat out of hell back to England.

Alec knew something was wrong as soon as he pulled the plane up.

"Fisher, I've got no elevator control."

"Did we take a hit?" Fisher asked.

"I don't think so. I didn't feel anything."

Fisher leaned over to examine the controls. After a few minutes, Fisher and Graves disappeared into the belly of the plane to see if they could work out the issue. Flak was heavy over the target—perhaps it was something they could fix.

In his head, Alec strategized what he would do if they met night fighters on the way home, without the ability to change the altitude of the aircraft properly.

Through the intercom, he warned the gunners to keep their eyes peeled.

Fisher returned and said with a shrug, "I can't explain it. There's no structural damage that I can see." He crouched next to Alec, and they worked through their options. There was no way to land the plane without elevator control. No simple, safe way.

"We could use power and trim settings," Fisher suggested. "It would work in theory."

Fisher began talking him through how they could manipulate other controls to bring the aircraft down.

Alec hissed in indecision. It was an entirely untested idea. "I suppose we can practice by trying to land on clouds on the way home, assuming we don't meet any unfriendlies."

Fisher shrugged again. "It's that or the ocean."

Alec announced the plan to the rest of the crew

"Wouldn't it be simpler to ditch into the drink?" Jonty asked.

But none of them liked their chances of surviving at this time of year. The Mae West life jacket might help them float but couldn't do anything about the hypothermia that would set in immediately.

They all agreed. Bailing out over the channel was their last resort. They'd try to get within radio range of the aerodrome, practicing the unconventional landing to see if it were even possible. Fisher left to do one final physical check, just in case he'd missed something the first time.

Alec hadn't managed to follow Oscar's advice before. What did he say? Turn your heart to God and let it speak?

He managed to do it now, his heart bellowing a silent prayer for them all to live through this.

He did more than that.

He prayed like Jonah in the belly of the whale.

He bargained.

CHAPTER THIRTY-FIVE

Control Tower, RAF Bottesford
5 March 1943, 11:51 p.m.

Queen Bee insisted her radio operators be sturdy types. "It might take the men nerves of steel to do what they do, but it isn't exactly a picnic waiting around while they do it," she'd said when Maggie had first met her.

Maggie felt the truth of that tonight. She knitted through several balls of yarn in her spot by the radio, listening constantly for the aircraft to return, as though her attention might bring them home sooner. When Bob Burgess called in, the entire room activated with her. Nancy rang the bell to scramble the ground crews, intelligence officers, transport corps, and medical team into action.

"Bedrock to A Able. You're first back again, Bob. Welcome home."

She heard the screech and monumental thud of the Lancaster landing, then tuned her ears in to listen for the arrival of other aircraft. She coordinated each of the planes as they arrived, directing them to increase altitude or land, as the situation called for it.

Relief washed over her in waves as, one by one, they landed and taxied away from the runway to their final stop. The engines subsided, and the air crews bounded out to give the aircraft over to the ground ones.

Y Yankee.

L Love.

F Freddie.

Down they came.

After twenty minutes of frantic activity, Maggie paused to breathe, keenly aware she still hadn't heard Alec through her headphones. She glanced at the board and saw that only two aircraft didn't have a landing time recorded.

Next to her, Nancy answered the ringing telephone and announced that someone had made an emergency landing at the Scampton airfield. Maggie watched her write the landing time next to G George.

Just Alec and his crew to come.

Maggie stared at the empty space on the board and prayed the prayer that countless other women prayed during this war. *Please bring him home, Lord.*

Next to her, Lieutenant Grant looked solemn. They watched the minutes tick by on the clock.

Each time the telephone rang, Maggie hoped it was good news about a safe landing at another aerodrome. Each time someone entered the tower, she looked up, expecting the newcomer to bring news from one of the intelligence officers speaking to the crews as they returned.

Then she heard the sound that made her heart leap—Alec's voice over the radio.

"Bedrock. This is Maggie. We've got a problem. The elevator control is not operational. No idea why. We think we can still land her but will need you to clear the long runway. Over."

She looked at Flight Lieutenant Grant next to her, who leapt into action, giving orders to alert engineers to help troubleshoot the problem.

"Roger that. Can you circle? The operational commander is alerting the engineers. Over."

"Negative, Bedrock. There's no fuel. We practiced on the way home. We only have one shot at this, but we think we can do it. Over."

Maggie looked helplessly at Grant as he ordered the long runway be cleared. She heard his conversation with the engineers. None of what he said sounded positive. Alec seemed confident about his ability to land, but if the elevator control suddenly gave out, how fragile was the rest of the aircraft? Could it survive the stress of a hard landing?

Grant nodded to Maggie.

"Bedrock to Maggie. You can land on the long runway." Then she added, "Don't mess this up. Over."

"Maggie to Bedrock. I won't. I promised my girl I'd take her to the cinema. I couldn't disappoint her. Over and out."

Maggie gulped in her next breath, unnoticed by the rest of the tower as all attention turned to the runway outside. Nancy scrambled ambulances and fire tenders. People around her listed all the things that could go wrong.

She stood up, keeping her headphones on, latching her focus on the plane about to land on the runway.

Lieutenant Grant handed her binoculars with a grim face. "Are you sure you want to watch?"

Every single person in the control tower knew they might be about to watch their friends hit the ground and explode in a ball of flames.

Please, Lord, bring him home.

Her soul cried out the prayer as she watched the distant aircraft grow bigger in the binoculars. At first everything looked normal. But the descent was irregular as Alec manipulated the controls to lose altitude in fits and starts.

She gasped, grabbing Nancy's arm as the plane dropped suddenly, before recovering. The engines sounded strange as he engaged and disengaged them.

Please, Lord, bring him home.
She held her breath as they flew close to the ground.
One wrong move at such a low altitude and they'd be goners. The final thud was loud and inelegant, but a cheer went up from the people around her, and she realized there was no crash, no explosion.

Out on the airfield, the crew didn't bother trying to taxi away from the runway. They shut down the engines and bailed out.

The fire crew swarmed over the plane. Her heart beat in her mouth as she tried to make out figures in the dark, with only the dull runway guide lights to give her any clue about who was who.

She counted the crew into the transport and let out a strangled sound. Seven men, praise God. She sucked in a breath and tried to make the sound that came out of her sound like a sigh and not a sob, sinking down into her seat with her head in her hands. Lieutenant Grant touched her arm.

She looked up at him.

"Go," he said.

She didn't need to be told twice.

She fled the tower, taking the steps two at a time, and pedaled her bike like a madwoman across the aerodrome.

Alec knew he needed to scramble out.

Instead, he sat in disbelief.

They hadn't hit the ground and burst into flames.

They weren't dead.

He knew Fisher was thinking the same thing. They'd both rode the same wave of desperate fear as they'd worked together to land the crippled plane.

"Let's get the hell out of here," Fisher said. If Alec's throat wasn't dry, he would have replied. Instead, he jolted into action, tearing out the communications and oxygen connectors from his flight suit.

"Hardie!" Alec reached out his arm to haul Hardie up through the cockpit. They clambered out the hatch in the roof. When their feet hit the ground, Hardie and Fisher ran to put some distance between themselves and the aircraft in case she still had one more surprise left in her.

Alec hung back to make sure all his men were out. He saw Jonty and Boyd drop out of the hatch.

"Graves! Staunton!" he shouted.

"Over here!" one of them called from behind him. They were already with the others, a safe distance away. Alec ran like the blazes to join them.

The airfield, clear just a moment ago to give them room to land, was now a sea of fire crews and ambulances. Heat wagons and meat wagons, he usually called them, but he couldn't even muster a joke. When he reached the others, his legs gave way, and he sank to the ground next to Graves who, he realized, was praying.

Martin MacPherson hauled him to his feet and shook his head at Alec. "You're one lucky man, Alec Thomas."

Alec was beginning to think luck had nothing to do with it. As heavy hands clapped his back in congratulation, he remembered the bargain he'd made.

Get us out of this alive, and I'll do anything, be anything, you want me to.

He'd managed the prayer in the sky, but somehow words failed him now.

Riding back across the airfield in the crew transport, his eyes sought out the control tower in the distance, where he knew Maggie was.

The debriefings would be long tonight, but after he got through them, nothing would stop him from seeing her.

―――∞―――

Outside the briefing room, she flung her bike to the ground. If they didn't let her in, she knew she would break the door down to get to him.

She burst into the room, staring wildly at the men in there, searching for his steel-gray eyes and cocky smile. He wasn't there.

"You right, luv?" someone she didn't recognize asked.

She fled back through the door, frantically trying to figure out where he could be.

Her breath caught in her throat when she saw him climbing out of the crew transport. He looked slightly wild with his hair ruffled from his headgear. Other airmen surrounded him, clapping him on the back, eager to talk about his narrow escape. She suppressed the sob that welled within her as she ran straight toward him. Every part of her being wanted to fling itself at him. Somehow she managed to stop herself about a foot from where he stood.

But he didn't hesitate.

Without a single thought for decorum, or protocol, or process, or who the blazes was watching, he lunged toward her, reached his arms around her waist, and pulled her into him, his lips on hers. Relief, and a burning desire to stay pressed against him like this forever, surged through her as she clung to him, holding his lips to hers.

How long were they in this embrace? Seconds? Minutes? She didn't know.

She didn't care.

Nothing, neither the other people around her whistling and whooping nor the ticking of time itself, felt real.

Nothing except him.

Her heartbeat pounded in her ears as they kissed. Or maybe it was his heartbeat. They were so close and beating in sync, so it was impossible to tell.

His arms around her—so solid and, praise the Lord, alive—lifted her off her feet for a moment. Only when they touched the ground again and he pulled his lips away from hers could she regain any other senses.

He rested his forehead against hers.

"I thought we were goners, Mags," he whispered.

"I thought you were too."

Now she felt how cold he was. His lips, his forehead, his hands, even his clothes were like ice against her skin. It brought her to her senses enough to remember they were most definitely not alone.

In fact, a small crowd gathered around them. She blushed, but he didn't seem to care what people thought. Those strong arms pulled her back into his chest. She buried her face into his neck and breathed in the sheepskin smell of the Irvine jacket intermingled with the scent of his cigarettes and cologne.

"Well done, Thomas. Remarkable flying tonight. Well done."

Wing Commander Palmer coming out of the briefing room and calling out seemed to make Alec realize where he was. Reluctantly they stepped away from each other. But he kept her hand in his and squeezed it. There was so much to say that couldn't be said here and now.

"Well, thank you for your assistance in the landing tonight, Corporal," he joked.

The crowd around them chuckled.

Palmer approached and slapped him on the back, oblivious to Maggie's presence. The steady hand of his superior on his back guided Alec into the briefing room.

"Sir, I . . ."

Duty called. He couldn't protest as his superior officer led him away.

The crowd of men dispersed—to the briefing room, the mess, or their dormitories—leaving Maggie standing in the cold night, her fingertips to her lips.

She was most definitely his girl.

CHAPTER THIRTY-SIX

RAF Bottesford
6 March 1943, 6:37 a.m.

Each time he got close to drifting off to sleep, a recalcitrant part of his brain jolted him awake, reminding him he shouldn't be alive. After a few hours of trying to stop his mind playing tricks, he rose. He wouldn't be missed until well after noon, so he left a note for Jonty to cover for him. He took one of the aerodrome's bicycles and rode along the bridle paths into the village. Taking the main road would be faster and much less muddy, but he wanted some thinking time before he got to his final destination—the church.

He wasn't sure what to expect on a Saturday. Maybe especially devout people went to church on Saturdays as well as Sundays. Hopefully, the place wouldn't be teeming with people. The only person he wanted to run into at the moment was the bug-eyed priest.

He found Oscar Williams inside the church, sorting through hymn books and laying them on pews for the following day's service.

When he looked up from his work and saw Alec standing awkwardly in the vestibule, his face flashed with a welcoming smile. "Hullo there, Alec!"

Alec nodded his greeting. "Can I speak with you?"

"Of course." The clergyman laid down the pile of hymnals and stretched his arm out to indicate for Alec to come in. They sat in the first few rows. Alec squeezed awkwardly into one row facing forward. Oscar sat in front of him, turned on an angle with his elbow resting on the back of the pew.

"I prayed last night," Alec said. "I didn't mean to, not really. But I did."

He explained the terrible flight home and the remarkable landing. No doubt Oscar thought he was rambling as he unpacked the unlikely events of the previous night, in fact the last few months, trying to make sense of the sheer number of improbable survivals he and his crew had seen.

"This is the thing. Every time we fly out, there is a fifty-fifty chance we won't come home. Maybe the odds are slightly better if you've had a bit more experience in a kite—unlike the newer blokes—but still, it's pretty grim. Even if you don't get shot out of the sky, there's still a thousand random things that could happen. Like what happened to Barnes. Or a few months ago, Joe Bailey's faulty headgear meant he asphyxiated during the flight home. But the odds of me surviving *all* the things that have happened in the last few months are impossible. A live incendiary bomb in the fuel tank? We should have been blown to kingdom come! And last night's landing was a one in a million shot. No! A billion."

"You are wondering 'why me'?"

"People are dying all across the world for this war. For noble reasons and for stupid ones. Accidentally and suddenly. Barnes and Bailey were good men. But here I am walking away unscathed. It doesn't make sense." He paused. "I suppose you are going to give me the line that the Lord works in mysterious ways and expect me to be happy with that."

"Well . . ." Oscar smiled. "I'm not going to deny it. And I personally find it a comfort to think there is a reason behind all this suffering—even if it is a reason I will never know or understand or may very well be irrelevant to me. But I can see that is not why you are here."

"I bargained with my soul last night." He knew he sounded desperate. "Like Jonah did in the whale."

"Ah, I see."

"I told God that if I survived, I'd go anywhere, do anything He wanted. Now, I'm a man of my word. I just . . . don't know what to do next."

When the last word came out as a sob, Alec realized, to his embarrassment, that tears made their way down his face. The one time he had prayed and he had bloody well signed his life away to God.

Oscar grinned broadly, picked up one of the Bibles from the pew, and opened it.

"Come, Alec. Let me show you."

When Queen Bee found out Maggie had been in Alec's sleeping quarters when he was sick, she received her first formal reprimand. She risked serious disciplinary action sneaking back to his dormitory now. But she wanted—no, needed—to see him.

She knocked tentatively, remembering how his febrile delusions spurred her to take charge of the people around her regardless of the consequences. Right now, after everyone saw them kiss last night, she felt sheepish, like a naughty schoolgirl.

"Come in," she heard a voice call from within. When she didn't obey, Jonty Ables opened the door.

"You've come to see Alec?" He wore a too-knowing smile.

She ignored the whistle from behind him and nodded.

"He's not here, I'm afraid. He's gone to church."

He laughed at her confused look.

"It seems one kiss from Maggie Morrison is such a spiritual

experience that it can turn a man to God," Jonty teased, barely able to get the sentence out without a laugh escaping.

"I should have let you burn, you know." She glared at him, ignoring his deepening laughter and the guffawing from the men behind him. But she could still hear it as she strode away.

Why had he gone to the church? Possible answers to that question turned themselves over in her head. In all the time she'd known him, he'd only been to church once, and she was fairly sure now he'd just done that to impress her. But she knew he'd been speaking with Oscar and she'd seen him reading the Bible in hospital. Maybe last night's brush with death had something to do with it.

She walked into the Map Room, greeted by the familiar chatter of the BBC that Grace had playing as she worked. At midday a stern newsreader reported the success of last night's operation over Essen. As was usual for the BBC, the news kept up morale by focusing on the important strategic outcome of the operation. They'd managed to cripple the steel-making capacity of the Krupp factories.

This no doubt cheered the British public up, but everyone at the aerodrome knew it meant searchlights would be more numerous and flak would be heavier the next time they flew. The Germans weren't idiots. This first play revealed their hand, and now Gerry would do everything he could to stop them the next time they flew over the Ruhr.

How many more times would she sit safely in the control tower, sending Alec out on operations and praying through the night he returned home? How many more close calls would there be? The very thought of it drove her to take out her knitting needles.

She was almost out of wool. She'd cast on a new project the day before to give her something to focus on other than the terrible memory of a stranger's face looming over her. Since then she'd finished knitting a beanie, a pair of socks, and was halfway through a blue scarf.

Maggie tried to maintain attention on the needles and wool, but the blue-gray yarn was the same color as Alec's eyes, and her mind kept wandering. She rested her head on one hand and let her mind be tempted away from her knitting to the much more pleasurable memory of their kiss in the early hours of the morning.

Grace glanced over at her. "I've heard the rumors, you know."

"Hmm?" Maggie replied, still partly in her reverie.

"Half of Bottesford is talking about you throwing yourself into Alec's arms last night, but I'm still waiting for you to tell me about it."

Maggie blushed, but her smile reached every corner of her face. "I didn't throw myself into his arms!" she protested.

"I want to know everything."

Maggie explained the whole night from the tension in the control tower to the blissful few moments before WingCo stole Alec away.

"Have you spoken to him today?" Grace asked.

"No—he wasn't there. Apparently he'd gone to church."

Grace raised her eyebrows. "Interesting." Maggie saw a scheme form in Grace's eyes. "Why don't you come with me into the village after I finish here? You can see if he is still there while I run my errands."

Maggie glanced out the small window dubiously. "I doubt the weather will hold."

Grace shook her head. "Doesn't matter. I have the car."

———∞———

When Alec walked out of the church, he felt as though the vice pressing on his chest over the past few weeks had loosened. There was something new about him that he didn't have words for yet. Something about his spirit was singing, despite the gray clouds.

He really did look like a wreck when he arrived back at the aerodrome. It had drizzled on the way back, and thick mud clung to the cuffs of his trousers. He'd need to see to his uniform and shine his shoes immediately or risk sanctions from his superiors for not being presentable.

Jonty was in the dormitory, watching as he peeled off his socks, changed his trousers, and started work with the boot polish. "You had a visitor while you were out."

"Oh, who?" A casual question, but he could tell the answer from the smirk Jonty wore. The thought made him bite back a grin.

He thought back to the way his conversation with Oscar ended. He had come clean about the kiss, but also confessed how differently he felt about Maggie compared to all the other girls who'd come his way during the war.

Oscar had nodded. "I do hear all the gossip, you know. And I take particular interest when it's about a woman whom I regard as a younger sister."

"Just a sister then?" Alec asked awkwardly.

"Yes." Oscar's answer was firm. "Her father would like things to be otherwise, but she has—and always has had—a very clear idea of her own mind. Remember everything we discussed today, Alec. If you love her, you'll take it to heart."

Oscar's words rang in Alec's ears all the way back to the aerodrome. But now as he worked at shining his shoes, the memory of the kiss crept into his mind. After last night's drama, his crew were stood down from tonight's op, so the day was technically his own. He smiled like a fool as he made plans to see her.

"WingCo's looking for you too."

Jonty's words drew Alec out of his daydream. He couldn't catch a break. Duty kept snatching it away.

"Thank you for coming," the senior officer said as Alec entered WingCo's office, indicating that Alec should stand at ease.

"That was top-notch flying last night. Incredible stuff. I think you should meet Wing Commander Gibson. He's forming a new squadron at Scampton. Only wants the cream of the crop for a one-off operation. I think you'll do the job nicely."

"Scampton, sir?"

"I want you to drive up tonight and meet him. They're flying back one of ours tomorrow so you can return as a passenger with them the following day."

"Tonight?" He groaned. When was he going to get the chance to speak with Maggie?

The wing commander heard the change in his tone. "Will that be a problem, Thomas?"

Alec weighed up his options. On one hand, he would be a fool to pass up an introduction like this. On the other hand, his tour was technically up. He wasn't sure he wanted to have a conversation about joining elite squadrons that would just mean flying back into harm's way. Especially when the conversation cost him the chance to continue that kiss.

"No problem at all, sir," he lied.

"Hello? Oscar?" Maggie called into the church from the vestibule.

He hurried out from behind the organ in response. "Maggie! What a surprise!"

"A good one, I hope."

"Yes, of course. I've been speaking about you already this morning. What can I do for you?"

Her heart quickened, and she tried to make her voice sound casual. "Oh, who have you been speaking with?"

Those big-brother eyes of his danced behind his glasses. "I think you know, Maggie. In fact, I think that's why you are here."

If he hadn't been such a dear old friend, she might have protested. But she rolled her eyes mockingly. "How do you know everything? Did they give you some kind of spiritual powers to divine thoughts at the seminary?"

He chuckled. "Not exactly. But I don't need any superpowers in this case. It was clear from the moment I saw him that he was in love with you."

She couldn't decide whether she should beam or scowl.

"He told me what happened last night. Do you want to talk

about it?"

She wavered. It would be nice to hear Oscar's thoughts, especially if he had recently spoken to Alec. "No," she decided. "I just . . . I thought I might find him here. Is he all right?" That was what she really wanted to know.

"Yes. Very definitely. In fact, I believe you'll find he's a new man."

Maggie narrowed her eyes at her friend, but her heart leapt inside her chest. "That's very cryptic, Oscar!"

"I suppose it is." He paused. "Well, go on! Go and find him!"

She gave him an exasperated laugh and ran back to Grace's car.

CHAPTER THIRTY-SEVEN

Barrowby Lane, Bottesford
6 March 1943, 2:30 p.m.

"This rain is blinding!" Grace complained as she drove at a snail's pace along the country road.

The earlier drizzle had turned into a soaking downpour. The wipers scraped in vain but did nothing to make the road any more visible.

"Should we pull over?" Maggie suggested. "It will pass soon enough."

Grace looked for a place where the road was wide enough for another car to pass and pulled her vehicle over safely. She stopped the engine, and they sat for a few moments, listening to the rain drum against the roof of Grace's father's car.

Maggie watched the drops trace blurring patterns outside the glass as she turned Oscar's words over in her head. She hated that Oscar was so obtuse about the whole thing, but was strangely comforted too. She knew that if Oscar was worried about her stepping out with Alec, he would tell her.

Yet he hadn't. Even after having some kind of insight into Alec's state of mind, Oscar still encouraged her toward Alec.

She grinned. She really was Alec Thomas's girl.

"So spill the beans—what did the vicar say?" Grace asked, obviously tired of sitting next to her friend's silence.

"He told me to talk with Alec," she said simply. "It all felt very mysterious, actually." Maggie sighed. "Apart from that, there's not much more to say."

"Oh really?" Grace's eyebrows were raised again.

"Really."

Eventually the rain stopped falling in sheets and resumed its drizzle against the windscreen. Grace turned the key in the engine, but instead of it rumbling into life, it let out a rhythmic wheeze, refusing to turn over.

Grace grumbled and swore under her breath.

"Come on, you stupid piece of machinery."

"I don't think abusing it will get it to cooperate."

"Martin did try to tell me it was having troubles this week." Grace tried the engine again.

Something caught Maggie's eye through the blur of the wet windshield. A dark-haired girl, just a slip of a thing wearing a green-and-brown Land Army uniform, stumbled into the middle of the road. Another taller woman, dressed the same way, appeared from the hedgerow behind her. They grabbed each other's hands and huddled together

"What on earth are they doing?" Maggie muttered, half to herself. "If other cars don't have the sense to stop, they'll be run over!"

Maggie peered more intently through the window and saw their expressions. They looked stricken with fear, and the way they were glancing around told her something was very wrong.

"Wait here." Maggie grabbed the umbrella Grace had stowed on the backseat. She turned her collar up, opened the car door, and stepped straight into a puddle, splashing cold, muddy water up her legs.

As she approached, she saw more clearly that both the Land Girls staggered wide eyed with terror. The older, larger one looked around wildly, as if she couldn't tell which way to go. She kept her arms protectively around the younger one. Maggie could hear the smaller girl crying in low, trembling sobs.

"Hello!" Maggie called. "Can I help you?"

They hadn't seen Maggie yet, and they swung around with a scream. Two terrified faces looked back at her, but Maggie's jaw dropped when she saw the smaller girl's face clearly for the first time.

"Rosie? What on earth?" Maggie couldn't finish the sentence. "You're supposed to be in Wales with Clara!"

As recognition flashed in the girl's eyes, she surged forward, throwing her arms around Maggie's neck and clinging to her like a wet, shivering monkey.

"What are you doing here?" Maggie could barely articulate her thoughts, given the number of questions exploding through her mind.

"I ran away. Like you. Except I kept writing letters. To you and to Mrs. Bickham and Father." Rosie's explanation came out through panicked huffs of breath.

"You're not even old enough to be part of the Land Army."

"We need to go! He'll find us!" The other Land Girl's eyes were as wide and frightened as Rosie's.

Maggie felt the woman's fear right down to the toes of her puddle-soaked shoes, but she wouldn't run helter-skelter down a rainy country lane with two bedraggled Land Girls without more information about what on earth she was running from and with whom. "Who are you?"

"This is Bessie."

Bessie ignored the introduction, trembling pathetically. "He'll be coming."

"Who'll be coming?" One of so many questions bouncing around in Maggie's head. She was about to call out to Grace to ask if she had any blankets in the car so she could bundle the hysterical girls up and get them dry, when a man's voice sliced through the air.

"You can't get away. I know this place better than you girls, and I can do this all day."

Maggie felt sick to her stomach as she whipped around to confront the voice's owner. Cold terror surged through her when she found herself staring into the same face that had wakened her two days ago. Her arms flew protectively around her sister. Bessie shrieked and hid herself behind Maggie.

The man—what had Chris Fisher said his name was? Stockton?—whose face at first mirrored Maggie's own shock, changed his expression into a brutish smile. "Hello, Maggie."

Maggie wanted her voice to work. She wanted her feet to move, but they were rooted to the spot. She willed her body to do something—despite its obvious memory of the fear from that terrible morning.

"Stay away." The mighty shout she tried to muster came out as a dry whisper.

"You're a beast!" Rosie shrieked. She wrung Maggie's coat sleeves in her hand.

What had this man done to her sister to make her so scared?

Stockton snarled at Rosie. "You shouldn't have snooped, you little snitch!"

He shifted his gaze back to Maggie. "I'm sorry it has to be like this Maggie, but they aren't meant to go into that barn."

His voice wasn't repentant. It was menacing. The three women shivered together. The viciousness of his smile deepened as he advanced upon them. Every hair on Maggie's body stood on end, preparing her to run. She backed herself and the girls away.

Before she could grab the girls and make an escape, she saw a flicker of movement behind Stockton. Grace crept up behind him with the car's jack raised in her hand, ready to strike. No one had noticed Grace slip from the car, weapon in hand. The predator was still so focused on his prey that he didn't see the blow coming.

Grace brought the jack down hard on his head. Stockton crumpled to the ground.

All four women watched him fall. Grace dropped the jack, her face white. Trembling, she bent over Stockton and checked his pulse.

"I think he's just out cold."

Stockton groaned, confirming he was alive.

"Not out cold then," Grace said. "Come on—we have to get back to the aerodrome. But we'll have to walk—the car won't start."

Grace tugged on Maggie's elbow, who in turn stretched her arm protectively across Rosie's shoulders and urged her forward. Rosie looked back at her friend, whose hand she was still holding, and pulled her on too.

Less than half a mile down the road they heard the rumble of a lorry over the patter of rain. Maggie froze in her steps, looking at Grace. Possibilities swirled in Maggie's mind. Perhaps he'd been picked up by another farmer and was now intent on chasing them down the country lane. Perhaps a police car had found him and was on its way to arrest them.

Rosie shivered in Maggie's arms.

"It can't be him. It's coming from the other direction." Her voice didn't match the certainty of her words.

Before they had time to hide, a USAAF troop transport truck rumbled around the corner. Grace waved it down. When it slowed to a stop beside them, a young private wound down the window and leaned out. "Say, can we give you ladies a ride? You look awfully wet!"

"Oh, I don't know. It's quite pleasant once you get used to being soaked through." Grace forced gaiety into her voice as she glanced over her shoulder. "Can you take us to the aerodrome?"

"Sure thing." The private grinned. "If you don't mind sitting in the back with the boys. There's no room up front."

Maggie followed Grace's gaze down the lane. Now was not the time to be thinking about propriety and protocol. Soaked and trembling as they were, the four of them couldn't outrun him, even if he was dazed by Grace's blow. She nodded for Grace to accept.

"That would be perfect," Grace said with her most polite smile, almost as if she were accepting an invitation to afternoon tea.

"Climb on in!"

Many people, including Alec, had choice words to say about the US Army Air Forces. But whatever flaws they might have, their politeness in the circumstances was impeccable. Every one of the seven men in the truck held out his hand to help them.

"Maggie?" said the one whose hand Maggie had grabbed from the many in front of her. She met his eyes—a striking greenish-gray she recognized from New Year's Eve.

"Caleb!"

He grinned. "Seems I'm always rescuing you from trouble."

"It's very good to see you again." She meant it with all her heart.

The men in the back of the transport looked as though they hadn't quite grown into their features yet. As the gears ground the lorry forward, several men offered their jackets to the wet women. Maggie accepted for Rosie and Bessie, but she and Grace made do with a blanket stretched over their knees.

Wrapped in a borrowed jacket and sobbing miserably, Rosie looked so small. Maggie's brain kept formulating questions she couldn't ask in front of all these strangers.

"Did anyone ever tell you boys it was rude to stare?" Caleb said.

The others sat straighter and did their best to keep their eyes forward.

"What happened to you ladies?" Caleb asked.

Maggie didn't remove her arm from Rosie's shoulders.

"Car trouble," Grace said with a tight smile.

Maggie thought she owed Caleb an explanation after he'd been more than helpful twice now. She gave him some details as they bounced along the country road. He nodded gravely and sent a sympathetic smile to Rosie and Bessie.

As he handed her out of the vehicle at the boom gate of the aerodrome, he kept hold of Maggie's hand.

"Maggie, I don't suppose I can write you, can I? Now that I know where to find you?"

"That's very kind—and you've been very kind to me several

times now—but it's probably best not." She bit her lip, feeling bad at letting him down. "I'm seeing someone."

"Let me guess—an Australian with a mean right hook?"

She nodded, unable to hold back her smile despite everything that had just happened.

"Well, he's a very lucky man." Caleb smiled.

As the truck drove off and the bedraggled women, two of them wide eyed with wonder, walked up the drive of the aerodrome, Maggie said to her sister, "You realize you have a lot of explaining to do."

———∞———

RAF Bottesford
6 March 1943, 3:45 p.m.

The wing commander insisted Alec take Jonty with him and get on his way to Scampton before the light failed.

Alec had asked the others in his crew to tell Maggie where he was.

"Sure," Staunton teased. "Same message as the one you gave her last night?"

Alec gave his navigator a look that made it clear that if Staunton ever spoke about his girl like that again, he'd get the same treatment as Hardie.

His girl. He was sure of it now. If he could just get a minute alone with her.

As he approached the boom gate, he slowed the vehicle for four unkempt, thoroughly soaked women walking along the side of the road toward them. He did a double take and stopped the car when he realized two of them were Maggie and Grace.

"Maggie? Are you all right?" He slid out of the car to find out the story. "You look like a drowned rat. What happened?"

She turned to the girl under her wing. "Stay here with Grace for just a minute, will you?"

She led him away from where the others could hear and began telling a story that made his every muscle tense. Stockton had tracked her down again.

"Did he hurt you?" He fought the urge to hold her safe. His muscles relaxed, but only a little, when she shook her head.

This was not the kind of conversation he wanted to have. He wanted to pick up where they'd left off during the night, before telling her everything he'd spoken about with Oscar. Perhaps he looked like he was about to do just that, because she gave an awkward shrug and inclined her head toward the other women.

"My little sister, Rosie, is just over there."

Hadn't Maggie said something about Rosie being in Wales? She took him by the elbow and guided him farther away from the too-interested stare of said sister.

"I'll give you lovebirds a minute," Jonty called. "But then we have to leave, Alec."

The one person he'd wanted to see more than anyone and the moment was being cut short. He took her hand and squeezed it, with a glance over to where Rosie stood watching everything.

"I've been asked to take a meeting at Scampton." Maggie glanced dubiously at the cloud-covered sky. "Jonty's driving me there. It's just overnight. But after that I finally get my six days' leave. We can go to the cinema, or dancing, or whatever you want."

"I'm sorry, Alec. I don't think I can. I have a feeling that I am going to have to take some leave to sort out this difficulty with my sister."

His hopeful heart sank. He allowed disappointment to write itself across his face, and he dropped his eyes to the ground.

"But it's not that I wouldn't love that." She bent her head, trying to catch his eye again. "In fact, I'm counting on having your full attention when I get back. We have a lot to talk about, I think."

He wanted to kiss her again then and there, sisters be damned.

But Jonty piped up. "Right you two. It's cold out here. Let's go, Alec."

Alec settled on leaning in close and kissing her cheek. Even soaking wet she smelled like soft, delicate wildflowers.

He took several steps backward toward the car so he could keep his eyes on her as long as possible, grinning as he did.

―――◆∞)

When they saw the state of the Land Girls, the WAAFs in the kitchen prepared some cocoa for them without asking questions. The girls now sat at one end of a large table in the mess, sipping the hot drinks, with additional blankets around their dry outfits. Amy had them giggling despite their predicament, with stories about the men she had dated. Maggie wasn't comfortable with the conversation, but she had bigger problems right now.

Rosie had explained everything once she felt warm and safe. How she had got the idea from a column in *Women's Illustrated*. How she'd told Mrs. Bickham she was shopping, when really she'd caught the bus to Warwick to where the Land Army had a regional office. How she'd lied about being eighteen, every moment thinking the Land Army representative would catch her out. How she had gone to great lengths to intercept the post every day for two weeks while waiting for her letter to arrive. How once Father loosened his grip she had convinced him to let her go to the seaside with Clara's family.

"I'm not even sure if Father knows where I am yet. Clara and I were quite clever about hiding things from him."

Bessie supplied details about the Stocktons' farm, including the stash of stolen goods they'd found.

"They can't stay here," Maggie declared to Grace in a violent whisper. "What will Queen Bee say?"

"What will Queen Bee say about what, Corporal?"

Maggie and Grace spun around to see Hillary Carver looking sternly at them both. Maggie had no choice but to come clean. She relayed the story Rosie and Bessie had told about the chest of stolen goods.

Queen Bee looked over to the girls drinking cocoa. "I want a word with them in my office," she demanded before stalking away.

Maggie prepared the younger pair for an inquisition. "I don't know what you do in the Land Army, but in the WAAF, when the Queen Bee calls, we have to look presentable." Maggie tried to be lighthearted as she pulled back Rosie's hair from her face and straightened the extra uniform she'd lent her sister.

Grace did the same to Bessie, who was dressed in something of Amy's.

"She's not nearly as fierce as you think she's going to be," Amy called as they stepped out of the mess toward Carver's office.

Once in Carver's office, the Land Girls spent the next half an hour describing what they had seen in the Stockton's barn. Bessie, who'd been at the farm much longer than Rosie, spoke the most, but Rosie filled in details where she knew them.

"Clive spent most of his spare time tucked away in there. Got very touchy if anyone tried to see what he's doing. We weren't allowed to go anywhere near that barn. Not that we wanted to go near him—he gave us the creeps. Rosie was the one who suggested we stick our noses in."

"I was just curious. I thought we could sneak in and take a peek while he was asleep," Rosie said.

"It was about quarter past two this morning when we snuck down in our overcoats. We went straight to the back corner of the barn, where he has this chest full of things."

"What kind of things?" Carver asked.

"At first I thought it wouldn't be anything valuable, because there was no lock."

"What was in the chest?" Carver pressed the girls to give specifics.

"It was just an odd assortment of everyday items," Bessie said.

"A collection," Rosie added.

"Yes. Like a collection."

"Be specific, girls," said Carver. "What did you see?"

Bessie pulled her mouth over to the side as she mentally sifted through the items. "Hairbrushes and razors."

Rosie nodded along as Bettie gave the catalogue.

"Paper weights, a radio transmitter, what looked like some kind of a flight helmet, and even a mink stole."

"One single woman's stocking," Rosie added.

Maggie shivered, knowing she was missing one of those.

"He'd sorted everything so that like items were grouped together, which was how we knew the stuff wasn't his. I mean, six ladies' hairbrushes?" Bessie said. "And a stole?"

"But he'd chosen things that were valuable as well as beautiful," Rosie said.

"Maybe he was planning to sell them, because it seemed like what was in there would be worth a lot of money. There was even a gold cigarette case!"

"Did he catch you looking?" Maggie asked.

Rosie shook her head. "I found this in his stash." She reached into the pocket of her dungarees, slid something silver out, then showed it to Maggie on her outstretched hand.

Maggie's silver compact. The one she thought she had lost with the inscription from her parents—*Both brave and beautiful.*

"We confronted him. I said you were my sister. And you would never give away something so important to you. So I knew he had taken it."

"What happened?" Maggie whispered, gripped by her sister's tale and terrified for what she was about to say next.

"He came at me." Rosie explained how she had run for the door, knowing she had the advantage because the kitchen table was between them. "He almost caught my arm, but I dodged and knocked over a chair. Bessie tipped a bucket of dirty dishwasher over him, and we bolted as fast as we could. I knew you were here, Maggie. I knew if we could find you, we'd be safe. And we did." Rosie smiled through tears of relief.

Maggie reached out to pull her sister into a hug, but before she could do it, Wing Commander Palmer entered the room. He insisted on looming over Bessie and Rosie as they wrote out everything they'd seen in the stolen chest.

"You're sure about the radio transmitter? And the flight helmets?" Palmer asked when they were done.

"I don't really know what they were," Bessie admitted. "But that's what they looked like to me."

Maggie, who sat with her chair close to her sister, saw the look Palmer and Carver exchanged. When the girls finished their writing, he took the lists and left the room. Queen Bee took a few extra details from the girls before asking them to wait outside with Grace.

"Your sister has got herself into a fine mess, Corporal," she said when the door clicked closed.

"She's sixteen, ma'am," Maggie said by way of explanation.

Carver grimaced. "Have you called your father?"

Maggie shook her head. "Not yet. Can I use your telephone?"

"Yes—and you're right, Corporal Morrison. She can't stay here. One night and then I expect you to escort her home. Try to talk some sense into her as you do. Fathers across the country have enough worries without their children running off doing stupid things like this."

"Yes, ma'am."

"But don't worry—we'll see to Stockton. Neither you nor your sister will have to worry about him."

Maggie smiled weakly as she reached for the phone on Carver's desk and picked up the receiver. "Kenilworth 6-5-1 please," she said to the operator.

Her father's anxious voice greeted her on the other end of the line. "Margaret, have you seen your sister? She's run away. Left a note but—"

"I have her, Father." She spoke simply and authoritatively, like she did over the radio when she was working. "She's safe, and I'll bring her home tomorrow."

She gave a brief explanation, leaving the most distressing details for the in-person discussions that would inevitably follow.

"Oh thank God." He gasped, as though the wind was being knocked out of him. "Oh, Maggie."

She imagined her father on the other end of the line sinking onto the chair in his study—the deep wingback one with the blue cushion her mother had embroidered all those years ago—and leaning his head in his hands.

She longed to reach out and hold him, but here at the end of the receiver she felt further away from him than ever.

"I'll see you tomorrow. I imagine we'll be on the four o'clock bus."

"Thank you, my dear. It will be good to see you. Both."

Her hand trembled as she hung up the receiver.

RAF Scampton, Lincolnshire
6 March 1943, 6:05 p.m.

Alec was in a bad mood going into the conversation. He'd spent the hour-long car trip to the Scampton Air Station listening to Jonty's incessant chatter and being plagued by mental images of Stockton accosting Maggie in the rain. By the time he'd arrived, he felt ready to let someone have it.

He'd been told Wing Commander Gibson was a brilliant, relentless pilot on his third operational tour. But Alec thought Gibson was up himself. That was what they would say back home. Not much older than Alec, Gibson had just become the RAF's youngest-ever wing commander. His first task in this new job was selecting air crews for his new squadron and training them for some kind of secret operation.

They met in a cramped office in the upstairs loft in an aircraft hangar. Gibson's desk was near a window that looked down over the main floor of the hangar, where the undercarriage of a Lancaster was being modified. The smell of welding equipment hung in the air as the clunks and bangs of the work filtered up to the office.

Gibson barely looked up when Alec walked in, his golden-haired head bowed over several service records, of which Alec presumed his was one.

"Are you the one they sent from Bottesford?"

"That's right," Alec said.

"I don't want you."

Stunned at being dismissed before he even walked in the door, he stared at Gibson in disbelief.

"Are you still here? I said I don't want you. Goodbye."

Gibson must be an excellent pilot, because it wasn't his warm, friendly leadership style that had people clamoring to work with him.

"Now listen here." Having happily survived his first tour, Alec wasn't sure he wanted to leap straight into another, but he was certain he didn't want to be dismissed out of hand. Especially not when coming all this way ruined what was certain to have been an extremely pleasurable evening.

His words, completely out of line when talking to a superior, made Gibson look at him properly for the first time. "I would be on my second tour if it weren't for being transferred to babysitting duty just before winter. My crew and I have the most aiming point photographs in all of 467—and equal first in our last squadron. And two nights ago my crew and I landed a Lanc safely without any blasted elevator control. So if you want the best, then I think you'll find that we are it!"

"Modest too. I see?" Gibson said.

"To a fault." Alec's sarcasm made Gibson smile.

"No elevator control, you say. How on earth did you do it?"

Alec gave the particulars, leaving out any mention of the downright terror he'd felt and the praying he'd done to sway the outcome.

Gibson considered him as he spoke. "All right, I'll take another look."

"That's it?"

"What more do you want? I'll be in touch with your WingCo if I want you."

He felt cheated, like he was being talked down to by some little prince.

Alec saluted as he left the office, but out of habit, not respect, and didn't look back as he strode away. Not even when he heard Gibson walk out onto the landing outside his office door and give the ground crew a dressing-down fiercer than Hades himself.

———∞———

As the train pulled away from the station, Maggie finally had the privacy to extract more details from Rosie about Father. Alone in the compartment, they didn't need to worry about the listening ears of strangers. Rosie explained how their father had restricted every single part of her life without replacing it with any kind of fatherly love. How she'd felt so suffocated by him, she had to find a way to get out.

"He loves you, Rosie. That's all. With Mother gone and me away, you are all he has. I think he was desperate that nothing would happen to you."

"That's just it, Maggie. You were away. You don't know what it was like!"

"If you could have heard the sound of his voice last night when I called him, Rosie, you'd understand."

"Don't talk to me like I am a baby who doesn't understand the ways of the world. I know a good deal more than you think."

"Clearly not enough to have any sense! Running away and joining the Land Army at sixteen is neither sensible nor rational, Rosie, whichever way you try to factor it."

The train stopped at a station to take on new passengers. Rosie sank back into the hard train carriage seat as a guard helped settle a small, swallow-like lady into their compartment. When Maggie spoke again, she kept her voice to a murmur.

"The Land Army? You don't even like gardening, Rosie!"

"It's exactly what you did! Father begged you to stay, but you wouldn't. You made it seem to Father like you were needed to serve your country, but your letters home were filled with stories of dances and trips to the pub with friends."

"I'm not allowed to write about the other bits!" Maggie gave

Rosie an apologetic smile. "I suppose I did go on a bit. But I thought you'd like the details."

"While you were off having fun in the WAAF, I was at home making tea for Father while he shut himself away in his study. He wouldn't even talk about Mother but expected me to step into her shoes. The way he retreated so far, it was like he had died too."

"I'm sorry, Rosie. I didn't know that—"

"And now I find out that you left out the juiciest bits. You barely said anything about the handsome pilot you've been kissing. Amy had to tell me!" She gave Maggie a wicked grin.

Maggie felt her face flame. "Amy Snee knows nothing." She kept her voice prim, biting back her smile. It would not be repressed.

"So you haven't been kissing a Clark Gable look-alike? Because that's what she says."

"Once! And he'd just narrowly escaped death, so propriety didn't come into it."

"And is he really the handsomest pilot in Lincolnshire?"

"He's so handsome." Maggie sighed.

"Well, there's another hour at least before I have to face the music with Father, so you've got time to spill all the details."

Scampton RAF Station
7 March 1943, 10:00 a.m.

As WingCo suggested, he'd arranged for Alec to hitch a ride back on a scheduled transfer flight. The aircraft that was diverted away from Bottesford two nights ago was being returned to its home.

He'd been put up in the barracks at RAF Scampton. Despite the unfamiliar surroundings, Alec's sleep was deep and satisfying. No nightmares, just enjoyable dreams about Maggie's beautiful smile.

In the morning, he met up with the pilot who would ferry him home. A relatively young chap, but Alec happily volunteered as fill-in flight engineer for the short trip. It would have taken Jonty an hour to drive home last night, but this would feel like mere minutes in the sky.

Still, he couldn't stop himself from observing his chauffeur's every move—checking and double-checking every routine, every button, every switch. An occupational hazard, not a judgment on his traveling companion. He liked being in control. If anything went wrong, he preferred to be in a position to do something about it rather than sit around watching.

Perhaps the shortness of the flight made the less experienced pilot let his guard down. Alec knew something was amiss when they came in for the landing. At first he thought his problem was not being in control himself. It didn't feel the same not being in the pilot's seat. But then he realized the speed was wrong too. They were coming in too hard.

He braced, utterly helpless from this position in the fold-out seat.

This was the moment that haunted his worst nightmares.

A great white flash, then nothingness.

But it wasn't entirely the same as in his dreams.

When he woke from those terrors, he heard the snoring of a dozen men around him.

Now, as he came to, he wasn't in his bed.

The white flash hadn't dissolved into an RAF dormitory.

The black around him wasn't a moonless night.

It was smoke.

Thick smoke that tore through his lungs with every breath.

"Banks!" he called, disoriented. Blinded by the acrid smoke, he felt around the cockpit.

Banks groaned, and Alec groped around until he could lay hands on him and give him a shake to rouse him properly. They both had enough experience to feel their way out to the emergency hatch even through their coughing.

He expected to feel relief when he escaped into the open air.

The choking feeling let up a little, but not enough to stop him from sinking to his knees on the tarmac.

He knew his brain was trying, but he couldn't make it send signals to his legs to propel him away from the aircraft. Banks managed to, but Alec couldn't make it happen for himself.

His chest heaved, and black spots appeared in his vision. *Need to get up. Need to run.*

Black spots? Or more black smoke—he couldn't tell.

Black smoke, aviation fuel. Not a good combination. He smelled them both as he tried to get the message to his legs to run. All he managed was a coughing fit.

More black.

He couldn't see what was happening but felt the heat from the explosion burn up his back before he passed out.

CHAPTER THIRTY-EIGHT

Letter from Alec Thomas, Lincolnshire, England
To Mrs. Moira and Miss Elizabeth Thomas, Sydney, Australia

6 March 1942

To be read in the event of my death,

Dear Mum and Lizzie,

Last night I made it through the last op of my tour.

At the beginning of the tour, I wrote you a letter like this one, to be sent in the event of my death. It sat on my pillow every night I flew. Thank God you never had to read it, but it came close several times. Especially last night.

In the whole time I've been here, I never updated the letter. I guess I didn't want to tempt fate. But I'm updating it now, because some things have changed.

Remember I wrote to you about Maggie? She forgave me, Mum. I'm sure I don't deserve her. She is the most wonderful, beautiful, intriguing, clever, feisty woman . . . and I love her. She's the reason I'm going to stay in England and do a second tour. I'm on my way to talk to someone about that now.

I want you to know, if you do get this letter, that I wasn't afraid. My soul is taken care of in a way I never thought it could be after everything I've done. Faith is a wonderful thing! If I am to die, I want to leave you with this encouragement: Your foolish son and brother knows the Lord and is at home with Him.

As the Good Book says, "Do not let your hearts be troubled," and, if you do get to meet her, take care of my beautiful Maggie for me.

I love you all so much it hurts,

Alec.

The Vicarage, St. John's Church, Kenilworth
7 March 1943, 4:30 p.m.

When they arrived back to their family home, Rosie was sent straight to her room.

No embrace. No expression of the relief Maggie knew her father must be feeling.

Rosie looked crestfallen by the way he simply pointed sternly to her bedroom with an "I'll deal with you later" look.

But Mrs. Bickham drew Rosie into her arms, and they walked up the hallway together. Maggie was sure a supply of tea and biscuits would be heading Rosie's way.

Maggie steeled herself for a hard conversation as she sat opposite her father in the study. Not in the comfortable wingback chair her mother had occupied when chatting cheerfully with her husband. Maggie sat in the hard wooden chair meant strictly for parish business matters.

She expected to deflect some kind of tirade, but instead her father looked broken. He'd never looked so small behind his desk as he did right now.

"She's hurting, Father. It wasn't easy for a daughter to point out the errors in her father's ways."

He nodded. "The truth is, I don't know what to do. I miss your mother terribly. She was the one who knew how to understand you two. But to me it's a mystery."

"It doesn't have to be, Papa. But you do need to look up from your books every now and then. You can't refuse to let her leave the house but ignore her while she's in it. What did you think would happen?"

He looked at his older daughter with new eyes. "You have the same insight as your mother." He sighed.

Maggie felt a little braver. "There is something I don't understand, Father. Why are you not taking comfort in the promises of the Bible? My assurance that Mother met her Maker trusting in Jesus means that I can move forward with—well, not without sadness, but at least with confidence that all is not lost. You taught me that faith. Why has it deserted you?"

Her lip trembled at the end of her speech. "Dear girl"—his voice sounded choked—"you have accused me of not looking up from my books in these past months. But in fact what I have been doing is wrestling with this very question. Poring through them, looking back at the evidence, trying to come to terms with my own doubt." He looked ashamed.

"People think that as a vicar I must have a perfect kind of faith. But if such a thing exists, it was your mother who possessed it. The war was challenging enough for a doubter like me. The way it is ripping apart the moral foundations of our society and . . ." He waved his hand to stop his thoughts from going down that tangent.

"The world that I know was being torn apart well before your mother died. She knew I was flagging in my faith and always did her best to encourage me. When she died so suddenly, it felt like God ripped away my very last support."

He cried now, but she let him continue.

"Job was able to be faithful through such trials, but it turns out I am a much lesser man. And how was I to admit to my two faithful daughters what a hypocrite I had become?"

Maggie took the Bible that sat spread open on her father's desk. "May I?"

He nodded, and she turned the book around to face her. It was opened at Job, and no doubt had been for many months now, but she flipped to the New Testament.

"Rosie told me the Bible was open in Mother's lap when she found her." She found 1 Thessalonians and turned the book around to face him. "Look what it was open to. 'Do not grieve as people who have no hope.'"

She read through Paul's description of the triumphant return of Christ and hope-filled promises that the living and the dead would one day see each other again. "Mother must have known she was going to die. She opened this as a message to you."

She looked up to see tears rolling down his face. She closed the Bible and walked around to the other side of his desk to embrace him as he sobbed.

"Did Carver let you use the telephone?" Maggie asked Grace.

"No, I'm phoning from home so I don't have to worry about permission. It's just, I wanted to tell you that there's been an accident."

Dread gripped Maggie's heart.

"The Lanc Alec was in crashed on landing. He wasn't flying, but it was a freakish thing anyway, they just overshot a little, and there was a fire, and . . ."

"Is he alive? Is he hurt?" Maggie's panicked voice ricocheted across the telephone lines.

"Yes, darling, he is alive. But his lungs aren't strong, you know, from the bronchitis he had, and he inhaled a lot of smoke."

"Where is he?"

"He's in the hospital at Grantham. We thought you should know. Jonty said that last time you visited him, he made a miraculous recovery, so we thought . . ." Grace trailed off.

Maggie assessed the possibilities. He was alive, thank God. But how serious was the damage to his lungs? Smoke inhalation could be fatal on its own, and she'd seen just how sick he'd been earlier in the year.

Her heart lobbed up a silent prayer to help her know what to do. The memory of him convulsing with fever tore at her. But things with her father and sister still felt so precarious. She wasn't sure it would be the right thing to leave them after so short a time. She begged Grace to find out more from Jonty or to see him for herself.

"Tell him I love him. So he knows, in case . . . you know." She didn't want to say it.

"Of course I will, darling."

Maggie could tell her friend was in tears on the other end of the line.

"There's another thing. I also wanted to tell you that the police raided Stockton's farm."

Maggie listened intently as Grace recounted how the police used the information from Rosie and Bessie to locate all the missing items. Bessie, escorted by police officers so she could pack up the personal items she and Rosie had left in their garret room, helped the police locate the chest in the barn.

"Everything that has gone missing in the past few months has been returned to its rightful owner. But it's not just petty theft that he's being charged with. Several of the items are more than personal effects. He stole pieces of flight equipment and had a radio transmitter. He'll be charged with sedition."

A shiver traveled down Maggie's spine. The penalty for a guilty verdict in such a case was death. Even though the memory of Stockton's vicious face still gave her nightmares, she didn't wish that on him.

"Is everything all right with your father?"

"It will be." Maggie sighed. "I thought I'd have more time with them, but if Alec needs me . . ."

Grace left her with a promise that she would call again with more information. Maggie set down the receiver with a heavy heart.

Over the next few days, she raced to the phone each time it

jingled, barely able to answer with her bated breath. She fought the urge to call the aerodrome or the hospital with frenzied knitting.

However, as much as she walked around with a constant prayer for Alec's recovery, as much as she missed the camaraderie of her friends and her work, she couldn't leave yet. She still had business here with her family. She had to step into her mother's shoes and have long, hard conversations with her father about grief and doubt and hope. It fell to her to talk Rosie through the consequences of her deceit.

"Why aren't you punishing me?" Rosie asked. She'd been called into their father's study after one of his many long phone calls with the Women's Land Army and the Bottesford constabulary. She sat small and contrite on the wooden chair in front of his desk.

"My girl, I accept that I drove you into such drastic action. That action led you to leave the safety of this house, where you were terrorized by an unstable man. I think that is punishment enough, don't you?"

Rosie sat in silence, eyes bouncing between Maggie and their father, waiting for him to say more. Maggie knew her sister was expecting to be locked inside until she was twenty-one.

"I hope you will accept my apologies for not comforting you as I ought after your mother passed away?" It came across as a question.

The words were like a polite request delivered to a parishioner, but they were delivered with deep feeling in his voice while his eyes pleaded with Rosie. Tears welled in Maggie's eyes.

"I should have surrounded you with love and pointed out the great hope that the Scriptures give us. But I found that I couldn't." His voice choked on his last word.

"Please, Father, don't cry."

Maggie knew her father needed to cry, but the sight still broke her heart. She pulled Rosie to her feet so they could both wrap their arms around him and cry together in a healing embrace.

CHAPTER THIRTY-NINE

When Maggie threw open the front door, it was only the second time Alec had ever seen her out of her WAAF uniform. Even dressed in a simple green cardigan and floral blouse with her hair tied loosely, she was the loveliest thing he'd ever beheld.

"Are you an idiot? An actual, verified idiot?"

He stood rooted to the spot on the threshold, dumbstruck by the accusation in her voice. He'd been in hospital. He couldn't possibly have done anything to deserve this. He dropped his grin into a frown.

Then she threw herself at him, wrapping her arms around his neck and pressing her whole body into him as if to prove his very existence. The force of her embrace, as wonderful as it was, made him cough, causing Maggie to let go.

"So you are glad I've come?"

"Why aren't you in hospital?" More accusation filled her voice.

"Because my medicine is here."

She answered him with a kiss so deep and heartfelt, only Jonty poking him in the ribs could make him emerge from it. He looked up to see a gray-haired man with a white clerical collar looking sternly at them both. The crash hadn't killed him, but her father just might, judging by the look on his face.

Maggie was brave under the fatherly gaze that made him uncomfortable. She didn't let go of his hand and welcomed the airmen into a small sitting room at the front of the house. Her father's gaze, penetrating from under his deeply frowning eyebrows, didn't stray from Alec.

Maggie made the introductions. "This is Alec Thomas, Father. I told you about him. And this is our friend Jonty Ables."

Well, at least she'd mentioned him to her father. He wasn't going in cold.

Alec held out his hand and tried to smile, ruining his charm by coughing. The older man studied him severely and shook his hand firmly.

"Actually, as lovely as it is to see Mags, ah Maggie, Margaret"—he glanced at Maggie's failed attempt to conceal a smile, probably because he'd never called her Margaret before—"I've actually come to see you, sir."

The older man stood silent. He indicated with his hand that Alec should follow him into his study. Maggie's eyes traced them out of the room. He saw her face, confused and amused at the same time, as her father shut the study door behind them.

This was the bit Alec had prepared for. He'd already practiced what he would say on Jonty, who'd listened with the irrepressible lights in his eyes shining like it was Christmas, laughing at Alec's expense. A lot.

Maggie's father still hadn't spoken. By now, Alec suspected silence was being used to keep him off guard. It was what he would do to a man he'd just discovered locking lips like that with his sister, after all. The older man sat behind his desk, but Alec stood. He understood he needed to launch in and speak first. It was like flying blind in a cloud—and it was more terrifying here than over Berlin.

He managed to get out what he'd practiced with Jonty.

That in the time that he knew Maggie, which he understood wasn't a long time, he'd quickly come to love her. That he thought she cared about him too. And he'd come to seek his permission to ask Maggie to marry him.

Still the older man looked at him, cold and stern. So he continued. "Each time I get into the cockpit, I take a bet each way on my returning in one piece. But if I am going to die during this war, I would very much like to die with Margaret Morrison as my wife."

The stern expression eased a little. "If you are going to die, I think you have more important things to think about than marrying my daughter. What will happen to your soul when you die, Mr Thomas? You might think this is a professional enquiry given that I am a clergyman, but actually my main concern is Maggie. Our family is all too aware right now that our only comfort in the face of death is Jesus Christ."

He'd held his breath while the other man spoke, relieved to have an answer for him. "I've never been a religious man, sir. I have avoided church and fled from anyone who tried to broach the subject for a very long time. But this war has made me . . . I can't explain it exactly. It's like I've been untouchable all the way through it in the most incredible and unlikely ways when all my friends are being shot down around me in equally improbable ways."

He gave some details about his service during the war, including the brushes with death. "Let's just say that one night it all came to a head, and I told God that if he rescued me, I'd do whatever he wanted." He recounted his conversation with Oscar Williams.

"He told me I shouldn't think about what I could do for God but what He had done for me. Of course, I'd heard those things before, but I'd never understood them until that moment. I've never felt so alive as when Oscar prayed with me to ask that the Lord forgive me and help me trust Him in my very core."

"Oscar Williams, you say? At Bottesford?" Something about the reference to Oscar seemed to seal the truth of his story in the older man's mind.

"He visited me several times while I was in hospital recently."

He waited under Maggie's father's gaze for a long time. Then he saw the tears in the older man's eyes.

"I was once in your position—a man with a new faith asking to marry the wife of my youth. We were very happily married for twenty-four years until . . . recently. I hope that you and Margaret will experience the same happiness."

"So you give your permission?"

"I give my permission."

"What are they speaking about in there?" Maggie wondered aloud, sitting gingerly on the edge of a sofa.

Jonty sat opposite her in an armchair, trying to hide his smug awareness behind his dancing eyes.

She kept her eyes on the door to her father's study and absent-mindedly picked up a knitting project from the basket next to the sofa. That door was closed for what seemed like a long time. She drilled into it with her stare as though concentrating hard enough might make it open. Her hands worked away with the needles without her brain thinking about what she was doing, while Rosie fussed in the kitchen, making tea.

"He's very handsome," Rosie said as she brought in a tea tray. "Oh sorry." When she caught sight of Jonty, she refrained from saying any more.

"It's all right. We all know it. Even before he put on the uniform, it was clear that no one else would stand a chance with the ladies next to him," Jonty joked. "But I'll be a married man soon myself, so I don't mind."

Maggie's concentration was so fully on her father's study door, she took a second or two to register Jonty's words. "What? To whom?" she said with a lack of manners that would appall her mother, had she been here.

"Katie Baines has agreed to be my wife," he said.

Maggie's jaw dropped. "Katie?" So many questions filled her.

Questions she couldn't ask with her little sister here.

"Yes." Jonty seemed to know exactly what her eyes were asking. "Next week, actually. We're both very excited about marriage and, you know, family. And with a war on, we thought, why wait?"

"Oh, Jonty!" She was so happy she could hug him. "With your good heart, I know you'll always be happy."

A glow of happiness emerged from the study with Alec and her father. She looked expectantly at Alec, but he didn't seem to want to look her in the eye. Instead, he looked straight at his friend. "Jonty, we're going now."

Jonty fumbled with his teacup in his haste to stand up and follow Alec out the door.

Maggie stared after them, perplexed and hurt, until her father put a hand on her shoulder.

He looked kindly at her. "I expect he'll be back soon."

In a few hours, he was. She answered the door to two grinning airmen and couldn't hide her exasperation. "Are you going to tell me what this is about?"

He didn't say a word.

He simply grabbed her hand and led her into the garden at the side of their house, where he sat her down on a low stone bench. Her mother had loved to sit here during summer, soaking in the glorious garden her husband maintained. Today, the garden was cold and muddy, but mercifully it wasn't raining, and signs of spring were desperately trying to show themselves.

Alec sat next to her on the bench. When he realized she didn't have a coat on, he gave her his. Then he took her hand and poured out his heart about the bargain he'd made with God. About praying with Oscar. About how he'd come to know exactly what Jesus's death meant and how he didn't understand everything about it, but he was sure his life was different now.

He recalled every feeling he'd ever had about her, how he couldn't sleep on the night he'd met her because she'd filled his dreams with her loveliness. How she'd been the most challenging and perplexing creature to get to know in the first place, but once he'd started, he didn't want to stop, and how he hoped that she would never make him stop, and if she agreed to marry him, he'd never have to.

She sat listening to him, wrapped in the warmth of the lambswool and feeling as if she glowed from the inside out.

Suddenly, he knelt on the muddy ground at her feet and produced a small ring with a tiny stone in a dull platinum setting on a very thin, delicate band. "It's just glass, I'm afraid. But I can get you a better one after the war."

"I don't care about the ring. Only you."

"So you'll marry me?"

"Of course I will." She leaned forward and kissed him deeply, drinking him in, like she'd been aching to since that horrible night last week, before leaning her forehead against his while he slipped the ring on her finger.

The Alexandra Theatre, Kenilworth
16 March 1943, 8:00 p.m.

Maggie enjoyed the past four days more thoroughly than any others since her mother's death. Jonty returned to Bottesford, but Alec had a billet in the village. Each morning he arrived early, and he stayed late into the evening. They almost forgot there was a war on in the happy domestic bubble they created. She delighted to see Alec get to know her father and sister, and she watched as her father guided Alec in his new faith while nursing his own bruised one.

Alec brought joy into their home again. When he sat in her mother's place at their small dining table, he filled it with an energy that lightened them all. His presence helped them draw closer to one another, closing the space that had developed over the past few months.

On his final day of leave, Alec took her to the cinema, as he'd promised. The film was terribly sad and gloriously romantic. She watched it with her fingers laced with his and didn't want it to end.

After the rest of the audience left, they sat alone in the theater. Maggie dabbed her eyes with the handkerchief he'd supplied halfway through the film.

"I thought you liked the cinema, Mags," he said, seemingly confused by her tears.

"I love it." She sniffed.

"Right. I was trying to find the right time to tell you this. I was hoping you would be . . . less emotional when I did." He paused. "I've been posted to Scampton." He hurried on. "I didn't know until today. I spoke with them on the night you left. They are forming a new squadron, and they want experienced pilots for some kind of specialized work. Jonty told them where they could find me, and they left a message with the landlady to call them."

Maggie's heart sank.

"I suppose there was little chance that we would be allowed to stay on the same station once we were married anyway," she admitted. "The RAF frown upon that."

They talked about the possibility of a station at a training school for him. She didn't want to think about him flying more operations over Germany. "Is it a Pathfinder squadron?" she asked, terrified to know the answer.

"No, not the Number Eights. In fact, the squadron still doesn't have a name yet. 'Squadron X' they are calling it."

They meandered back to her doorstep, enjoying their last quiet moments before they had to return to the aerodrome and report for duty. They were catching the same train back to Lincolnshire the next day but it seemed important to draw this moment out.

As a goodbye, he drew her into his arms and cupped her face in his hands so he could look into her eyes and speak to her soul. "Before I met you, Mags, I could only think about surviving from one operation to the next. But now I have something to actually live for."

"That's because I'm your girl, Alec Thomas," she said, her lips straining for a kiss.

"You're my girl."

FIRST CHAPTER FROM

THE MAPMAKER'S SECRET

21 May 1943
RAF Medmenham, Buckinghamshire, England

"You want me to do what!"

Lieutenant Jack Marsden wasn't using the polite, respectful tone he usually took with his superiors. But considering the idea just presented to him, there was nothing else to say—and no other way to say it.

"It's unconventional, I know." Lieutenant Colonel Robert Lewis, the most senior American officer at this British photographic interpretation unit, should have been on Jack's side. Instead, he leaned back in his chair and continued laying out his argument. "But most of the time you'll be involved in the same kind of work you do here. And from what I've seen, you are well suited to the task, Jack."

"Well suited? Sir, I do this intelligence work for my country, but my real training is in medicine, not espionage." He usually kept quiet about his former life as a doctor in front of his superiors, worried he might get pulled away from a desk and put in a clinic.

Two British civilians, MI5 he suspected, from the way they were talking, stood behind his commanding officer, bestowing such stern looks he wanted to laugh. One of them, introduced with a single name, Petrie, looked at least ninety, with white-gray hair covering his solid head. The younger one, Wilson—although Jack didn't know if that was his first or last name—stared with merciless, fox-like eyes.

"Lieutenant, you are an urbane, single, intelligent man who knows all about cartography, and right now that's what we need." The older man compensated for the perfect stillness of his body with the deliberate energy of his precise accent.

"I'm not single, sir." Jack indicated the wedding ring on his left hand.

"She's dead, Jack." Warrant Officer Alvin Harris, his *supposed* friend sitting in the chair beside him, piped up.

Jack glowered at him.

"It's been four years." Alvin spoke more gently this time.

So this was an ambush. That was why Alvin was here. There was no other reason for him to be at a meeting like this, other than to get Jack to play ball.

"Your country is asking this of you, Marsden. You did sign up to serve your country, didn't you?" the Lieutenant Colonel said.

"Not as a spy." Intelligence reports were one thing—what they had just proposed was completely different. "Don't we have some kind of euphemistically named department—Strategic Services, isn't it?—who can help you out?"

He wanted to keep protesting, but the way the others stared at him, he knew he faced a losing battle. He looked down at the unopened dossier in his hands and sighed. "Explain it to me again."

"Bartondale is a new cartography facility set up by the Air Ministry." Wilson spoke for the first time, his sly eyes studying Jack from behind round spectacles. "Hitler began preparing for war as soon as he took power. But he wouldn't allow maps to leave the country. Up-to-date maps are very hard to come by. As a result, the accuracy of our bombing was compromised. You've seen the results in your work here. Bartondale is the fix. Similar to this place, it hosts a range of specialists on site—intelligence officers, cartographers, artists—all of whom make sure our maps marry up with the most recent information, and in a form that is easy for the pilots and navigators to use. I should say that all this is top secret and everyone in this room"—he looked at Alvin directly—"is bound by our Official Secrets Act and the Treachery Act, both of which you signed on the way in, not to mention a word."

Everyone nodded without thinking. Secret-keeping was a matter of course these days.

Wilson continued. "In the months that it has been open, the Germans have anticipated several of our air raids. They've been ready for us with extra antiaircraft measures and have brought several aircraft down. Lives have been lost." He paused, to let the gravity of that statement sink in. "We've traced the link back to Bartondale."

"And you have a suspect?" Jack ignored Wilson's dramatic flourish.

"Open the dossier and you'll see."

Jack flipped open the file, and his attention zeroed in on the photograph paper-clipped to the first sheet of information. A woman with Rita Hayworth–style good looks and golden brown hair. She smiled elegantly at the camera in a studio photograph, wearing a Women's Auxiliary Air Force uniform.

"Who's the broad?" Alvin leaned over Jack's shoulder and gave a low whistle.

"Grace Deroy. She's a WAAF corporal." Wilson motioned to the file. "As you know, we have requisitioned the country houses of wealthy families all over the country for this kind of work."

Jack needed no more proof of what Wilson was saying than to look around him. RAF Medmenham was a grand house with glorious views toward the River Thames. Lewis' office had probably once been some old lady's sitting room.

"Bartondale was recently requisitioned from Grace's family, but she insists on working there. Actually, she lives on site in a caretaker's cottage."

"We think she could be working with the Nazis." Petrie lobbed the comment into the conversation like it was a precision grenade.

Jack raised his eyebrows as he flipped through the dossier. His eyes skimmed the typed report about Grace Deroy, understanding a little more about her home and family. Then he came across a photo of Grace, younger this time, grinning up at an athletic young man. His dapper suit and shiny Oxfords told of elegance and breeding.

Jack frowned at the picture and looked closer. "I know this face."

"That's Andrew Hastings, otherwise known as the Duke of Clarence," Wilson replied. "Although he wasn't the duke when that picture was taken in forty, because his father was still alive then."

Jack remembered. He'd seen this guy walking with the king in newsreels several times since he'd been posted here. Jack couldn't recall all the details, but the guy was some kind of businessman or art dealer as well as having all the privileges of being a member of the British nobility.

"His father was openly sympathetic to the Nazi cause before the war." Petrie took up the story. "He was one of the peers to urge negotiation and even capitulation to the Germans. We suspect his son inherited his views when he inherited his land and title. That picture was taken while the couple was at Oxford, when the pair were close."

Jack had been on English soil long enough to understand that "close" was a euphemism.

"Can't you just transfer her away if you are suspicious of her?" Jack asked.

Wilson glanced at his older colleague, who picked up the story.

"Not to put too fine a point on it, but her father is a high-ranking officer in the RAF. Her brothers are also in the air force. If she is up to something, it may go further than just her, and we don't want her relatives getting wind of our suspicions."

"They want to embed you in the mapmaking facility, Jack." The lieutenant colonel came to the point. "You'll work there, just as you do here, but your real job will be to get close to her and work out if she is the traitor."

Hopefully, the lieutenant colonel wasn't using the same euphemism as the Brit.

"With respect, sir, isn't there someone else? A surveyor or engineer, even someone with a little more experience in espionage?" That was a much more acceptable question to ask aloud than some of the others firing through his brain. Ones like, *Is this really how we plan to defeat the Nazis? With harebrained schemes?*

His CO shrugged. "I already told them that and suggested several other candidates, but they seem to think that you are the kind of guy she might like, which will make things go faster. They think she'll open up to you, especially if you get *close*."

He did not like where this was going. Not one bit. He scrambled for another excuse, one that Lewis could appreciate. "Don't the Air Ministry hate us? Resent us for having the firepower but not being under their command? What makes you think they'll just let me in?"

"They'll do what I tell them to do." Petrie's tone left Jack in no doubt of his power to pull strings behind the scenes.

"I'm sorry, but you've chosen the wrong man for the job." Jack closed the file and pushed it back across the desk.

"We aren't ordering you to seduce the girl." Wilson was backpedalling. "Although, you have permission to try."

Jack hoped his stone-faced expression told Wilson how he felt about that. He doubted he could help with such a scheme. Since his wife died, he was out of practice when it came to romance. She was the only woman who'd ever fallen for his charm anyway. Even then, they'd both been bashful on their wedding night. He was literally the opposite of a Casanova.

Not that he would say that here.

"Your CO tells us that you have deeply held religious convictions. They might help you tease out some of the contradictions in her character."

Jack ignored the pang of guilt that description caused.

"Your work here will help you in your day-to-day job there, and you already know about the whole mapmaking process. You understand the technical side of the work there. You are a unique combination, Lieutenant."

Jack tried objecting in a new way. "My father was the surveyor. He ran the mapmaking business, not me. Are you telling me there isn't anybody else in the US Army with more qualifications—one of the navigators maybe—who could do this job?"

"We want you, Lieutenant Marsden." Petrie's uncompromising stare skewered Jack. He had no way out.

"I don't have a choice, do I?"

Everyone else in the room, including Alvin, shook their heads.

"You'll be serving your country, Marsden. And there are worse ways to do it." The lieutenant colonel looked toward the door.

Jack nodded, said his farewells, and pivoted toward the exit, hoping that his grimace remained private.

"I'll be in touch with more about the specifics next week," Wilson said as Jack left.

Once outside, he turned on Alvin. "How could you do that to me, Alvin?"

"Do what?" Alvin feigned innocence too well.

"You were part of an ambush!"

"C'mon, Jack. Live a little. An English country house. A pretty girl. It's not every day you get orders like that! And did you see her, Jack?"

Alvin's whistle left Jack in no doubt what he thought about the picture of Grace Deroy, but Jack's own stomach churned. How could he possibly be the right man for a job like this? Besides, the ring on his finger reminded him of his promise to his wife. Not many men wore a wedding ring, but he had been delighted to accept the gift. He happily weathered the jokes about being shackled to her—because he was, heart and soul.

"You aren't cheating on anyone," Alvin said.

Jack didn't even know he'd been playing with the thin, gold

band on his left hand. He changed his tone to playful to shake Alvin off.

"I'm just disturbed this is the Allied plan to bring down a Nazi stooge, maybe even a whole ring of them. It relies on me, a widowed ex-doctor and definitely not a spy, whose sole romantic interest includes one woman, 'getting close' to someone who may or may not already have the Duke of Clarence as a lover."

He paused so that Alvin understood he thought the whole thing was incomprehensibly foolish. "What could possibly go wrong?"

Learn more about *The Mapmaker's Secret* at https://jennifermistmorgan.com/mapmakers-secret/

ACKNOWLEDGMENTS

The first and greatest acknowledgment must go to my grandfather, Allan Fisher, who served with RAAF 467 Squadron as part of the New Zealand Air Force during WW II. Just under half of the 125,000 men who flew with RAF Bomber Command died. They weren't career soldiers. They were young men—barely adults, some of them—who believed it was right to defeat Hitler. To fly out each night knowing there was a fifty-fifty chance of coming back is so incomprehensibly brave, it often moves me to tears.

Many of Alec's lucky escapes come directly from the pages of my grandfather's flight logbook. Researching his service, I came across an account of a crew who attempted to land their Lancaster without elevator control, all while the pilot's girlfriend looked on from the control room. (I now believe the account I read was from *Never a Dull* by Bill Manifold, but at the time I had no idea.) In history, things did not end well. So I wanted to write the couple a happy ending. And that's where this story began. For more historical notes, go to https://jennifermistmorgan.com/.

Writing a story is one thing—turning it into a book is quite another. I wouldn't have got there without the following people: Bronwyn, my first reader, who didn't think the story was awful and kindly edited the first draft; Roseanna, who inspired me to lean into the hope at the heart of the story, for her generous-spirited mentorship and beautiful cover; Rachel McMillan, my agent, for believing in me and being a wise ally through the process; Mindy, Jess, and Narelle—thanks for being part of my support crew and sharing the writerly ride; Keith and Anais, for my lovely cover photograph and for not thinking I was spambot when I asked to use it; Dori Harrell, for her wise guiding hand as editor; and to all the people, too numerous to name, who encouraged me and shared the ups and downs on this twisting, turning path to publication.

Finally, my beautiful family. Firstly, Mum and Dad, to whom this is dedicated. I love you both so much. Thanks for everything ever. And to my husband and kids, my favourite people. You are all awesome and I love you to bits—thank you for allowing me time to play with my imaginary friends. Sorry for those moments when they put me in a bad mood. To God be the glory.

WANT MORE FROM JENNIFER MISTMORGAN?

Finishing School
Inverness, Scotland, 1944

In her final weeks of training at a Special Operations Executive Finishing School, Amy Snee's last chance to redeem her career is to parachute behind enemy lines as an SOE wireless operator. She just needs to master Morse code.

Stuart Lewis teaches radio operations, knowing that his bright, brave students won't last more than six weeks behind enemy lines. Can he bring himself to teach Morse to his high school crush, when it means losing her forever? Or can he give her a fighting chance at love?

With rigorous historical detail and compelling characters, this sweet historical romance will delight fans of Sarah Sundin (*Until Leaves Fall in Paris*, *When Twilight Breaks*) and Roseanna M. White (The Codebreakers series) alike.

Read for FREE only by signing up to Jennifer's "Nom de Plume" newsletter at https://jennifermistmorgan.com/subscribe/

Loved *Heart in the Clouds*?
Please consider leaving a review at the outlet where you purchased the book!

Printed in Great Britain
by Amazon